Dear Betty

While I Was Away

Please Enjoy

BILLIE HUANTE

Billie Huante
1/9/11

authorHOUSE®

AuthorHouse™
1663 Liberty Drive, Suite 200
Bloomington, IN 47403
www.authorhouse.com
Phone: 1-800-839-8640

First published by AuthorHouse 3/5/2009

ISBN: 978-1-4389-3884-4 (sc)

Library of Congress Control Number: 2009900588

Printed in the United States of America
Bloomington, Indiana

This book is printed on acid-free paper.

Dedication

My thankful appreciation to Margaret Crowder for the many hours she donated to my novel and passed away recently at age 97 before realizing her dream of seeing my novel in print.

I also want to thank my son, Jack Edwards for the editing of my novel from first draft to final copy and my dear friend, Ann Fraser, who labored for hours at trying to make sense of what I was trying to say and still remain my friend.

Chapter 1

Bruce wheeled his Outback into the reserved parking and locked the doors. The wind was messing with his hair, as it does most every morning at this time, when he strides toward the business office. He slowed to a stop about midway to the front door and turned to find BJ and Bobbitt in the sales office looking at him through the plate glass window. With a dimple in each cheek and a whistle on his lips, he returned their wave and continued on his way.

The article in the newspaper this morning about weapons of mass destruction brought the threat of a Middle East invasion to mind. The terrorist attack on September 11th still makes him madder than hell and if it means going to war this year or a year from now, so be it.

He turned to the window before digging into the pile of paper work on his desk, to take in the vast array of colors, makes and models of new Subaru's. He marveled at the pop and son neon sign, Lawson and Lawson Subaru, and grinned at the memory of twelve years ago.

"I was a sixteen year old know it all when Pops made me partner," he chuckled, "but the ole man sure took me down a notch or two when he put a mop in my right hand and a bucket in the left and told me to learn the business from the floor up."

Once his masculine frame was settled into the chair with his lap under the desk, he shuffled through the stack of invoices. A hiss of sorts sounded between his teeth at the nine new sales. B J Jackson's signature was on the first three. "Way to go, Billy Joe."

Sheila Larken? Ah yes, my main sales lady could charm the britches off the male species, but the feminine spouses held tight to the purse strings making life somewhat difficult for the pretty sales lady. She made two of the nine sales, a Subaru Legacy and the used purple Sporty Subaru Impreza. "Hot, hot, hot," Bruce applauded the buyer of the purple eye catcher. "Lana Elkington," he let the name roll across his tongue. "The lucky broad landed a big one here, a real honey of a catch."

Tony, John and Lester each sold an Outback. "Good job guys," he looked around to the sound of his own voice. Hmmm must be losing it, he thought and set about verifying the credit ratings of each customer to find eight of them an easy sell. "But this one," he shook his head and positioned the invoice in front of him. "A first time charge and no co-signer." A hand to his chin while pondering the reasoning behind Sheila's intent, he shook his head and searched his mind for the right finance company. He felt beneath his chin again and yep, just as he thought, a nest of stubble he'd missed with the razor this morning.

"Excuse me Sir," a voice interrupts his train of thought.

His expression changed from who to *WOW!* What the hell is this thing rattling around in my chest? He smiled and locked in on the eyes of a fine looking young woman?

"May I help you?" he asked and pointed to the chair across the desk from him. "Please, please have a seat."

*   *   *

Chapter 2

Bruce couldn't help but wonder what the hell she was doing here and him feeling pretty much as he did the first time he asked a young lady to the movies. He was only fourteen at the time and now, a man of 28 and feeling much the same with nerve control as he did back then. He looked at her while trying not to stare at her eyes. Were they hazel with blue flecks or blue with...?

"I came in last night in search of this place and bought a car," she giggled and appearing somewhat ill at ease, took a deep breath and settled back into the chair.

"You bought a car?" Bruce pulled his eyes away from her face and shuffled through the invoices in front of him. He stole a sneak peek at her eyes again, only to find her long lashes hugging the color of mystery.

"Which car did you buy?"

"The purple Impreza."

Quickly turning his attention away from her tantalizing smile, he fingered the scatter of invoices. "Oh yes, here we are," he smiled across at her and down again to the invoice in front of him. "Your first charge, I see."

"Yes, it is." A look of confusion crossed her face. "Is there something wrong?"

"We usually get a co-signer on a first charge."

"That's not the reason I came in today. Uh...Sheila told me to come in and talk to you about the job opening for assistant bookkeeper."

"Oh!" he said and turned to the file cabinet. "Let me get you an application."

"Sheila gave me one and told me to bring it in today."

Bruce wasn't sure how it happened, but her purse tumbled from her lap to the floor. He moved out from behind the desk and settled into a squat alongside her, where a scatter of feminine gadgets lay at her feet.

"No, no." With a hand up to stop him, she smoothed out the folds in the application and held it up without looking at him. "I'll pick up this mess while you look it over."

With the feeling he was having scaring hell out of him at the moment, he leaned forward to sneak a sly peek across the desk to see if she was wearing a wedding ring. Her marital status still in question, he placed his hand on the desk palm side up. "Ugh… The Miss Lana Elkington in your application meets favorably with the qualifications I'm looking for."

Lana returned to her chair and with a shy like glance across the desk and gripping the purse in her lap with one hand, she reached for his hand with the other.

"My name is Bruce Lawson, by the way," he squeezed her dainty hand in a handshake and wanted to warm the chill of it next to his lips. "When can you come in?"

"Anytime, today…tomorrow…next week, whenever,"

she answered. "I just quit my old job a couple of days ago," she smiled across the desk and pulled her hand free to finger the paper in front of him. "It's all in the application there."

"Hmmm," he mumbles, a wolf after his prey. Guess I better watch how I handle this urge to wrap my arms around her, to taste and feel her lips on mine. "Better be on my best behavior," he said with a chuckle. Her long fingernails fascinated him, but left him to wonder how she managed the typewriter and adding machine.

"I work really hard, Mr. Lawson, and will learn whatever you throw at me," she spoke assuredly. "My aim is to become an asset to you and your business,"

"Are you available to come in tomorrow morning at 8?"

"Yes Sir," she smiled. "Sheila has already explained the benefits."

Having her underfoot all day and hiding the way I feel will not be easy, he reasoned with himself. "Another thing we must get straight before we can work together," he smiled and locked in on her eyes again to find them hazel with flecks of green. "We don't use the Sir word around here."

"I'll try to remember that," she smiled and appeared nervous again.

"Why don't I show you around today and give you an idea of what your position will be," he suggested in hopes of keeping her around for an hour or so longer. In the doorway of her office, he stopped and turned to find her almost rubbing up to the backside of him. Hiding a near to surface chuckle, he pointed to the desk. "The chair might be too low, try it out."

Almost as if she knew what to do, she rolled the chair up to the desk and smoothed her palms across the desk blotter. She reached for the adding machine and pulled it toward her.

"Pops will bring filing in every so often...oops I lied, Pops and I will fill your work basket every day." He pulled up a chair and sat down across the desk from her. "There will be lots of proofreading and correcting of mistakes made by Pops and myself."

"A lot of filing I see and yes, I do type." She tossed her long blond hair to one side and smiled up at him. She walked over to the file cabinets, pulled the drawer open and warmed him with her tantalizing smile again.

He hadn't noticed her dimples before and stood his ground when she moved in so close he could smell the aroma of her perfume. "Well, how about us going to Pop's office? You will be his working slave as well as mine."

He knocked on the ole man's door and ushered Lana inside. "This is our new proofreading assistant bookkeeper."

Pops rushed around his desk and reached for her hand. "Happy to see that Bruce's taste in help, brightens up our drab maleness. Glad to meet you...?"

"Lana Elkington, Sir."

"Oh no, no, the word sir is forbidden around here, I'm just plain Pops, honey." He returned to his chair and sat down behind the desk. "Why don't you show her around the place and introduce her to the sales and service people."

After a brief visit with the service department, they returned to the office. "I hope you don't expect me to remember all those names."

"That will come with time. Let's take a walk around the lot and stop at the snack room for donuts and coffee." Much to his disappointment and way too soon, Lana drank the last of her coffee and stood up to leave.

"See you in the morning," Bruce said, as he stood to one side while she unlocked her car and slid in behind the steering wheel. Once her gorgeous legs were tucked inside, he closed the door and backed away to return her wave and watch the purple Impreza pull across traffic into the left hand lane and speed away.

*   *   *

Chapter 3

Lana returned his wave and pulled across traffic into the fast lane and sped away. Just the thought of seeing the handsome hunk again the next day made her squeal with delight. She noticed his ring finger right off. No wedding band, he must be single! "I'm gonna marry that man one day, oh yeah," she screams, "and that's a promise I intend to keep Mr. Bruce Lawson, you can count on it."

Her eyes locked in on the rearview mirror in hopes that someone would see the turn signal and let her crowd in. Bruce had completely occupied her head dreams and paying little or no attention to the streets, her turn was coming up fast.

The bumper-to-bumper traffic refused to recognize

the demands of her right turn signal. "Keep your mind on the traffic, stupid girl, and think about that scrumptious hunk later." she fussed and eased into the center turn lane for a U turn on the green.

Lana whipped into her parking space, locked the Sporty Impreza and raced up the steps and into the apartment to find her roommate Samantha watching television. She let the door slam shut behind her and raced across the room to flop down on the couch. It was impossible to keep the excitement from gushing out, but she sat there in silence.

"What... why are you grinning like that?"

"I met my husband today."

"You what?"

"Met my husband. Watch my lips Sam. I-met-the-man-I'm-going-to-marry."

"Oh!" At a loss for words, Samantha sat there with her mouth hanging open.

"He is sooo grooovy, and handsome. His eyes wrapped around me like a fleece of brown velvet. I get goose pimples just thinking about it! I thought for sure I was going to faint at just the sound of his voice!"

"This is just a rebound thing," Sam said. "Think about it Lana, does it make good sense to rebound from David and fall in love with another man and think of him as your husband?"

"None of it makes sense, but when he shook my hand, I almost had a heart attack."

"Who the hell is this man? Do I know him?"

"Remember me telling you about my interview for the assistant bookkeeper position?"

Samantha could only stare at this friend who was acting like a complete stranger. "I remember. But you've always been the levelheaded one. Come on, get up and follow me."

"Where?"

"Outside" Samantha teased. "Come on Lana, get up. Let's go see what you did with my best friend."

"Sam, please. When I get to know him better I'll

prove it to you. I love him and I'm going to marry him one day."

Lana's glow was beginning to flicker, thanks to Samantha, and she was starting to have second thoughts. David was my main man and I was in love with him... or was I? It's for sure my heart was broken when he left me for a woman who would give him sex, or did it?

The memory of Bruce, the warmth in his eyes and smile make me feel beautiful. "Maybe what I felt for David wasn't love, because if Bruce wanted to lay me in the floor, I'm almost positive I would have opened my legs and let him have all of me, as many times as he wanted," Lana said, and suddenly felt her face flush, like when she was a little girl and stood in front of a hot wood stove.

"Oh my God Lana, I love Richard and never have I felt like that, but listening to you is getting me all worked up and wet between my legs."

Lana giggled at what Sam said. "Don't you have

that sick in the stomach feeling when you see him?"

"I used to, but its different now."

"Do you want to have sex with him?"

Samantha laughed. "Richard and I have sex, dummy."

Lana looked at Samantha in disbelief. It was almost like meeting her for the first time. "You never told me. I thought we told each other everything. Did it hurt?"

"Yes, but it felt good too."

While wondering how it would feel to make love with Bruce, Lana's heart began to pound against her rib cage. Perhaps I should talk to mother tonight and ask for advice on how to handle this out of control feeling about Bruce before I go in to work tomorrow. "Let's go see mother and dad, there's probably something good cooking on the range or in the oven."

"Got a date tonight with Richard," Sam said. "How about you come with us, maybe it'll calm you down, who knows, you might even find a handsome young man to get your mind off this guy."

"Thanks Sam, but no thanks." Lana grabbed her purse and keys off the table. "I'm going to mothers. You guys have a good time and I'll see you later to-night."

*   *   *

Chapter 4

Bruce sat at his desk for over an hour with Lana's purchase invoice on the desk in front of him. The pretty lady must be single? She wasn't wearing a wedding band. "I'm gonna marry that woman and that's a promise, Miss Lana Elkington," he muttered and kissed her signature on the employment application.

With purchase invoice in hand, he kissed her signature there also and since she was now an employee, he figured the 10% above cost allotted employees. Getting back to the other invoices, he reached for the phone to sell the eight purchases to their financial institution. Once the phone was in the cradle again, he fingered his light brown hair and appeared deep in thought until the tantalizing scent of Lana's perfume grabbed his sense of smell.

He whirled around to find Billy Joe standing in front of his desk instead of the lady on his mind, and pushing aside his disappointment he motioned his black salesman into the empty chair. "What have you got for me Billy Joe?"

"This is for a new Forester," BJ chuckled and tossed an offer on the desk. "Hated to bother you with his ridiculous offer, but told the man I had to bring it to the boss and would get back to him with a deal he couldn't refuse."

After taking a quick glance at the figures Bruce chuckled and shook his head. "No way, B Joe." With pencil in hand, he scribbled numbers on a piece of paper. "Show him the figures here and play it up as the best deal ever offered by this company," Bruce chuckled again and held the counter offer out to B Joe. "You made a pretty good chunk of change in commissions last night my man. Good work."

"Yeah, I'm gonna need it for sure," he admitted

openly. "With a new baby coming and all," Billy Joe turned with a laugh and looked back at his boss from the door. "I'll get back to you with the sales invoice, ha."

"You probably will," Bruce waved to him outside the window and caught sight of the old man. "Hey dad, what the hell brings you in here?"

"With the new employee coming in tomorrow," he raised his eyebrow and winks at his son. "I may take your mother on a cruise, our anniversary you know."

"It's about time you give mom a piece of the good life." Bruce moved around his desk to sit on the corner of it and look down at his father. "Where?"

"We fly in and out of Florida to San Juan, where we catch the ship for a ten day Caribbean cruise with excursions and island hopping along the way."

"Don't worry about taking time off, go show mom you got some good stuff left," he gave the ole man a shoulder punch.

"While I'm here may as well take Lana's application

son, and add her to the payroll."

"We can handle things around here Pops, no problem."

"The young lady is the right age son, how about the rest of her?"

"Dad!"

"Joshing son, just joshing," pops raised his left hand in surrender. "A grandbaby for mama and me to spoil might be fun."

Bruce waved the ole man away while thinking about Lana and trying to come up with a plan in which to handle these tender feelings. With eyes shut tight, he found the love of his life easy on his mind and could feel the scent of her perfume surrounding him like dainty arms around his neck. Her presence and fragrance was all around him and daring to hope she had returned he opened his eyes to find Sheila smiling down at him.

"Well...did you hire her?"

"Yes I did. She has all the qualities I'm looking for, and a little more."

"How does she like the car?"

"Loves it, I guess. We really didn't get around to that."

"Better get back to work. See you boss," Sheila left him with a wave and a kinky smile.

*   *   *

Chapter 5

Lana found the door was locked and stole a peek in the front window to see her dad sitting at the table. She put a thumb to the doorbell and loved the sound of musical chimes inside the house, vowing to have door chimes like that when she marries Bruce.

The door opened and Lana moved into the safety of her father's arms for a hugs, kisses and words of sweet endearment.

"Hello sweetheart," Mother Elkington said while waiting at the table with open arms for her only child. She pointed to the kitchen range. "Roast beef tonight, honey, help yourself if you're hungry."

"You're going to have to teach me how to cook some hungry man dishes."

"Is that a hint dear? You and David kiss and make up?"

"Remember that assistant bookkeeper position I was telling you about? Well, I got it and my new boss is, oh! So handsome."

She returned her daddy's smile and made a request, one that was almost too embarrassing to make. "Close your ears, daddy, because you don't want to hear what I'm about to say."

"What makes you think that, Sis? Do you think I'm too old to hear what my beautiful daughter has to say?"

"Yeah, I do, because today I'm coming down off that pedestal you put me on. I found me a new man and he has won me over, body and soul."

"Honey, I have owned your mama's body and soul from the first day we met. Are you pregnant?"

"Daddy! For heaven's sake, we just met, but it could happen any day now cause all he has to do is look at me and I feel completely out of control." Lana looked at her father but couldn't read his expression. "I have never felt like this before."

"You're my daughter and whatever you do, my love for you will never change, but I wish you would wait until I give you away to this man."

Confused by the grin on her mother's face, she quickly glanced down at her plate. "This pot roast is so tender I can cut it with a fork." She turned to her father, to find the same sly grin on his face as well. "What's going on here mother? Daddy?"

"You want to tell her mama or do you want me to?"

"Tell me what?"

"Well dear, what I said about me and your mama is true. We fell so madly in love on our first date we couldn't help ourselves."

"Daddy! Did you and mother make love on your first date?"

"Not only that, my daughter" mother said and smiled at dad. "You were conceived on that first date. You are our love child and every time we look at you, it brings back our wonderful first night together."

"And what a night it was, Sweet Thing," Elkington said as he came around the table to hug and kiss the top of his daughter's head.

"You never told me," Lana said and laughed at the thought of her coming to tell them her secret. "Meee, a love child? Wow!"

"Who is this young man, dear?" her father needled.

"He and his dad own the Subaru Dealership in Troutdale. I start work tomorrow morning." Just thinking of him sitting at his desk, the way he was when she went into the office, made it hard for her to breathe.

"Love at first sight is hard to come by honey and when it does it nearly floors you," mother said and looked to dad for confirmation.

"Was it love at first sight for you and daddy?"

"That it was, baby."

"Do you think he might feel the same way?"

Elkington shrugged his shoulder. "If he does, you'll find out soon enough."

She grinned at her father and wondered what

tomorrow will bring. Her heartbeat became so rapid she could feel the throb of it in her throat, making her breathing sound like a gasp. "Don't know if I like falling in love."

"When it's all out in the open and you know how he feels, the wrinkles of doubt will smooth out," mother said and smiled at her husband.

"But mother, you said the first time you and daddy had sex, it hurt as bad going in as a baby does coming out, remember?"

"What mama is saying dear, the pain is not worth a romp under the covers with just any meatball."

* * *

Chapter 6

Lana returned to the apartment she shared with Samantha and noticed Richard's outback parked nearby. Thinking her entrance might meet with an embarrassing situation, she knocked before barging into the room.

"Hey, Lana, just the gal I've been waiting for," Richard said. "Me and Sam want you to double date with a friend of mine."

"I'm not much for blind dates, Richard."

"He's really a swell guy, I swear," Richard crossed his heart and followed her to the kitchen. "We joined the National Guard together and hell, if I was a woman I could go for him in a big way."

She pointed to the glass in his hand. "That looks good."

"I'll mix you one and me another," he said and downed what was left in his glass. "Sam's in the bathroom," he called back over his shoulder. "How about it Lana, want to try a date with my friend tomorrow night?""

"I don't know Richard, tomorrow's my first day on a new job and I might not make a very good first impression on your friend."

"He's a good catch for any woman," Richard chuckled and held the drink out to her. "I know you two will like each other."

"This is just what I needed," she said and followed the first sip with a second. "I'll have to think about it." She took the mixed drink to her bedroom and wondered what Bruce would think about her going on a blind date. Would he go on one? A good-looking man like him probably wouldn't have to. Damn, I hadn't thought of that, he may already have a special someone. Heartbroken with the very thought of it, she walked out of her bedroom to find Samantha waiting in the hallway.

"Come on Lana and make it a foursome tomorrow night. Richard's friend is a really nice guy. I could go for him myself if I wasn't already hung up on Richard."

"Okay Sam, I'll go," she said and turned for the bathroom. "What time?"

Samantha yelled down the hall to Richard and after Lana heard his 7:30 answer, she went into the bathroom to take a shower. She dried off and lets the towel fall down around her feet in front of the full-length mirror. Massaging her body with sweet smelling lotion in all the reachable places she wondered what it would feel like to make love in the shower, and the thought of being naked in the shower with Bruce made her tingle all over.

She closed the door to her bedroom and hopped into bed with a short prayer for immediate sleep. "Please Lord, Amen."

"Goodnight my darling, until we meet tomorrow morning," she whispered into the darkness and could feel her body tremble with anticipation. She put a hand between her legs to put pressure on the throb of excitement. "Goodnight little puss, we have met the man who's worth the pain, now go to sleep and one day soon he may honor us with his love tool."

*   *   *

Chapter 7

The sound of a door closing brought Bruce around to wave his good friend into the office. "Hey Richard, my good buddy," he pointed to the empty chair across the desk from him and frowned at his watch. "What the hell you doing out and about this early?"

"Samantha and I have a new gal for you to meet...a real looker"

"Before you ask, the answer is no, definitely not!"

"Come on Bruce, her and Samantha are best friends. You won't be sorry, I promise."

"If she's so good, how come I've never met her?"

"She finally broke up with this spoiled rich boy, a real loser believe me, and has agreed to the blind date. Please Bruce, don't make me break her heart."

"Unless she's a cute little gal with short black hair, a twinkle in her eye, a dimple in her chin and plump ruby lips, I'm not interested."

"Hey," Richard laughed. "I know a little gal that looks like that, but she's hung up on a friend of yours."

"Just sporting, but you know how I hate blind dates."

"I know ole buddy and I promised never to do it again, but..." he smiled across at Bruce with a whistle and moved his hands in an hourglass shape.

"That good huh? Reminds me of the gorgeous lady I met yesterday, Bro," Bruce said and moved his hands to match Richard's hourglass shape. "Just the thought of her brings unrest to my stomach, but she's sure as hell easy on my mind, thought about her all damn night."

"Well...?" Richard asked, with a smile and a sparkle of mischief in his brown eyes. "This gal has long blond hair and hazel eyes, better than last time."

Bruce reluctantly agreed to the date and watched the backside of his friend walk out the door. He shook his head, must be losing my mind to go along with this dumb idea. He shook his head again and turned his attention to the paper work on his desk. The National Guard meeting tonight suddenly came to mind and feeling the need to remind Richard, he turned to the door just as it opened.

"By the way," Richard said. "The meeting tonight has been called off. You probably have an email to that effect from Commander Markham on your computer. See you tonight, a little after 7:30."

Bruce thought of the day when the two of them joined the Army National Guard. Age 20 and hell bent on fighting for our country. He laughed at the memory of hell and hard work during basic training.

For the past seven years all had been quiet until this shit about weapons of mass destruction and a possible war in Iraq. Bruce shrugged his shoulders at the thought of a war looming in his future. "With Lana here to help, dad will more than likely be able to handle the business without me," he thought aloud. "Guess I better see if my gal can handle the work load before I go traipsing all over Iraq."

✳   ✳   ✳

Chapter 8

A glance at the time brought a quick adrenalin rush. The pile of paper work, sorted and stacked in front of him, was ready and waiting for Lana's arrival. Bruce looked out to find Billy Joe and John Babbitt standing in the parking lot taking a cigarette break.

The purple Impreza pulled into the lot and parked alongside Sheila's outback. There was a sudden jolt of electricity to the main circuit in his heart, sending a surge of blood through his body like a runaway train.

Billy Joe rushed up to her and the two of them became lost in conversation until John Babbitt joined them and reached out for her hand. With a wave to the two salesmen, Lana turned toward the office.

Bruce met her at the door and pretending the jolt to

his heart hadn't happened, introduced her to the paper work on his desk. Once her knees fit snuggly under the desk, he pulled his chair dangerously close alongside to explain the work assignment. The manner in which she took the papers and began to work them up came as a surprise.

Her perfume brought on another adrenalin rush, sending his male hormones scampering for cover. With the need to escape the flush of her nearness, he excused himself to the restroom. He returned to his seat more in control of his sexual urge, and watched the magical hands of this wonder woman performing miracles.

"Would you like to check my work before I start another set of sales papers?"

"Very good, let's finish this before we start on another one. I called the credit bureau earlier to find Mr. and Mrs. Prescott's purchase an easy sale to our financial institution." He centered the invoice on the desk in front of her. "Are you game?"

She looked up at Bruce with a smile of sorts and

reached for the telephone.

"The man you will talk to is a Mr. Alan Ranger." He scribbled the name on a note pad and pushed it in front of her. "Alan is a pleasant man and will talk to you through the sale one step at a time."

Lana dialed the number in front of her and inhaled deeply just as someone picked up the phone at the other end."Hello, Mr. Alan Ranger please?" She looked around at Bruce with a fearful look in her eyes, but her smile said otherwise. "Hello Mr. Ranger, Lana here with Lawson and Lawson Subaru."

"Yes I am, since yesterday." She smiled into the mouthpiece. "Thank you, I hope so." She read off the invoice and answered questions with a sureness that surprised even Bruce. He caught her smile and the twinkle in her eye and knew right off, she did a good sale.

"Was that hard?"

"I really hate to admit this, to my boss especially, but I was scared shitless and couldn't control the tremor in my voice."

"Well my dear lady, you could have fooled me. Scared shitless, huh?"

"I'm sorry Sir, I shouldn't have said that, it just slipped out."

Bruce looked around behind him and back again to Lana with a shrug. "I thought perhaps someone important might have snuck in unnoticed because the Sir word is strictly forbidden around here."

"I'm sorry Bruce. Let's take a break to the coffee room and I'll buy."

"You're on." He followed her and without awareness of what he was doing, put his arm around her waist and it felt good...real good. I will marry this woman, he vowed, and make her an important part of my life and my business.

He pulled out a chair for her and took up the one next to it. He couldn't help but feel she was sizing him up. "Care for a donut?"

"Yes please, a maple bar," she smiles.

"A favorite of mine too."

When he finished his coffee and maple bar and was licking the sticky off his fingers, he stood to his feet. "You ready?" he said and upon her answer with a nod, he slipped her arm through his.

*   *   *

Chapter 9

Bruce tossed a new set of paper work on the desk in front of Lana. "These sales are the ones Jim Lancaster put into the computer last night. The forms are signed and ready to be filed. See the icon 'CONTRACTS' there on the desk top?"

"Yes. Do you want me to click on it?"

"Yes and move down to yesterday's date. Double check these forms to see if they have been entered correctly. I've never found a mistake in his work but." He smiled at the pretty lady seated across the desk from him, fascinated with the beautiful manicured nails and the speed with which they flew across the keyboard.

"They look good to me, but then I don't know if I know what to look for."

"Close out the screen and now on the desk top again, look for the icon 'FORMS' and click on it. Let's take this sale that Jim worked up and find the forms he used. You will receive sales information from Russ Littlejohn every day, remember him?"

"Was he the Indian, or should I say...I don't know what to say, but yes, I think I do."

"You will notice certain numbers on the Oregon Motor Vehicle Purchase Order form are fixed. Type in the buyer information, new car info trade-in info and itemize each step from the purchase invoice and let the computer do the rest."

She put her hand to the seat next to her. "Sit here with me while I enter this sale."

Bruce was amazed at the speed in which she completed the first form. He looked it over and finding all spaces filled and decimal points positioned correctly, he smiled. "Good job… print it and let's have another look."

"When will Mr. and Mrs. Lambskin come in to sign

the papers?"

"Just as soon as you have all the forms ready...now press the return arrow and click on the next form."

Lana had no more than completed the final form when the Lambskins stepped into the office and sat in the chairs Bruce pulled out for them. Lana placed the first form to be signed across from her and smiled at the couple. "This will only take ten minutes or so and we will have you on your way in a brand new Legacy." She went on to explain each form to the couple, tore the customer copy out to put in a folder and the rest she put aside for proper documentation.

Bruce backed out of his office and went to hers. He hooked up her new computer and played around with it to ensure the computer expert had it up and running properly. He returned to his office to find a new couple signing papers. Holy Cow! How could I ask for anything more, he wondered and stepped into the room to stand beside her. A kiss now and then perhaps, he thought and felt flush when she answered his thoughts with a smile.

He picked up the paper work and returned to Lana's new office. With phone in hand and all but the last button punched, he let her sell the three charges to their financial institution...

"Are you busy?" Lana stood there, oh so beautiful and smiling down at him. He cradled the phone and looked at the folders she tossed on the desk. "You want to look these over?"

"Go into your new computer here and check for any mistakes you might have made." He chuckled and let her have the chair but stood nearby to look over the finished forms.

"How did you set it up so fast, the computer I mean?" she asked.

"It was programmed and ready but not hooked up. These forms my dear, look great. I can't believe the speed in which you picked up, what I thought to be difficult."

"Thank you, Sir Bruce," she laughed.

"Are you hungry?"

"Do you always make your people labor through the lunch hour?"

He looked at his watch, apologized and offered to buy her lunch.

"Oh no, it's too late. I have a dinner date tonight."

"Yeah, me too," Bruce said and wondered about her date for tonight. Is he special? Could she be in love with someone else?

"Since we both have dates with special people," she smiled sweetly. "We should get busy and tackle the pile of paper work here on my desk."

"I don't know about special people, but we better get a move on."

Later, the work finished and filed away, Bruce walked Lana to her car and waved, keeping an eye on the back of it until it disappeared from sight. He wondered about her date tonight and felt a tinge of jealousy. Feeling the need to talk, he went to Pop's office.

"Come in son, come in and sit down."

"She is one smart lady, Pops. I am really hot for her and I don't know what to do about it. If I let her know how I feel, it might scare her off and that would be a huge loss for all of us, because she can handle that computer better than I can."

"Just don't rush it son, you got lots of time to pursue the young lady."

*   *   *

Chapter 10

The living room, in dire need of maid service, met him at the threshold before he shut the door and entered the room. With an armful of clothes, fifty percent clean and the other half dirty, two pairs of shoes and the Oregonian, he opened the closet door and tossed them inside.

He backed out into the room with a clothes hanger in each hand, his favorite shirt on one and a pair of black slacks on the other. Shaved, showered and ready, he looked at the clock to find it half past seven at the very same time a knock sounded at the door.

"Hey!" Bruce looked over Richard's shoulder and into the back seat to catch a glimpse of his date, but tinted windows foiled his attempt. "Do the girls want to come in for a drink first?"

"Not now, we'll have cocktails at the restaurant before dinner and from there, we take the pretty ladies to the dance floor for a warm snuggle."

Bruce wasn't so sure about that, but locked his front door and dropping the jangle of keys in his pocket, he followed Richard to the car.

*   *   *

Chapter 11

Lana's heart began to beat wildly when she caught sight of Bruce walking toward the car. Her eyes held to his face when he opened the door and froze momentarily. Wondering why this handsome man is going out on a blind date, of all things, she smiled up at him. He must have lots of women after his beautiful body. "Hello Mr. Lawson," she trembled slightly at the nearness of him.

What the hell is with this Mr. Lawson shit, he wanted to say, but slid in beside her and heard her sharp intake of breath when he put her cold hand to his lips. "Hello Lana, fancy seeing you again so soon."

Lana tapped Samantha on the shoulder. "Sam, this is the man I was telling you about, my new boss."

"Is this the lady you were telling me about?" Richard asked.

"Yep, in the flesh," he smiled at the pretty lady and she was quick to return his smile. "You did reeeal good this time Richard, but don't do it again because I'll be too busy," he smiled down at Lana again and bumps his shoulder to hers.

"Lana told me about her new job and she was quite taken by you Bruce," Samantha called into the back seat.

"Samantha!" Lana shrieked with embarrassment. "Our man talk is just between you and me, remember?"

"Sorry Lana."

She lookd down at the hand on the seat between them urging her to close the distance between them and thought she was going to pass out. "Don't let this get you down because men say sweet things about the beautiful women they meet. Take today, I told Richard about you and how hot you were."

"You didn't."

"Oh yes indeedy."

Richard found a parking space near the door and wheeled his car into it. "Well, here we are," he called back over the seat. "The Cattle Company."

They were caught inside with a line waiting to be seated. Richard stepped up to the lady in charge of reservation. "Graves for four."

They had no more than sat down when the waitress steps up to the table with menus for each of them. Richard ordered a bottle of merlot and looks for a nod in agreement from Bruce. "Did I ever tell you about my millionaire friend in Fresno?"

When the bottle of wine appeared, quickly followed by the salad and bread, the foursome settles back into their seats while waiting for Richard to fill each glass and make his quick salutation before taking a greedy sip. "He owns the Aladdin Bar and Lounge now and invited me to spend some time with him at his cabin in Bass Lake. We'll have to look into that Bruce, who knows, it might be fun."

Bruce answered, but it sounded more like a grunt

than a yeah.

To shield the tenderness of falling in love, Lana fondled the menu, making sure she had it right end up while pretending to read. *How the hell can I work for this man and hide my feelings from him?*

Bruce tried not to stare at the beautiful lady seated next to him, but earlier…when she hurriedly snatched up the menu and remembering they had skipped a lunch today, he felt to blame for her hunger. He stole another look to see her rubbing her arms. "Are you cold?"

"A little," she answered and just as he put his arm around her shoulder, the steaks replaced the salad bowls. He caught her sneaking peeks at him through dinner and wondered at her curiosity.

Bruce sat back away from the table to let the busboy clear away the dirty dishes. His stomach felt queasy, but it wasn't from hunger, it was the close proximity of the lady seated next to him. He slipped his credit card on the tray with the ticket and turned back to Lana again.

"It is a little nippy in here."

Richard began talking about his friend again. "His employer made him partner in the bar business and when the man died, he left everything to Larry, making him a multi millionaire." He tried to grab the ticket away from Bruce. "This is my party, bro."

"Your turn next time."

"Okay, first round of drinks on me when we get to the Dew Drop Inn," Richard said and helped Samantha on with her coat.

Bruce followed his lead and helped Lana on with hers. He slipped an arm around her waist and when she laid her head on his chest, he wondered if she could hear the rocky unrest in his heart.

Bruce opened the back door and watched Lana struggle with holding her dress down when she moved to the center of the seat. He smiled at the invitation in her eyes and quickly slid into the back seat before she had second thoughts and moved to the far side of the car. He put one arm around her shoulder and a hand across her stomach to pull her snug against him for body warmth. She laid her hand on his knee and it was good.

Bruce lowered his head to where his lips were so close he could smell her sweet breath and wondered, will she or will she not touch her lips to mine for the kiss I have waiting for her? He caught a flutter of confusion in her eyes before she accepted his invitation and the sky suddenly filled with fireworks on the 4th of July.

He pulled her snug against him and turned to the window, fighting the urge to confess his feelings for her.

"Is something wrong?"

"No dear, everything's right with the world as far as I'm concerned," he kissed her nose to make light of what he was feeling and looked up when Richard pulled into the parking lot and parked near the entrance of the Dew Drop Inn.

He opened the door and stood waiting with his hand out to help Lana out of the car, tucked her arm through his and reached around her to shut the door.

*   *   *

Chapter 12

Once in the dance hall, the ladies went to the restroom while Richard and Bruce found a table near the dance floor. The singer was no Andy Williams, but who the hell gives a damn how good the man sings *Moon River*. All I want is the feel of this woman in my arms. He saw her coming his way and waited with his hand out to the beautiful lady, who apparently had eyes only for him.

The dance floor was crowded, but what the hell, they didn't need a lot of room. It felt so right being here with the woman he loved, but he worried too about scaring her off. Pushing all caution aside, he put his lips to her ear. "Do you think we can work together without eating each other up or am I taking too much for granted?"

She stood on tiptoe to whisper in his ear. "Not for me."

He waltzed her around the floor. Why stop now, he argues, may as well go all the way. "I intend to marry you woman, don't know when or where, but you will be my wife one day."

Lana inhaled sharply and leaned back to search his face. "I'll be more than happy to share my life with you."

"Richard's in love with Samantha," Bruce said with thoughts of a double wedding on his mind. Like Siamese twins we are, Richard and me, why not have the same wedding day? "Does Samantha love Richard?"

"Oh yes, without a doubt."

The dance ended and torn between waiting for another dance with Lana or hitting Richard with a thought that was almost too daring to put in words, he laced Lana's arm through his at about the time the band started to play and waltzed her to the table. He sat down and leaned forward with both elbows on the table to look Richard in the eye. "I know we talked about when we were married, what we would do and where we would vacation," he waited for a reaction. "Why don't we marry these ladies?"

"Damn Bruce, this is kind of sudden," Richard said with a look of disbelief. "Are you serious?"

"Damn right, you and Sam have been a couple for a longtime now and I..."

"You meet a girl and want to marry her the same night?" Richard shakes his head. "The friend I've known for half my life would never ever make a snap decision of this importance."

Bruce sat there, his eyes on Richard, telling him more than words ever could. "I met this lady and fell in love with her yesterday."

"I know our little women are sweet and lovely to look at but," he makes eye contact with Samantha. "Why the hell not? How about it Samantha Harris, will you marry me?"

"Oh my God Richard!" she leaned toward him and put her hand to his brow. "This is kinda sudden! Are you sure?" Disbelief filled her eyes until she glanced around to see Lana nod her head. "Yes, yes, before you change your mind."

Bruce smiled across the table at his two friends and turned to Lana, letting his eyes linger on her face. This is so right, he thought, I could close my eyes and still feel the perfection of our love. "I want to spend the rest of my life with you, Lana. Will you marry me?"

"Yes, I will," she whispers softly and could read in his eyes how complete their life will be, living together as husband and wife.

"Why are you two so quiet?" Richard asked with a look of confusion "You having second thoughts about this idea of yours?"

Bruce pulled his eyes away from Lana. "Are you crazy, man? Why the hell would I let this lady get away?" He palmed her hand and walked her to the dance floor. He pushed her away to take in first one dimple to the right of her smile and another on the left and look deep into her hazel eyes with blue flecks. Feeling the unrest of his male hormones, he pulls her to the front of him with a groan and found her delicate neck with lip nibbles. "My love for you will be complete the day we stand before the minister and exchange vows."

"I am so lucky," she whispered, "to have met you."

"You're lucky! Oh baby, if anybody's lucky it's this man," Bruce said and remembered the times he thought he was in love. Thank God for unanswered prayers and the high power of knowing the difference between love and that other feeling he thought was love.

With arms around each other and their feet unaware of the floor beneath them, they moved toward the table. Bruce scraped her chair legs across the floor until it was touching his and sat with his arm around her shoulder while she snuggles against him with her head on his shoulder.

"All right you two lovers," Samantha murmured.

"Let's get back to the double wedding."

"Wedding plans are the bride's responsibility, don't you agree Bruce?"

"I agree," he answered. "Just don't make it a long drawn out affair."

*   *   *

Chapter 13

Richard sat waiting behind the steering wheel, his car idling while Bruce walked the ladies to the door. When he settled into passenger's seat and slammed the car door, Bruce noticed the frown on Richard's face. "What's up Bro, having second thoughts?"

"Not me, but hell Bruce, you only met the lady today."

"Oh no Richard, I met her yesterday and fell in love with her the same day. Tonight was the awakening of that love."

"For a man who's always been hard to please when it comes to women, what the hell happened? You sure it's love and not a sexual thing?"

"It's not infatuation, if that's what you're thinking.

Her eyes Richard, damn... Did you look at her eyes?"

"What happens if we're shipped to Iraq?" Richard stared straight ahead at the traffic. "What the hell do we do about the wedding? I read more in that email from the captain than was in print. Why did they cancel our meeting tonight?"

"There could be numerous reasons," Bruce argued. "It'll probably be a year or more before they get their shit together and know what the hell they're doing, but if they ship us out, I want my cake fully frosted and waiting for me when I come home."

Richard parked the car near Bruce's apartment and let the motor run while they talked. "I have a couple of weeks before the folks leave on their cruise and if Lana is willing, I want us to be married before then."

"I can think of worse things than being married, but...what the shit," Richard gave Bruce a fist bump to the shoulder. "I'm ready if you are."

"If we go to war with Iraq, dad's gonna need help. Seriously Richard, I kid you not, Lana can handle the job now, but I want a year or more to live and work with her before I leave."

"Tell you what Bruce, let's sleep on it. Tomorrow might be a good day for a wedding," he chuckles softly. "Maybe spend a couple of days in Reno for a honey-moooon."

It took the men six days to convince the girls to get married in Reno and one day for them to buy their wedding dresses and load their luggage into the car.

*   *   *

Chapter 14

Bruce lifted the veil and trembled as he looked upon the beauty before him. In slow motion and ever so gently his lips found hers. He took the feminine softness of his beautiful wife into his arms and accepted the complete package as his very own. "I promise to hold fast to my wedding vows and to love you all the days of my life."

"I have never felt as right about anything in my life as I do in our marriage," she touched her lips to his again. "And I promise to love you for as long as I live and into the hereafter."

Standing outside the bridal suite with his delicate bride in his arms, Bruce fed his key into the lock and kicked the door open with his foot. He backed into it and upon the click of the lock, carried his lovely wife to the bed and lowered the two of them onto the edge of it. "Have I told you how much I love you, Mrs. Lawson, and how easy you rest on my mind?"

"Yes you have and I love you back more." She kissed his cheek and giggled like a schoolgirl. "Have you ever made out with a virgin?"

"Can't say that I have, why?"

"I'm going to the bathroom to change," she kissed him on the lips and struggled out of his arms. "I have a surprise for you my darling," she called over her shoulder.

Lying in bed with his eyes on the bathroom door, Bruce waited patiently for his surprise. Lana suddenly appeared in the room but tortured him with a slow shuffle toward the bed. He smiled in spite of it and hungered for the beauty beneath the thin white negligee.

His heart was pounding like crazy and he found it hard to breathe. Gently pulling her into bed, he snuggled her partly beneath him, his lips moving from her lips to her ears and down her neck to the shoulder. The struggle with animal control was near to impossible and his fingers felt much too large and clumsy for the delicate ties. Like magic, her negligee suddenly fell open and caressing the wonder before his eyes, he kissed her breast, first one nipple and then the other. He could feel her tremble beneath him.

"Honey, be gentle with me, please," she whispered and drew in her breath sharply when she felt his hand between her legs.

"I will baby, I will," he whispers thickly between nibbles down her stomach.

Oh my God, she moaned silently and rolled to her back. With her legs wide apart she reached out for him wanting the feel of him inside her. "Oh God, honey."

Fighting the urge to break through the forbidden cherry in a hurry and trying not to cause her pain it was all over before it began. He'd managed to sink about half his erection inside her before turning control over to the throbbing escape of happy sperm cells.

I'm sure as hell proud to be the first with her, but never realized how damn hard it was to make love with a virgin. Her silence concerned him and wondering if she was crying, he put his arm around her and palmed her stomach. "I'm sorry honey."

"I love you, darling," she said. "Maybe tomorrow morning I can do better."

"It was my fault sweetheart...I couldn't hold it." He held her close and kissed her goodnight. "I love you Mrs. Lawson."

"You were so gentle and patient my darling husband and I love you more now than I thought possible."

*   *   *

Chapter 15

Six months into the marriage, and seeing very little of Richard and Samantha since the double wedding, Lana entered her husband's office with two cups of coffee. "Is there a laborer in here wanting a cup of steaming hot coffee and a woman with a twenty minute break on her hands to join him?"

He took the cup in one hand and put the other hand on her stomach. For a couple of months now she's been gaining weight, but how the hell do you approach a woman about her weight without making her self-conscious? If I ask if she's pregnant and she's not, how do I explain the reasoning behind the question, oh what the hell? "Is there something you haven't told me? Like a secret I don't know about?"

"I was curious as to how long it would take you to notice how fat I'm getting," she laughed and turned around to model her figure. "You like?"

"You're pregnant?"

"Do you want me to be?"

"Come on, honey, tell me."

"In about three months, my darling husband, you'll be changing diapers and holding a bottle to the mouth of a little boy or girl."

"Oh my God! Here honey sit down," he fought against her resistance and forced her into the chair in front of his desk and cleared a corner of it to sit down. Dumfounded as what to say next, he picked up his cup and while taking a sip now and then, her eyes flirted with him over the brim of hers.

She looked at him expectantly. "Are you excited?"

"I'm damn excited, too damn excited to sit still. Let's go tell Pops."

They barged in the ole man's office without knocking and Bruce turned Lana sideways. "See anything different, Pops?"

Pops looked at the two of them with a frown, but with a look of excitement in his eyes. "I'd much rather you tell than have me guess."

"In three months you're going be a grandpa...we're having a baby," Lana said.

Momentarily stunned and unmoving, Pops suddenly pushed his chair against the wall and rushed around the desk. "Help her to a chair, son. A baby!"

"I don't want you men treating me like an invalid," her voice rose into what sounded like an order. "That's why I didn't tell you, I'm a normal healthy pregnant woman, so don't handle me with gloved hands, please."

"Oh honey, not even for a little while?"

They both laughed at the whiney sound in Pops voice but unaware of what they were laughing at, he continued in the same whiney voice. "There's not a hell of a lot of time left to pamper you dear. That's a Lawson baby you have in the cradle honey, my grandchild."

"Okay, but only for the last month," Lana said and

laughed at the facial expression on their faces. "There's a lot of work to be done, and I say we do it."

Bruce put his arm around her waist and walked her back to his office. He rubbed her stomach and felt the little bugger kick. "Is that what I think it was?"

"Oh, you mean that drop kick to your hand?"

This is all so aggravating, he thought with a touch of anger, months of being an expectant father lost and there's not a damn thing I can do to get it back. "Honey please, giving me a baby is a precious gift and you treat it so lightly."

Lana stood up to face him and ever so slowly and very very sexy...well as sexy as a pregnant lady can perform, she snuggles her and the baby into his arms. "I love you darling, but you'll never know how scared I was when the doctor told me I was pregnant. We never talked about starting a family." She stood on tiptoes to kiss his chin. "I have great news, darling, we're going to have a baby. I think we got pregnant on our wedding night."

Bruce shook his head and realized what a lousy husband he was not to have noticed the sparkle of motherhood in her eyes. "Lord Honey only three months left."

"I'm sorry, darling."

"Come to think about it Sweetheart, I didn't think I got enough of my tool inside you to home in on the sperm target."

"Oh yeah honey, one little bugger was like his parents, go after what you want and don't turn back."

*   *   *

Chapter 16

Bruce marked an X on his desk calendar, to find three weeks left to go before the due date. He was particularly interested in Lana's expression when she came into his office to sit down at the desk across from him. I love the way her stomach cradles my unborn child, he marveled, and the way she reached into the paper bag and comes out with a sandwich between her dainty fingers.

He burned his lip on the hot hazel nut mocha but flirts with her just the same, through the steam swirls above the cup. With the corner of his sandwich between his teeth, he bit down and searched the face of his very pregnant wife for signs of pain. She teases him with a smile like always, but this one was different somehow, more secretive.

"Are we having a baby?" He moved to her side of

the desk and put his arm across her shoulder. "Are we having pains? Here sweetheart, stay where you are. I'll call to let dad know we're leaving for the hospital."

"Calm down honey, we still have 31/2 weeks to go."

"Three. We have three weeks but who the hell's counting," Bruce said with a pen and paper in hand. He clears a part of his desk and answered the phone to find Richard on the other end.

"Well friend," he said. "A special meeting has been called for tonight. You probably have the details in your e-mail."

"Does it sound like we're going?"

"Yep," he answered. "But you know how it is, every-thing so secretive and all. I just hope to hell they don't send us to Iraq right away, at least let us get used to the idea."

Bruce waved to Lana when she stopped in the doorway before leaving for her office. He turned to the computer and logged in to his e-mail. He sat there for a while after reading the call to meeting, his mind on Pops and Lana and how best to approach them with the news. He needed more time to see his baby before he leaves, for chrissakes.

He loved Lana more than life itself and leaving the e-mail on the computer for her to read was a chicken's way. However tempting the chicken's way was, he faced her like a man and told her the news. Her acceptance of it nearly floored him.

"If you ship out, I will be with you all the way, and don't forget, there's always e-mail." She smiled up at him and suddenly without warning, her bravery fell apart. "Oh hoooney!"

"Please baby, don't cry." He held her close while she cried into his chest, his vision blurry with tears as well. With his face buried into her shoulder and tears mixed with his kisses to her neck; he repeated a part of their wedding vow dearest to his heart. "I will love you and only you for as long as we both shall live.

"What the hell?" Pops voice sounded from the doorway. "What happened?"

They whirled around to find him looking at them.

Bruce explained as best he could, and let the old man read the e-mail.

"I thought I was ready for this son, but...I don't know. It scares hell out of me."

"We'll know more after the meeting tonight." Bruce squeezed his wife's shoulder and stepped away to look at his dad. "I want you to take care of this little woman, should I have to leave. I know the two of you will have no problem with the business, but lonely is a sickness and only an overflow of love can help numb the pain."

He looked out the window to see rows and rows of new Subaru's and catches Billy Joe talking with a customer. Lord I'll miss this, he thought, Lana and my unborn child, the folks, oh shit, I haven't left and I miss them already. He felt a hand on his shoulder and looked around into the face of his father, to see the pain in his eyes and feel the pain in his chest.

"Let's not do this to us, we don't know yet..." Lana put her arms around her husband, and Pops threw his arm around both of them. "We may be getting worked up over nothing."

"Come by the house after the meeting tonight," pop suggested and turned toward the door. "Mama will want to see you. We should have dinner before you leave, one that will last you for awhile."

"We don't know that he's leaving yet, please...please, you're breaking my heart and there's time enough for that when the time comes." Lana turned away and covered her face with both hands. She dried her eyes, threw her shoulders back and sat down at her desk to busy her fingers and mind on work.

Bruce watched his father leave the office and at a loss for words he left Lana with a kiss on her cheek and returned to his office.

He was too antsy to sit still and left the office to spend time with his salesmen. Both sad and happy to see Billy Joe and Tony LaPause with customers, he sat down across the table from John Babbitt and told him the possibility of his going to war. Shortly after, Babbitt left and one by one, his crew of sales people came into the room to wish him luck.

"Hey boss," Sheila sat down beside him. "Is what I'm hearing the truth?"

"I'll know more after the meeting."

"How's Lana taking it?"

"Same as any wife I suppose. Official transfer orders may come through tonight and maybe not. Perhaps with a little luck, I'll have a week or so before the Government ships my butt out."

"The grapevine just reached me, Boss," Billy Joe pulled a chair up between him and Sheila. "Sorry for crowding in Sheila, but I have a customer waiting and I need a quick word with Bruce. Is what I'm hearing true?"

"I'll know more after the meeting tonight. I want you people to sell so many cars, my wife won't have time to worry about me."

Billy Joe grabbed his hand, "good luck boss, just want you to know, prayers from me and my church family will follow your every move."

* * *

Chapter 17

Bruce entered the accounting office. He'll probably forget the smelly paper, but the wonderful aroma of his wife's perfume will forever be etched in his memory. He stood in the doorway of Lana's office, his eyes on her fingers and the speed with which they play the numbers on the ten key.

She suddenly stopped and stared off into space, and feeling her thoughts closing in on him, he hugged her worries to his chest. Turning away from the door, he leaned against the wall in the hallway and reached for a handkerchief.

Silence fell in the room again before the pain in her words tore at his heart. "My love will surround you like body armor to protect you from the enemy and bring you home to me. Life will go on honey, but in a dull lonely way."

"When I close my eyes, I see you on the battlefield my darling and it's strange. Never being there before, I can feel the heat and the sand on my face. No matter where you are or how far it is, my love will surround you." She stopped to dry her eyes.

"Your pillow and unwashed pillowcase will be my bed partner while you are away and that's where your thoughts should be, but oh no my darling, not when you're on the battlefield! Stay safe and keep your mind attentive to your surroundings."

Unaware of Bruce in the doorway, Lana pulled a handkerchief out of her purse to dab at her tears again and blow her nose. "I love you my husband and will until the day I die," she moaned and returned to the work on her desk.

He peeked around to see a tear slide down alongside her nose and empty into the corner of her mouth. Her tongue flicked out to catch still another while she dabbed at her eyes again with the corner of her hanky. "There's plenty of time for this," she scolded softly. "That's it, I'm not going to cry anymore until after the meeting tonight and even then, I know I must be strong for you, my husband. I can't promise to be brave after you leave."

"I love you my darling," Bruce mouthed in silence and looked into the room again to find Lana busy at the computer. He slipped away and down the hallway to Pop's office to find the old man waiting for him.

"Hi pops, how's it going?"

"Come in Son." He nodded to the chair across from his desk. "Come in and sit down."

He eased down into the chair and looked into the troubled face of the older man. His arms ached to hold him and tell him not to worry, but that would be a lie. "Do you think you'll be able to handle things around here?"

"I don't want to talk about that now, just sit there and let me look at you. Have I told you how proud of you I am, the way you settled in here to make my dream come true?"

"Yeah, dad...many times and I know how you feel without you telling me."

"We have done pretty damn good around here, making a family out of our people and watching them grow with the company."

"I know, and I love every damn..." Bruce felt his throat choke on the words and stood up to leave but feeling the old man's arm around him he accepted the hug and gave one back. "I love you dad, and you better damn sure stay well for me while I'm gone."

"I love you too son, but it's you, who will be in danger every minute of the day."

"You know dad, it takes something like this to make you thankful for the wonderful life you've had, like the times I scraped my knee and mashed my finger, it wasn't always mother who kissed it well, you did too." He pulled out of the old man's tight embrace with a chuckle. "I remember the day I broke my arm..."

"You remember it! I'll never forget how helpless I felt,

when I couldn't fix it and had to take you to the doctor," he forced a laugh. "What time is your meeting tonight?"

"7 o'clock."

"Remember what I told you earlier, Lana will be at the house so no matter how late it is, she'll be waiting at the house for you to come pick her up." He backed up to the desk and sit down on the edge of it. "I'm not getting a whole hell of a lot of work done today."

"Nor I, pop," Bruce laughed and looked around to the person who belonged to the arms around his waist.

"I've been looking everywhere for you dear," Lana squeezed him hard before she let go and moved aside. "You know what I would like to do?"

"I can think of a lot of fun things pretty woman, what do you have in mind?"

"Come on pops, don't look so embarrassed, I wasn't thinking about that."

"I surrender sweet girl, but if it was me and mama, I know what she would want."

* * *

Chapter 18

With a fist bump to his shoulder, someone took up the chair next to Bruce at the National Guard Armory Meeting room, and brought him around to the feel of Richard near his ear. "I think I've come to grips with the inevitable and just as soon go now and get it over with."

"I wish the whole damn threat of war would just go away. Our baby will be a year old when I come home. Damn Richard, I'll be daddy and my baby won't even know me."

"Yeah, I'm glad Sam and I didn't have a baby. She wanted one, but I kept holding back for some unknown reason."

Bruce looked up to catch the down in the mouth

expression on Lt. Col. David Markham's face when he approached the podium. You could almost feel what he was feeling and guess what he was going to say. *"Well men, yes...we have received our deployment schedule."* He looked down at the paper in his hand and began to read. *"The soldiers of the 1st. Battalion, 162 Infantry will form up at the Armory in Gresham on Tuesday morning at 8 a.m."* The Col. looked up from the podium momentarily and Bruce could feel his eyes when they stopped on him before moving to Richard. *"The presidential call up in support of Operations places 710 soldiers in federal active duty. You will report to your mobilization station at Ft.* Carson, *Colorado by Feb. 13, 2003 and from there you are scheduled for maneuvers on the desert at Ft. Irwin. We will depart on the 13th here at the armory at 8 a.m. Your family members are urged to accompany you here for their goodbyes prior to your departure for Ft. Carson. You will be departing from PDX Security gate #14, vicinity of 82nd and Airport Way at 12:00 noon. Najaf, Iraq will be your final duty station. Are there any questions?"*

What the hell is there to ask, Bruce thought and looked down to the idle hands in his lap. I know a hell of a lot more than I wanted to know. He reached for the orders being passed around, kept one and passed the rest on. He stepped outside with Richard and huddled up with Jim Brown and Leonard Goodwin with his hand out. "Are you guys ready for this shit?"

"Not really, Lawson," Brown said, "and Shasha is a hell of a lot less ready than I am."

"Yeah," Goodwin agreed. "Janis almost had me talked into going AWOL."

"Well guys, I hate to run off with my tail between my legs, but being the bearer of bad news over the folk's dinner table, I may as well get it over with. See you at the airport in three days."

"Me too guys," Richard said and stepped up beside Bruce and began to count off their steps to the parking lot. "Hep two three four, hep two three four."

"Cut it out, Richard, we'll have enough of that later."

"Goodnight Bruce."

"Night Richard, the four of us should get together for a night out before we leave."

*   *   *

Chapter 19

Bruce tightened his right arm around Lana's waist and clears the thickness from his throat. "I didn't think three days could go by so fast, but here we are," he said, stealing a quick kiss from the woman who will fill his dreams and waking thoughts while he's away. "Waiting for the final boarding call to take me away from the people I love."

Aware of the arms around the three of them and the show of tears in Pops' eyes, Bruce nearly lost control of his pretense at showing a brave front. Lana pulled away and motioned her mother-in-law in to take her place.

Her eyes brimming with tears, mom gently pushed in between the two men. "Come on papa and let's let the children have some lone time." She reached up on tiptoe to kiss her son goodbye and give him a hug. "I love you son and please come back safely."

"Give me another of those famous mother hugs you gorgeous lady. I love you mom." He said and turned to his wife with a few words before the last call to board.

Pops smiled through the tears in his eyes and stepped up for one more hug. "I love you son and everything will be alright here, so you just keep your mind on the war and stay safe because I sure as hell need you at the car lot." Bruce kissed the old man's cheek and stepped back with the taste of salt on his lips.

Samantha stepped in to give Bruce a goodbye hug. "Keep my husband safe for me Bruce," she said. "You too my friend." Bruce stepped away from Samantha and smiled when he heard Lana asking the same from Richard.

"You gals watch after each other and be ready for two horny guys the next time you see us," Richard laughed and turned to Bruce. "We sure as hell got lucky when we found these two little gals."

He pulled Lana into his arms again and placed his hand on her stomach. "You can say that again, Bro." He placed a kiss on her lips that was to last until they were together again. "I love you dear, my darling wife," he said and stepped back. "Did you feel that?"

"I did I did," Lana laughed. "Your baby can feel his mother's sadness and is upset at your leaving before he is born."

"His…he? Do you know something I don't know?"

"No honey, it could be a she."

"I love you honey and I'll love it whatever it is," Bruce said and squeezed her tight. "Take care of yourself, okay?"

"Don't forget to let me know where you are so I can e-mail you every day and send you letters too and please honey, stay safe for me while you are away."

"I will darling, I promise," he kissed her again. "You will be with me every hour, every minute, every second of every day, right here," he put a hand to his heart.

Time had run out and the Sergeant was yelling, sending men scattering in all directions. "I love you darling," he whispered against her lips with a quick kiss and refused to let go of her hand. It took both Jim Brown and Richard to pull him loose and head for the gate.

* * *

Chapter 20

Bruce, Richard and Jim stopped at the ramp for a final wave before boarding the plane. Richard took up the first double seat with Jim in the seat behind and Bruce fell into the window seat next to Richard, and looked out at the place he wanted to come home to. PDX never looked so good as it did before the airstrip vanished beneath plane and they were airborne. Bruce closed his eyes to the pain in his chest and soon fell asleep.

The thud of the landing gear roused him out of a sound sleep. Caught up in the rush of adrenalin due to rapid loss of altitude, he closed his eyes again and waited with bated breath until the tires found the runway and the vibration of the thrust reversers settled down.

With happy feet on the ground, he and Richard joined Jim, Goodwin and the other men to find a seat on one of the busses nearby.

"Attention men. I am Captain Edwards and will accompany you to your final destination, at which time I will assign each of you a room number in our fabulous hotel. Your orders will be on your bunk.

Bruce favored the Captain with a laugh to his joke, as did his fellow passengers, but his thoughts were on family and home.

The driver stopped at the gate to show his pass and waited for the guard to wave him through. They hadn't gone far when again the buss stopped in front of three barracks. "When I call your name and building number," the Captain said. "You are free to leave the bus."

Bruce was the first name called and he tapped Richard's shoulder with crossed fingers when he left. He tossed his gear on the corner cot and curious as to who would be sharing his quarters, he picked up the orders Captain Edwards had told them about and sat down.

He slumped forward with his eyes on the door, and studied each face, as they entered the room and tossed their belongings on a cot. "Well men," Bruce said and looked around to find each of them waiting for what he had to say. "It says here, we have a medical appointment in forty-five minutes. A bus will pick us up in front of the tent in about 30 minutes."

"Should give us time to make our bed and unpack," the young man nearest the door said as he began to push his sack of foam into the pillowcase. "We were ordered to pick up our bedding and towels from the supply barracks at the first camp I was stationed at. This a hell of a lot better."

Bruce opened his footlocker to find a carrier for his toiletries and baby wipes. He folded and put the rest of what he brought with him into the locker along with his laptop. It had been awhile since he made a bed to government specifications but assured his bunk would pass inspection, he stepped back and wondered at Richards's whereabouts.

He turned to the men near him and looked around to find Brown and Goodwin had claimed cots near his. "Please allow me to introduce myself and two men who are from Gresham Oregon. I'm Staff Sgt. Bruce Lawson and this is Sgt Jim Brown here and Pvt. Leonard Goodwin. The three men shook hands and turned to shake hands with the others as each of them stated their rank and name.

"I'm Pvt. Eldon Longview, sir, from Forest Grove, Oregon."

"Private Robert Wilson here from St. Helens, Washington."

"Sgt. Robert Davidson from Hillsboro, Oregon."

"Pvt. Vernon Roosevelt from Salem, Oregon, and no, I'm not related to either president," he laughed and the group laughed with him.

"Pvt. Jess Mackey from McMinnville, Oregon. Since me and a friend of mine joined the Guard together, do you think we might be able to exchange lodgings later?"

"I have no idea Mackey," Bruce said, his mind on Richard again. "When you find out let me know. I have a good friend somewhere around here also."

"Sgt. Don Brandon here from Portland, Oregon, and I wonder who the hell is responsible for sending us to Colorado. Here we are, bound for a hotter than hell country and they land us in a place that's cold enough to freeze our nuts off."

"Damn good question Brandon," Bruce laughed, as the thought had crossed his mind also. "You'll have to question someone with more answers than me, cause I sure as hell don't have one for you."

"Sgt. Jack Edminston here from Zig Zag, Oregon."

"We had snow in Gresham a couple of nights ago before we left," Bruce laughed. "How about you, Edminston?"

"Six inches at the house when I left," he chuckled. "Had a hell of time getting out."

"Pvt. Albert Martinez from Portland, Oregon."

"Buck Pvt. Buck Jamison from Salem, Oregon.

That's not saying much for an old guy, but I can't seem to hold onto my stripes for more than three months at a stretch."

Bruce laughed as he shook the man's hand and noticed he was indeed an old man. "Well, that's about all the time we have for introductions, so what do you say about us trying to find the medical building?"

Chapter 21

Bruce cleared Medical on a good note, but still had to get through the Active Duty Doctors after lunch. He was a little concerned about their taking a different look at him than the Reservists in Oregon, but then...if they don't want me, he thought, my little lady sure as hell does.

"How about we walk to the chow hall for lunch?" he suggested and remembering earlier when the blast of cold slammed into them outside the Medical Building, he donned his coat and pulled the collar up around his neck before leaving the barracks.

He turned to the hand on his shoulder, hoping to see Richard, but it was Martinez on one side and Brandon on the other. "I smell food," Martinez said and turned up his nose for a better sniff. "Smells pretty good even to a Mexican."

Brandon inhaled deeply and shook his head. "Smells a little like cabbage to me," he said and questioned Bruce with a look. "Yep, sure does and I'm not a cabbage lover."

"I'm so damn hungry I can eat anything, even turnips and Lord knows I hate turnips with a passion," Bruce laughed and joined the others at the end of the chow line. "It's been six hours without food and I sure as hell miss my ten minute donut break at the car lot. Just the thought of his coffee breaks with Lana was making him homesick in the worst way.

After lunch, Martinez continued with Bruce's remark. "A car dealer huh? I'm into renting shoes and bowling lanes, myself."

"Been a long time since I had my fingers and thumb in the holes of a bowling ball," Brandon said. "Bet I could still roll a mean ball."

"What's your average?" Martinez asked.

"Two fifteen on a twenty game count. We'll have to look on the map, maybe they have a bowling alley here and we can go whip up a game or two."

"Damn, Senior Brandon, I could use a man with your talent on my team when we get back home, where was it you said you hail from?"

"Portland, Oregon."

"Oh si, me too," Martinez said and trailed the two men to a table.

Bruce looked around the room for Richard but spotted Brown instead and motioned Martinez and Brandon to follow him. "Hey Jim, have you seen Richard?"

Taking a quick glance around the room Brown shook his head. "Sorry Lawson, but he seems to have disappeared," he said and shoved a bite of cabbage in his mouth. "This is almost as good as back home and the macaroni and cheese is pretty good for Army grub."

Martinez pushed his plate away and Bruce followed suit. "We don't have a heck of a lot of time before our meeting with the next set if doctors," Bruce said as he pushed his chair back and turned for the tray drop.

* * *

Chapter 22

Bruce hopped out of the bus to join the long line in the front of the Soldier Readiness Program building. Two hours later, inside the front door and waiting in line again for a chair to open up so he could sit another two hours before his name is called to stand in line again in front of the desk. After five hours or so total, he faced the receptionist from his side of the desk and flatly refused to return her smile.

"State your name and destination, please," she said and scanned his card into the system.

"Sgt. Bruce Lawson, Iraq."

"Step this way Lawson," the first doctor said, looking at him and grinning like a Cheshire cat while waving a six-inch long needle like a fencing sword in his right hand. He was hustled down the express line to where two doctors, one on each side stabbed both right and left arm at the same time. There was a fourth medical man with a sick smile on his face waiting for him to lower his britches and he had no more than bared his butt when he felt the jab of what felt like a dull needle.

"I hate needles," he muttered under his breath and before he could pull up his britches a taunting voice from somewhere down the line, ordered him to wear them around his knees and to keep moving. He bent over for the fifth and sixth doctors to have their way with him and hardly felt a thing.

His butt throbbing and his arms not feeling so good, Bruce stepped into the waiting bus and to cushion his tender ass with care, he sat down ever so gently behind the driver to await the rest of the men. A glance at his watch told him it had taken five hours of waiting in line and another hour of getting shot up.

Playing it safe in case of a diarrhea attack, Bruce layered his clothes on the floor next to his cot for a quick exit before he crawled into the sack and closed his eyes.

Morning came at him fast and immediately following roll call at 0500 hrs, they climbed aboard the Central Issue Facility line bus to join the end of another line of 20 or more soldiers. Bruce caught sight of Richard up ahead and careful not to hit a shoulder that was probably as tender as his, he snuck up from behind with a pat to the butt. "Atten...tion!"

"Bruce!" Richard turned around for a full man hug. "I'll be damned! I've been looking all over hell for you. Why the hell did they break us up?"

"You got me. Do you have a Pvt. McDonald in your outfit?"

"Yeah," Richard chuckled. "Poor schmuck's been looking for a friend of his."

"That's Mackey and he's in our barracks," Bruce said and looked around to find Mackey looking back at him.

Richard reached out for another man hug. "You with a pretty good group?"

"I haven't exchanged names with all of them yet, but

yeah, a good bunch of men."

"Do you want to move in with my bunch or should I try to join yours?" Richard said. "I saw the Commander on my way in this morning."

"Either way is okay with me," Bruce said. "Come back in line with me and I'll introduce you to a couple of the guys."

*   *   *

Chapter 23

After three hours and twenty minutes of standing outside in the freezing snow, Bruce pushed Richard across threshold and into a building that was not much warmer, to wait another ten minutes in line before they reached the Central Issue Facility counter. Over the next five hours of station to station, his Desert Equipment was finally in his possession. He struggled with rucksack, hip pack, and duffle bags to join Richard at the bus stop. "Damn Bro, a hell of a lot more than we had to carry during Desert Storm."

"What's that guy up ahead selling?" Roosevelt asked.

"MREs," Brandon answered. "It's not half bad if you're hungry.

"What the hell is MRE's?"

"Meals ready to eat," Martinez answered. "Just squish em around and ole! A hot meal just like back home."

"How the hell do you know?" Bruce turned a look of surprise on Martinez.

"Oh Si, senior Lawson, I asked," Martinez laughed.

"In the barracks at last," Bruce mumbled and dumped the contents of his duffle bags on the cot. Desert fatigues, beige with browns and greens, a rucksack with removable packs, chemical suits with gas mask, mosquito netting, sleeping bag, boots and permethrin.

"What the hell is this permethrin sheeeit, amigo?"

"It's a chemical you add to your rinse water to keep the sand fleas, mosquitoes and other insects out of your britches," Bruce said.

"Hey men, we're due at the SRP office in about thirty minutes, where the hell is building 56?" Bruce called out to Brandon, the map-reader.

The men looked up when the Commander walked

into the room. "Good afternoon, men."

The men returned the salute. "Good afternoon, Commander Markham Sir."

"I have been informed of two men who request a change of quarters. Pvt. Jess Mackey, am I correct to assume you are one of the men?"

"That's correct, Sir."

"Gather your property together and follow me," the Commander said and while waiting, gave the men a glimpse into their future. "In two days at ten hundred hours, we will leave for the desert in preparation for insurgent warfare. You will learn more on the plane. He opened the door and held it open. "Sgt. Richard Graves, you may come into your new quarters and make your acquaintance with the men."

Once the Commander and Mackey left the barracks, Richard grabbed Bruce and pulled him into a quick man hug. "I'll unpack later after we return from the Soldier Readiness Program, our processing you know, financial legal stuff and insurance so we can get paid."

It was nineteen hundred hours before they were seated around the table to fill their gut and return to the barracks with happy stomachs. Bruce helped Richard unpack, before they hit the showers and the crapper.

*   *   *

Chapter 24

The bugle Sergeant turned barracks #84 into a danger zone at exactly 0500 hrs. There were 48 elbows flying in all directions. By 0700 hrs all 24 men were in the classroom where Bruce motioned Richard over to a table with two empty chairs. For the next eight grueling hours they watched slides on Muslin Culture.

Captain Petersen turned on the lights and moved the screen to stand in front of them for another two hours of warnings. "We can't emphasize enough the importance of immediate recognition to the improved explosives devices, better known in Iraq as IED's. The slides on what piles of debris to look for and avoid are to remain in your memory to be called upon during your tour of duty. Dead dogs stuffed with dynamite are not the only dead animals to be leery of."

"The Iraqis know their country, weather conditions, the desert terrain and what to expect. You will be fighting on their turf and you must never let your guard down."

"Creep targets are the hardest to detect, watch for eye and lip movement, and most importantly, hand reaction. Keep a safe distance from abandoned vehicles, if in doubt just walk away. Guard duty can be mind weary and lonely, but I'm sure if you stay awake and alert, you will have no problems."

"I have here a two-hour test." Captain Petersen placed a copy on the table in front of each man. "When you have finished you are free to leave. Wait across the street inside the PX for the bus."

Roosevelt left the test room first, followed by Richard, Brandon and Bruce.

Richard put a hand to Bruce's shoulder. "Have you

e-mailed Lana yet?"

"Oh yes indeedy, but haven't had a chance to see if she answered or not. What about you? Have you heard from Sam?"

"Not yet. I'll try again after chow."

An hour or so later and his stomach satisfied, Bruce opened his E-mail. "Oh Lord, Lana baby, how good you look, he drooled over the photograph she had sent him." He brushed at a tear on his cheek with the back of his hand while reading his e-mail from Lana.

He sent a quick answer and could almost picture her reading it. While trying to calm the pain and loneliness in his heart, he looked across the room to find Richard at his laptop.

"Looks like Sam and Lana had dinner with your folks last night, Bruce. Your dad and mom are fine and miss seeing our ugly faces. Sam still loves me, she says," Richard's laugh was far from hearty, as he laid his laptop aside to reach for his handkerchief.

Deep in thought about the danger of explosives, Bruce wondered at their future in Iraq while taking a hot shower and later, after he brushed his teeth and crawled into his bunk, the worrisome thoughts soon turned to a night of dreams.

*   *   *

Chapter 25

The alarm clocks, two of them as a matter of fact, went off way earlier than Bruce felt necessary. Forty-five minutes later however, when a shout of impatience sounded outside the door, he had a sudden change of mind.

"Good morning men. So good of you to join me for a brisk early morning roll call and a hike in the snow," Drill Sergeant Johnson said, as he let his eyes linger on each face with a devilish smirk on his face. "We will join up with the men from barracks E to form up four lines of 12 men to a row."

Bruce stared down at his feet, boots, socks, pants, shirt, hat? He looked around to see if Richard was fully dressed and back again to answer when his name was called.

Four military mini busses were waiting at the curb and as the first twelve names were called, they entered the first bus. Bruce was seated with Richard and across aisle sat Martinez and Longview.

"Well men, I am Captain Wilkins and our driver, Sgt Rawlins here, will take us on the scenic route along highway 115 and direct our attention to the sightseeing pleasure of his hometown of Colorado Springs so settle back and enjoy," Captain Wilkins said and held the mike out to Sgt Rawlins.

"I've been in this man's army a long time and this is the first time I've ever been treated like a tourist," Buck Jamison said with a laugh.

"Well I'm still just a baby in this man's army and already I think I'm gonna like it," Martinez said.

There was something about Martinez and his humor that Bruce found pleasing. "You better like it good, Martinez," he said and looked around Richard and across the aisle to catch the young man's eye. "Because

I'm certain we will pay big time for this pleasure."

Capt. Wilkins laughed and joined in the banter. "Don't judge a gift by the size of its bow, is that right Lawson?"

"Something like that Captain Wilkins, Sir."

"No matter what the end of the line has in store for us, may as well enjoy the sights of the here and now," Martinez said.

Bruce settled back in his seat to look and listen as Rawlins held the microphone up to his mouth. "To your right is the famous snow capped Pikes Peak."

The bus slowed to a stop. "This is the Garden of the Gods, hope you enjoy your two hour maneuvers here." Sgt. Rawlins said and opened the door.

Bruce looked around at the beauty, the towering red rock formation and stepped into line when his name was called.

"We thought you might like to see a part of Colorado Springs before you leave our beautiful state tomorrow morning," Capt. Wilkins said and waved his arm around the park. "Take over, Sgt. Johnson."

Bruce adjusted his backpack and upon the orders called back to them from Sgt. Johnson, began to fast jog in place and then forward with a left right…

"Your new name for today and on the battlefield is leapfrog," Sgt. Johnson called back over his shoulder. "Stay with me and do as I do."

The snow was foot-numbing cold and the icy wind blowing snow in his face made his eyes water and the tears freeze to his cheeks.

"This is just the start of a five mile march through Colorado's beautiful snowy pines. What do you do if you stumble into a minefield?"

"Freeze Sir."

"What else?"

"Retrace our steps, Sir."

"What do you do if you come across battlefield souvenirs?"

"Don't pick them up Sir, they might be rigged with explosives," Martinez's accent sounded above all the others, bringing a chuckle out of Drill Sgt. Johnson.

"Very good men and Martinez."

Bruce looked to the right just as someone lobbed a canister from out of the bushes and open fire on the unsuspecting men.

Sgt. Johnson, Bruce and several voices around them yelled. "Gas! Gas! Gas!"

The fear in Bruce was near out of control when he strapped on his gas mask and raced for the trees. He threw off his rucksack and fell to his stomach behind the snow bank. His heavy breathing was fogging up the inside of his gas mask to where he could hardly see what was in the sights of his M16. When a deathlike quiet fell over the area, Bruce threw off his gas mask and looked around at Richard but it was Roosevelt at the right side of him.

"End of test, men," Sgt. Johnson yelled. "A couple of you might have been shot, other than that, good work men."

"Holy shit!" Martinez yelled.

"There's a hamburger and hot dog stand about 20 minutes away and a place set up to eat." Sgt. Johnson accepted the yells of pleasure with a smile. "Restrooms are nearby."

"That scared me so bad I might have shit my pants," Roosevelt whispered. "Did you know about the planned attack?"

"Hell no," Bruce said. "Caught me completely off guard, but that's the way it is on the battle field and we must be ready for it. Good lesson Roosevelt."

"Don't worry none about me, Lawson," Roosevelt said. "If we fight together, I will be like your joined twin, a hitchhiker on your right shoulder."

They gave each other a knuckle on knuckle and slipped back into their rucksack.

Back in the barracks, and with the exception of one man, the leapfrog team was telling tales and laughing about the day's adventure. Unaware as to what was going on around him, Bruce only had eyes for his laptop screen. He read Lana's letter a second time and returned to the picture. The most beautiful female with the bulging stomach was looking back at him through eyes of gorgeous hazel. "Hey Richard, did Sam send you a picture of her and Lana?"

He looked around to see both Roosevelt and Richard looking at the screen. "I still think we have a couple of winners there and you're to blame," Richard whispered in his right ear. "Think my computer is dead. How about I borrow yours?"

"Sure thing Bro, soon as I finish my letter." He read the words as he typed and could almost feel what Lana would feel, the smile on her face and the perfection of her sitting at her desk while reading it. He closed his eyes and remembered the times she puzzled her way through a problem and her expression when she caught him watching her.

Bruce pulled on his rucksack and feeling a bit ridiculous, he strapped the gas mask to his leg and picked up his toy M16 only to pull them off again to take a shower and hit the head before calling it a day. He no more than reached the barracks and closed the door when the yells of gas...gas...gas sounded outside. Within seconds, Bruce was in his protective gear and looking over his shoulder to find Roosevelt looking back at him.

At the first sound of all clear and not a second sooner, Bruce shed the bulky shit and laid it out beside the bed for easy access. He lay back on the cot and pulled the covers over his head to sleep and dream away what was left of the night.

Bruce wasn't sure if he heard what he thought he heard, but he heard it again and tossed his covers to one side. "I hate bugles," he muttered and swung his feet out of the bed and into his pants. Shortly after, Johnson was at the door yelling the formation yell.

"How do you feel about a Colorado mile jog before breakfast?" Sgt. Johnson stood there bright eyed and smiling.

Twenty minutes into the jog, his stomach was grumbling for a hot cup of coffee, a side of bacon, two eggs, hash browns and toast.

"Lines on the left, jog in place and fall in behind the lines to the right. Hep two three four, hep two three four, faster men before they close the chow hall down."

"Oh hell Amigo my friend, Sgt. Johnson Sir, that thought ain't setting so good on my belly."

*   *   *

Chapter 26

Bruce looked up from his empty plate at about the same time Commander Markham rapped on the table with his knife. "Listen up men," he yelled for attention and waited until he was sure he had it. "A bus will pick you up for a three-hour first aid class but before you leave, pack all issues and leave them inside the barracks to be picked up later. A military caravan will transport you and your luggage to the airport where we will leave for the desert."

"Please," the Commander raised his hand to the commotion in the room. "No questions at this time, perhaps later before we reach our destination."

Bruce put his napkin and silverware on the tray and waited for Richard to do the same. "Are you men ready for one last jog in the snow?"

Immediately upon returning to the barracks, Bruce pulled out his laptop and signed in for his e-mail. There was a letter from Lana and one from Pops. He smiled at the name just below Pops. Billy Joe's letter was short and to the point. Pops was missing him and so was mom. He opened Lana's letter and let it touch his heart, but in spite of the spread of excitement through all parts of his body, it left him feeling unsatisfied.

Lonely for the feel of his wife in his arms with his baby between them, he laid his laptop aside and began pulling the contents of his footlocker out and onto the cot. He sat in the midst of it while stuffing his rucksack to capacity. After shoving what was left into his hip pack and duffle bags, he looked across the room to catch Richard doing the same.

He couldn't understand the Mexican muttering, but hearing the frustration in it, Bruce went over to offer his assistance. "Is this your first time out, Martinez?"

"Si. I think I feel like a poor little Mexican boy in

a Mexican man's britches, but I learn real good, senior, and when I get the hang of it, I never forget."

"Let me give you a hand here and it'll make it a lot easier next time."

"Don't feel bad, Alberto my man," Richard said and put his arm around the young man's shoulder. "Me and Bruce here had a lot to learn on our first tour of duty."

"Here you go, Martinez, the backpack will be heavy, same with your hip pack," Bruce warned and buckled the rucksack to his back. "Lean forward...good, now take a few steps around the room to get the feel of it. The only time you worry with the duffle bag is during transfers."

"Hey, men," Brandon called out. "The bus is here."

On the plane during takeoff, Bruce put his book aside and looked out the window to watch Colorado's snow covered Pikes Peak disappear behind them and tried but failed to see the Garden of the Gods and the trail of maneuvers where they almost froze to death. "Did you notice how the young men took an interest in the first aid meeting today?" he asked Richard but before he could answer, the Commander was calling for attention at the front of the plane.

He cleared his throat and waited for quiet to settle amongst the group. "Are you ready for action?" He grinned when the men's voices came back less than enthusiastic. "We are headed for the desert ovens with sand and dust storms to prepare you for the ills in Iraq." He searched the faces of each man as he looked around the plane. "A cluster of Iraqi villages, miles and miles from civilization awaits your fighting technique against trained enemy Iraqis who are ready to take us on."

"Sgt. Lawson here, Commander Sir. Will we be trained to fight with live ammunition?"

"You will know when you've been hit, Sergeant."

"Thank you Sir." Bruce looked around at the men and found Martinez looking at the Commander, with eyes twice their normal size.

"Senior, Commander Sir, will we receive weapons training first?"

"Your name, Private?"

"Albert Martinez, Sir."

"Yes Martinez. When you complete your training at Ft. Irwin, you will know more about the enemy than you thought possible and will become as familiar with your rifle as you are with your innermost self. You will know it inside and out and will value it with your life."

"I value it with my life already, senior Sir," Martinez laughed and looked around at the men who joined in with the laughter, including Commander Markham.

"I have here a map of the village. It will introduce you to the division between the good boys and the enemy. We don't want you to suddenly find yourself in the enemy camp. To be a captive in the Iraqi torture camp is...believe me men when I say you don't want to go there."

Bruce reached for the map handed him by the man seated in front of him and gave one to Richard before passing the rest to the men behind.   He found the enemy camps and turned when Richard said something, to see him pointing to a different area.

"Looks a little like tent city," Bruce said and noticed the number on each tent. He pointed to one of the tents. "This one has the same number as we had at Ft. Carson."

"Attention men," C.O. Markham said. "I have here your partner assignment. You are to sit together during the trip and by the time we land, I want you to know as much about your sidekick as you know about yourself."

Bruce took the packet of lists handed him, and passed the others back over his shoulder after giving one to Richard. He found the name of his partner and looked around the plane until he met the young man's grin. He was pleased with his draw, but hated to change seats. He looked at the list again to see if he recognized the man Richard was partnered with.

"Do you know this Roosevelt, your partner? What about my partner, Eldon Longview, do you know him?" Bruce looked around for Longview and jabbed Richard to point out where the young man was seated.

"He's quiet, but I think he'll make a good partner. I'll send him up here on my way back to sit with Roosevelt," Bruce said, just before he filled the aisle with his presence. He leaned down to enlighten Longview as to who and where his partner was waiting.

"Thank you Sir," Longview smiled and moved into the seat beside Richard.

"Well Roosevelt, do you think we'll make a great team?"

"I'll do everything in my power to make it so, sir."

Bruce palmed the hand of his partner and prayed for a lasting relationship and a safe return from the war in Iraq.

*   *   *

Chapter 27

Bruce took up the seat vacated by a man he hadn't met and stretched out with his headrest back and his feet under the seat in front of him. He put an arm behind his head and closed his eyes. "Tell me about your life Roosevelt, help me to know you like family."

"I joined the National Guard as the patriotic thing to do, like helping others less fortunate and serving my country. During the six weeks of basic combat training as an infantryman, I observed and learned how to share living quarters with men and how they interacted with each other. It was hard, believe me, the whole trial of basics nearly broke my back but I have come to enjoy being the man I am today."

"I did lots of hunting with dad and I was good," he

chuckled. "Even thought I was better than the old man with a rifle, but this war with Iraq scares hell out of me. I have doubts about the positive feeling I had when I joined the Guards."

"I met and fell in love with Alice just before I shipped out for six months of mobilization training at Fort Hood, Texas and only saw her twice before they sent me here for additional training. I was with Bravo Company, 2nd Battalion 162 infantry. If I could have had a little more time, I would probably have a more positive outlook on everything." Roosevelt looked across at his partner. "Are you awake, Sarge?"

"Yeah Roosevelt, are you ready to hear a little bit about me?"

"Sure am, Sir."

"First off, save the Sir bit for officers and drill sergeants, they love that kind of shit. I went into business with dad when I was sixteen, but the day I became an 18-year-old grownup I felt the same as you. I joined the National Guard with my best friend Richard when we were about your age."

"Ft. Benning, aha...never forget the great state of Georgia. A lotta pretty women there, but with basic and advanced individual training as infantrymen, there was very little time to enjoy the feminine fillies. I too learned how to work with others and develop trust in order to accomplish goals within a team. In the years that followed, and long standing traditions of service in Oregon, I was assigned to serve with the 1st battalion, 162 Infantry."

"My first tour of duty was with Richard in Kuwait during Desert Storm. I have since married a beautiful young woman who is pregnant with our first child, I sure as hell didn't want to leave her to go through child birth alone. Now that I'm here, my focus has changed to winning this damn war." He grinned across the seat at Roosevelt with a wink. "We'll do okay, young man."

"I feel the same way, Sarge."

Bruce laid back in his seat and closed his eyes again only to be awakened by the seat belt ding and looked around to see the men putting their seats up and fastening their seat belts. He pulled his seat back and looked around Roosevelt to see through the window but was unable to see anything of the territory below. "What do you see?"

"A lot of desert and a...well Sarge, a camel I think. A lot of tents, jeeps, trucks and hummers down there," he said and looked around at Bruce. "You know those little tent huts scattered on the desert where the Iraqi's live...it looks like the real thing, here...trade seats with me."

"Stay in your seat, Sir, we will be landing at the airport in ten minutes." Bruce settled back in his seat with a smile and nod to the stewardess

"Looks like a regular town now Sarge, city streets houses and businesses and yeah, there's the airport," Roosevelt looked around at Bruce, a question in his eyes.

"Well partner, looks like we gotta wait to find out what's going on."

"Army trucks down there Sarge?" He looked around at Bruce again, like a little boy waiting for someone to explain to him, what's going on. I bet they're waiting for us."

"That's too good a bet for me to take you up on, Roosevelt."

*   *   *

Chapter 28

Upon the grind before the thud of the landing gear and sudden descent of floor beneath his feet, he sat back to let the grip of adrenalin demand his attention until he felt the tires touch down on the runway. He stepped in behind Roosevelt to follow him down the steps and gather to one side on the tarmac to await orders. He looked around and sure as hell, a convoy was waiting with what looked like a gun truck in front. Protection???

What part of the USA are we the hell in, he wondered, and looked around for something, a sign, anything with a name on it. When Roosevelt looked at him for answers, he raised an eyebrow and shook his head.

It wasn't Kuwait, of that he was certain, not nearly enough hours in the sky, but the desert surrounding the airport looked a hell of a lot like Kuwait.

The drill Sergeant suddenly appeared from, who in the hell knows where he came from, and ordered the group into a formation. He called six partners in groups of twelve and ordered the first dozen into transport truck #1.

Bruce was pleased to find he was with his main bunk buddies from Ft. Carson, in truck #1. As they rounded a curve in the road, he caught sight of a gun truck at the end of the convoy and nudged Roosevelt with his elbow to bring his attention around to the gunner.

Excitement over, he leaned back against the side of the truck and looked around at the men. The young privates, their fearful expressions pulled at his heart. No older than eighteen, nineteen at the most. That is, all except for Buck Jamison, Bruce laughed out loud.

"What, Sarge?" Roosevelt asked.

"I was just thinking about old Buck," he said and called back over his shoulder. "You may get back a stripe or two before this is over, Buck."

"Don't count on it unless you'll be around to teach me how to be a sergeant," he laughed. "Who the hell knows Lawson, I might even make general and make you my second in command."

"I think we just ran out of paved road, look at the dust swirling in circles between our truck and the one behind us," Richard said, "and us without our dust masks."

Roosevelt pointed to several young radicals yelling at them and throwing rocks. "Sarge! Look!" he said.

"What the hell?" Bruce wondered aloud. "They look like Iraqis." Gunshots sounded and the men scampered further into the desert to scatter in all directions. One of them lifted his rifle to shoot, but when the sand kicked up around his feet, he lowered his rifle and fell . in behind the others. Bruce looked back around to the men, but found them towering over him and looking at what he saw.

"Damn." Richard was wiping the sweat out of his eyes. "It's hotter than hell in here."

Longview pointed to the side of the road. "That looks just like those little Iraqi huts I saw on television the other day."

Bruce lay back and wondered where in the United States they were. Not hot enough and not nearly enough sand for Iraq but he questioned the covered transports? Lana's lovely face suddenly interrupted his confusion, her lips moving but when he turned his ear toward her, he was still unable to make out what she was saying. Playing it safe, he thinks love thoughts her way, but she was gone as suddenly as she appeared.

He opened his eyes when the truck slowed to a stop and looked out the back just as it began to move forward again and saw miles and miles of rolled barbed wire and three feet high sand berms on both sides of the road and around what looked like a compound.

"Damn," Brown spoke up for the first time since

they left the airport, "looks to me like a prison camp.

"If that was a glimpse of the enemy back there," Bruce chuckles and looks in Brown's direction. "I suppose it might be for our protection."

"This is the tent city I saw from the plane," Roosevelt said and looked at Bruce.

Bruce smiled in recognition to the statement Roosevelt made and looked around at the tent buildings when they slowed down. He stood to his feet when the truck stopped, as did the rest of the men, ready to exit and have a look at their new surroundings.

Completely in the dark as to what they should do, Bruce kicked at a pebble and looked left to find the men from the other trucks looking as restless and confused as he.

The Sergeant heading their way looked to be in a hurry. "Good afternoon men, I am Sgt. Goodyear here to welcome you to Iraq," he followed his greeting with a chuckle. "This is Ft. Irwin and your days here will be filled with many surprises. Commander Markham has brought to my attention that you twelve men bunked together at Ft. Carson?"

"Yes Sir."

This is bldg. #84, your new home away from home. You are free at this time to enter and choose the same cots you had at Ft. Carson. Good luck men," he said and rushed up to the next group of men.

The bunkhouse is indeed, a carbon copy of the one in Ft. Carson, Bruce thought as he shed his rucksack and hip pack to let them drop on the floor alongside his duffle and sleeping bag. He spread out the same shitty colored bedding on his cot and picked up the orders. "Looks like we have the rest of the day off," he informed the others and wondered where in the hell Fort Irwin is located. "Maybe a walk around the camp would be a good idea."

"Well, what do ya know," Richard joined in and holding a newspaper up for the men to see. "This is the Mojave Desert gentlemen, just a short distance from Barstow and a hell of a long way from Iraq?"

"Those Iraqi's sure as hell looked like the real thing," Roosevelt said as he turned the corners of his bedding under. He smoothed his hand across it and stepped back for a look.

"Looks good, partner, good enough to pass inspection," Bruce said with a shoulder bump to the young man. "Maybe we should try our luck in Las Vegas while we're here."

"I've never been lucky at gambling but you can count us in, eh Amigo's?" Alberto's announcement was followed by a positive response.

*   *   *

Chapter 29

Bruce wondered if they had been gone long enough for his laptop to charge and smiled when his puppy icon appeared in the lower right corner with an envelope in his mouth. "Oh yes indeedy," he chuckled while centering his mouse pointer on the mail icon with a double click and a double click yet again on his wife's name to bring up her letter.

A picture of her smiling face suddenly appeared on the screen, so lifelike and yet so far away it was breaking his heart. Unashamed of the tears in his eyes and feeling her pain and loneliness as well as his own, he began to read.

My dearest husband;

I thought I knew how much I loved you before you left,

but honey, I didn't know what lonely was until I crawled into bed the first night you were gone. I helped Pops send you an e-mail, but I didn't read it.

He is so worried and lonely for you. Your mother is too, but pops... you are so blessed to have a father like him. My father is good honey, and I'm lucky to have had him to pamper me, but pops? Sorry honey, I had to wipe the tears out of my eyes. I don't know what else to say.

Other than work, my life has come to a standstill, nothing is important.

My donut at break is far from satisfying, doesn't even taste the same.

The guys at work told me to tell you hello for them and they miss you, especially, Billy Joe. He and his wife had a cuddly baby girl. Billy brought her into the office for me to see and hold. Our baby has really been active today, like it's trying to kick out of its holding pen. It's kicking now honey, wish you were here so you could give him a talking to. I'm not supposed to write long letters sweetheart so I'll sign off for now and hope to hear from you soon. By the way I want to name our baby Sari if it is a girl and Bruce

Junior if it's a Boy. What do you think?

   All my love, babe

   your wife, Lana.

He read it a second time and with a handkerchief in his hand to dab at the tears, he laughed at her smart ass remarks and turned back to his computer. He started her email with *"My darling wife"* and filling the bulk of it with mushy words of love. He ended it with more of the same. He opened pops mail and was reading it when Richard called out to him. "Hey Bruce, looks like the girls are still spending a lot of time over at your folk's house."

"Yeah, I'm not surprised, probably feels like a part of us is there with them," he said and turned back to finish pops letter. With visions of Lana in his mind, he signed off and left his laptop to charge again. "Sweet Jeeesus woman, I miss hell out of you."

*   *   *

Chapter 30

Feeling restless, Bruce stood outside the barracks looking across the desert beyond the rolls of barbed wire and could almost feel the enemy looking back at him. Someone leaned into the back of him and looking over his shoulder, Richard standing there looking back at him. "How about a walk, maybe check out the movie house?"

"Doesn't sound like our kind of movie," Richard said and waved the two men behind to join them. "Our two partners look lost, probably looking for us. Why don't we go on over to the PX, see what's going on there,"

Roosevelt and Longview caught up before they reached their destination and walked alongside the rest of the way. "Find anything interesting going on?"

"Beetle juice is playing at the movie house," Bruce answered. "Thought we would check out the fast food cafe. I've got a hankering for a platter of french fries."

"Who the hell knows," Richard laughed and continued to walk along the dirt path. "We might find a bowling alley."

Bruce followed behind taking in the sights, but his mind was elsewhere and he failed to make out what Roosevelt was saying. "What was that again?"

"Tomorrow we go for our weapons training," he said. "I'm ready to get the hang of it and learn what I need to know."

"They say we will know our rifles inside and out, so I imagine we'll be tearing down and putting them together until we can do it with our eyes closed," Bruce said and ordered two large baskets of fries.

"I went to the firing range a lot in Salem and received a pretty good score, but this will be more intensive and expectations a lot higher," Roosevelt said as he tossed the last two french fries in his mouth and turned toward the door.

Back in the barracks again, Bruce picked up the orders for tomorrow. Classes begin at 0600 hrs to learn the pros and cons of dealing with Iraqi prisoners and searching suspicious looking vehicles. After lunch is the Nuclear, Biological and Chemical training, in case of gas attacks, followed by the basic gun care and marksmanship with the M-16 rifle and M-9 pistol. "Breakfast at 0500 hrs tomorrow, in order to make our classes," Bruce announced to whomever.

* * *

Chapter 31

Brandon slammed into the barracks wearing a wet towel around his neck and laughing his head off. "You men are in for the surprise of a life time. The weather here is hotter than hell, and the showers are so damn cold it makes your chin lock up," he broke down in hysterics again. "The john..." Brandon rolled around on the bed laughing and talking at the same time.

Since Bruce couldn't understand a word of what Brandon was saying, he waved his partner over. "Now would be a good time to take a shower and check out the funny johns."

Roosevelt leaned forward and looked in the hole. "I Bet when they suck this crap out, the smell is so bad it could make you puke," he said and put a finger to his nose. "How in the hell is the best way to use this damn contraption?"

"When me and Richard were in Kuwait we straddled it like you would a urinal unless we needed to crap and then we squatted with our butts aimed at the hole," Bruce said and stepped in with a strip of toilet paper for a squat to find his knees didn't bend like they used to.

Roosevelt moved into the next stall. "Not bad," he said with a chuckle. "I went to Morocco with the folks when I was younger and their crapper was a hole in the ground. I was still small enough to fall through and it scared hell out of me, I can tell you that."

"I'm not surprised," Bruce joined the younger man in a chuckle. "Enough to give a boy nightmares huh."

"My brother sure led me wrong, Sarge," Roosevelt said and moved around to catch the door to the barracks. "He said sergeants in the army were mean sons a bitches."

"He was talking about Drill Sergeants," Bruce said and stopped at the door to look around with a grin.

"They are a bunch of sumbitches but show them a lot of respect and you have nothing to worry about."

"Those damn french fries didn't last long," Longview surprised everyone by breaking his silence. "Maybe we should hit the chow lines."

"Hey, Longview, you're getting this shit down pretty good," Bruce laughed and gave the younger man a fist bump to the shoulder.

They were early yet and in a line of twelve men, it didn't take long to fill their plates and find an empty table. "I'm glad to find what I heard about army stew to be far from the truth, Senior Bruce," Martinez said. "It's not so good as beans and tortillas, but for gringo food, it's damn good."

"I bet you can whip up a mean pot of beans, eh Martinez?"

"You betcha, Roosevelt, I been doing it since I was seven years old."

The twelve men left the chow hall in route to barracks #84. Bruce, Richard and their two partners left shortly after with soap in hand and towels under their arms and was surprised to find a shower open for each of them. "This water is cold enough to freeze a man's balls off," Bruce said through clenched teeth and considered himself lucky when he escaped with his intact.

He climbed into the sack soon after Johnson's lights out at 2200 yell. It was during the low murmurs of prayer, he caught a few Mexican words in the mix, and smiled.

*   *   *

Chapter 32

The alarm brought Bruce up on his elbow. With eyes squint against the overhead light he looked around the room. "Hey Brandon," he kicked free of his blanket and slammed his feet on the floor. "How the hell long does it take that alarm of yours to run down?"

Don reached out and pushed the button down. "Sorry Bruce, what the hell time is it anyway?" He said and pulled the pillow over his face to shut out the glare

"What the hell time did you set it for, man?" Martinez grumbled. "That's what the hell time it is, Amigo."

Four men were missing, four others waiting with bunks made and towel in hand, ready to hit the showers. Glad he had showered last night, Bruce shivered at the thought of suffering an icy shower this early in the day. He made his bunk and dressed to army specification.

After a quick review of the orders for the day, breakfast was number one and then off for full body armor, weapons training, basic gun care, breaking down, cleaning and reassembling the M-16 rifle. Range statistics on each man and his feel for various weapons.

"Keep your eye on the instructor when he dismantles his gun, the layout of each part and the order in which he reassembles the gun to its original shape."

Roosevelt's grin and wink, just before he turned away, left Bruce to wonder at its meaning.

After breakfast and while Bruce and Richard milled around outside while awaiting formation, Roosevelt and Longview moved in to join them. "Do you think one of them mean sons a bitches will march us to our first meeting?" Longview asked.

"Atten...tion! Drill Sgt. Gill Smith, here."

Bruce stood to attention in the first line of six when Sgt. Smith began roll call. He wanted to look around but answered to his name and listened to the voices of all twenty four men.

"First order of the day is a fast jog to the armory to pick up your weapons and Point Blank body armor. Flank left, hep two three four, hep two three four. Flank left and repeat after me, hep two three four."

"Hep two three four," they repeated in a loud sing along voice and continued to sing until they arrived at the armory. They were the first in line for weapons and ordered to stand at attention until all the men had been served. Bruce stood perfectly still until his name was called and he stepped forward for his M16 and stepped back into position. He caught sight of Sgt. Smith and an officer with him, but remained in line and at attention.

"Attention men, heads up!" All eyes turned to Sgt. Smith and the Officer with him. "This is Captain James Wilkins, your new Commanding Officer."

"Good morning men," Captain Wilkins said and waited for the usual response. He moved down the line with Smith in front of him handing out body armor to each man. "This is your new body armor. You will wear it at all times beginning now and throughout the day with exception of the bunkhouse and now, shed your shirts and slip into your armor with your shirt on over it."

"It is uncomfortable and it is hot, but it may be the difference between living and dying," he said while standing by until each man had his shirt buttoned.

Captain Wilkins opened his own shirt to display the armor beneath and called Drill Sgt. Smith over for a show of the same. "Inspections will be made when you least expect it so don't let us catch you with a naked chest."

"Captain Wilkins, sir?"

"Your name Private?"

"Alberto Martinez, Sir. Do we have to wear it to the outhouse and the shower stalls?"

"While taking a shower no, to the showers and outhouse, yes...anytime outside your barracks." The

Captain smiled at Martinez and his attention lingered on each face. "Alright men, I am here for you and will remain so throughout your tour of duty. If you have no more questions, I'll leave you in the hands of Sgt. Smith."

* * *

Chapter 33

Half the leapfrog unit entered the weapons-learning center and was sectioned into three groups of eight. "Sgt. Roberts here for the first group, Sgt. Washington will take the second group and Sgt. Rugby the third. We will be your instructors throughout the weapons training. If my group will follow me outside we will get down to business."

"This is the Browning 2.50 Caliber machine gun," he said and went on to explain the moving parts and speed with which to set it up and ready to fire, followed by an hour and half of questions and answers and the same go around with the M16 A1 Rifle with M203 40 MM grenade launcher.

"What do you think partner?" Bruce turned to

Roosevelt. "Did you ever practice with anything like this?"

"Never saw one before and I'm anxious to get my hands on it and try it out," he said and moved up beside Bruce.

Sgt. Roberts stepped to one side. "There it is men, any volunteers."

Roosevelt smiled at Bruce and stepped forward. "I'll give it a try, Sgt. Roberts," he said and pointed toward a white sign in the field. "Is that the target?"

"Your name, Private?"

"Vernon Roosevelt, and no Sir, I'm not related to either president."

"A fine name just the same. You have good eyesight, Roosevelt."

The instructor stood behind him with field glasses and after a succession of ten shots, he tapped Roosevelt on the head. "Very good Roosevelt and now, if you would fold it for the next man and step back?" Sgt. Roberts moved aside and talked into the field radio while waiting for the jeep driver to put up a new target. "Ready for the next man."

What the hell, Bruce thought, may as well get with it. He stepped forward, fell to the ground and had the gun ready in a reasonable amount of time, but not as fast as Roosevelt. He took his 10 shots, folded the gun and stepped back.

"Your name Sgt?" Roberts said and held the field radio to his mouth.

"Sgt. Bruce Lawson, Sir," he said and stepped back, looking at Richard and egging him on with a nod and a grin while crowding in alongside him.

The jeep pulled up to the target area with a new target and Richard stepped forward. After Richard, El-don Longview stepped forward followed by Jim Brown, Buck Jamison, Don Brandon and Albert Martinez.

"Si, Sgt. Roberts Sir, that was harder than my friends here made it look," Martinez said as he backed away and waited with the others to learn their scores.

The Jeep drove up with the targets and after a quick

study of each, Sgt Roberts looks up at Roosevelt. "If your battalion is set up for the M2.50 Caliber Browning machine gun young man, I am recommending you for the position."

"Thank you, Sir."

Sgt. Roberts looked down at his watch and motioned the men to fall in behind. Inside building #5, Roberts sat down on the floor with the men gathering around him. "Each day you will disassemble the firing mechanism including the bolt, the firing pin and this large spring. Wipe out the grime inside, as this will keep your gun firing smoothly."

"It is extremely important here in the desert where sand and dust infiltrate every moving part of your weapon. After cleaning and reassembling your gun you must then pull the trigger. Listen for the comforting click of the firing pin and only after the click, should you re-insert the magazine."

Roosevelt watched and listened, as did the other men, to the naming of each part. Bruce saw the confidence in his face and hoped it wouldn't rear up to bite him in the butt later.

"Alright men, pick a spot on the floor and show me what you know."

Bruce sat between Richard and Roosevelt, and praying he wouldn't make a fool of himself, began to tear down his gun and lay the parts aside. He was at a loss as to how Sgt. Roberts could keep track and hear all eight men at the same time.

Roberts smiled his approval when the last man held his weapon up for inspection. "Take this pamphlet outlining the test you will be taking and report back to me in room #81 after lunch."

*   *   *

Chapter 34

After lunch and a favorable score on the written gun test, the squad of eight left the exam room for the firing range. Bruce looked across his left shoulder to see Roosevelt's readiness with a test aim on his target.

Sgt. Roberts lined them up about the length of a football field away from their targets. "Each man is to fire six shots in his top target while standing, six shots to the middle while down on one knee and six shots to the bottom while flat of your belly," he said and looked down the line. "After the last shot, lay your rifle down and step away."

Bruce stepped back to stand beside Roosevelt. "You're for sure the pick of the litter," he said. "I feel lucky as hell, going to war with you watching my back."

The jeep in the field gathered up the targets and brought them back. "Good aim you got there Roosevelt, chewed up the bulls eye on all three targets," Sgt. Roberts said.

Roosevelt walked over to have a look. "Gotta give the old man credit for that, Sir, he taught me everything I know."

"My notation in the report says we are to train you on the lightweight M249 SAW and you, Lawson are to train with him," he said and reached into the jeep for the Saw, a link of ammunition and a magazine for Bruce's M16.

Bruce carried his weapon and ammunition to the location pointed out to him and waited to see Brandon and Martinez with their M16's take up their position wide to the right. Brown with his M16 and Jamison with a grenade launcher attached to his M16 A1 rifle settled in at the middle. Richard and Longview were to the immediate right.

Roosevelt smiled from ear to ear and looking like

a kid with a brand new toy, tucked the machine gun under his left elbow and the link of ammunition over his right arm.

Sgt. Roberts explained the importance of partners and the ability to work and think together as one mind and body. He went on to explain the field targets, cars and jeeps filled with Iraqi soldiers, civilians and children.

Bruce stepped back, but the warning Roberts was laying on them was like an extra brain cell in his mind.

"Be extremely careful," Roberts warned. "You will have only mini-seconds to decide whether to squeeze or not to squeeze the trigger. To error in your decision and kill civilians, especially women and children will count big time against your total score. Are you ready, men?"

Satisfied with their shouts of readiness Sgt. Roberts raised his right arm. "Keep your guns aimed at the target field." He let his arm drop and yelled. "Attack!"

Life sized forms came at them from the other side of the hill. The men fell into the sand behind a 2 foot

sand berm where Roosevelt positioned his SAW on the
bank. Bruce quickly fed the link of ammunition into it
and quickly snapped a magazine of ammunition into his
M16. He leaned into the berm and turned his rifle on
the advancing enemy. A grenade from Buck's launcher
stops the advancement of a cardboard jeep and with the
SAW shooter taking out the advancing enemy, Bruce
and the other five men picked off the scatter of Iraqis.

With the enemy laid out and the children still alive,
Sgt. Roberts applauded them. "Very good men, two
more weeks of war maneuvers will make you more than
war ready. Lawson and Roosevelt will work together
at the left side of the battlefield. Brown and Jamison
will form up at the center while Brandon and Martinez
cover wide right. Graves and Longview will move in
here, alongside Lawson and Roosevelt. Take a 20 minute break men, and shape up for the next attack."

The day ended with a three-mile uphill, downhill
jog and a stop at the chow hall. Long after dinner
and down for the count, Bruce was too damn tired to

check his e-mail and with two more weeks of this shit, he would be too damn sore to battle the Iraqis. After a quick shower and a stop at the john, he felt somewhat better when he got back to the barrack. He laid out what he needed in the event of a gas attack, fell back on his cot and was asleep before his head hit the pillow.

*   *   *

Chapter 35

Damn that bugle to hell, Bruce thought as he swung his feet around and onto the floor. It was 0500 hrs and rush hour in the barracks with every man for himself. He did a quick check of his corner bunk and rushed outside for the not yet awake and before breakfast formation.

"What the hell is this, Longview?" Sgt. Smith yelled and yanked the young man's pant leg up to show the improper tie of his shoelaces.

Longview fell to a double time squat and tied his shoelaces. "Sorry sir, Sgt. Smith Sir."

Bruce almost laughed, not so much at Longview, but every man, including himself, looked down at their feet.

"Very good," Sgt Smith said. "Fall out men and enjoy your breakfast."

Out in the field at 0800 hrs for maneuvers in full dress and rucksack, sweat was leaking from every pore. Bruce crawled on his stomach while trying to ignore the sand sticking to the perspiration on his face. Roosevelt was keeping pace to the right of him, their toy guns ready to fire ink bullets. Richard and his partner were six yards or so further right with eyes trained ahead, looking like it was a matter of life or death.

"I'm so damn thirsty, I can hardly swallow," Roosevelt whispered.

"Me too, but your water has to last out the day, just don't pass out on me."

"The Gods sure smiled down on me when I drew you for a partner," Roosevelt said. "Just hope he keeps an eye on us in Iraq."

"I sure as hell hope I can measure up. You surpass what I could have hoped for in a partner."

"What about your friend, Graves?" Roosevelt

asked, but followed Bruce's lead and raised his gun to aim at what looked like a man with a gun. He hesitated, at which time Bruce raised his gun and squeezed the trigger.

"I didn't think I would do that," Roosevelt dropped his head to his arm.

"That's why we're out here, to toughen us into killing machines."

"Don't know if I can kill a man."

"It's kill or be killed and I'm depending on you to help save my ass as well as your own. Bring your head up Roosevelt, the enemy is still out there just waiting to paint your chest with a blob of ink."

"Right Sarge, it's them or us and I sure as hell don't want to see you on the ground with a bullet hole in your gut."

"That's the spirit, now let's go get them gun toting Iraqis," Bruce said and turned away from the hero worship in the young man's eyes.

*   *   *

Chapter 36

With forty-eight men living in one barracks, friend-to-friend chats were hard to come by. Bruce felt drained and needed some down time with Richard. He sauntered over to where his friend lay on his cot with a book. "How about a walk?"

Richard looked at his watch. "We got 20 minutes before curfew."

Bruce stood there looking down at him. "Is that a yes or a no?"

"Hell yes, I've been wanting some one on one time with you."

They stepped outside and heard the door open and close behind them. Bruce looked around to find his shadow and Longview behind them.

"Don't mind us Sarge," Roosevelt said. "Me and Longview needed a breath of air. We'll just saunter along behind just in case you might need us."

"Me and my old buddy here need some down time together."

"You just go on ahead Sarge. Me and Longview here need to plan a strategy of attack on the battle field tomorrow."

"Very good Roosevelt," Bruce looked across at Richard to find him grinning in the moonlight. "Do you have your gas mask?"

"Hell yeah and full dress too," Richard said. "That's a damn good man you got there for a partner. Longview is quiet, but don't let it fool you, he's ready to take on the Iraqis."

"I was worried whether or not he was going to hold up his end."

"Without a doubt, Longview cut down those cardboard figures today before I could aim my gun. He's so fast on the draw it makes me feel like a man too old for this shit."

Bruce looked around to find the two young men okay. "Tomorrow's for real. Just hope our two weeks training has made us fit for battle, hate to think of lying dead in the hot sun if I'm shot," Bruce chuckled. "Maybe my man will drag me into the shade of a sage bush."

"There won't be many of those in Iraq, so guess we better not get shot," Richard laughed. "We'll be fighting Iraqis tomorrow who know the lay of the terrain and they're gonna fight like hell to keep from dying on their own turf."

"They have the advantage alright, same as the Iraqi army we'll be facing soon." He felt Richard's arm around his shoulder and put arm around Richard's waist.

"Are you scared, Bruce?"

"A little up tight perhaps, but with Roosevelt as a partner, I feel like we could whip the whole damn world."

"I guess it's best we're not partners. I would for sure

lose it if you were shot and blame myself for letting it happen," Richard's voice cracked.

Feeling choked up, Bruce tightened his grip around Richard's waist. "I know two little gorgeous females who are expecting us to come home safe Bro, so the choice of whether we make it or not has already been made. You ready to turn back?"

"Probably should get a good night's sleep," Richard said and motioned the two young men behind to turn around.

Bruce heard Brown yelling his name from the doorway and broke out in a run. "Come quick Lawson, you got a telephone call."

He grabbed the phone out of old Buck's hand and put it to his mouth. "Hello!"

"Honey…can you hear me?"

"Yes sweetheart, what's wrong?"

"I'm in the birthing room, the baby is coming and I wanted you here with me." She stopped talking and he could hear her taking short quick breaths.

Bruce started to pant and puff with her, but the doctor's voice in the back ground, he strained to hear what she was saying. "Did the doctor say the baby is coming?"

"Yes honey, she told me to push with the next pain…here it comes."

"Push honey, push," he said and all became quiet for a second or so and then he heard his baby cry.

"You can stop pushing Lana, we have the baby," the doctor said, Bruce could hear her and waited with bated breath to hear if it was a boy or girl.

"Oh honey, Dr. Miley held our naked baby up for me to see!"

"Well, what is it?"

"A beautiful baby girl, with everything intact," Lana began to laugh and cry at the same time. "Honey, we have a girl."

"A girl," Bruce whispered and then turned to the men around him with a yell. "It's a girl!"

"Is Samantha there with her?" Richard asked and

reached to take the phone.

"Just a minute Bro," he said and dodged the phone away from Richard. "Is Sam in the room with you?"

"Yes and she wants to tell Richard something. I have the baby in my arms now and the doctor is cleaning the birthing machine between my legs so I'll let Sam have the phone."

"Hello, Sam," Richard said and smiled at Bruce. "Yes darling, I love you too and would like to talk longer but we have over talked our limit," he said and let Bruce have the phone.

"I love you baby, guess I can't call you that anymore little mama," Bruce said and smiled at the men hovering around him. "I know you do sweetheart and I miss you too. I'll be looking for e-mail pictures. I want to say goodbye before they cut us off and yes I'm proud of you sweetheart." He replaced the receiver to the cradle and beamed at Richard.

"I'm glad you left your wife pregnant, gave us a chance to talk to them on the phone. How did the call get through, Jim?" Richard said.

"Have an idea the Captain let it slip through." Brown said.

"Knowing my wife, she probably wouldn't take no for an answer," Bruce chuckled. "I'm a daddy and I don't even have a cigar."

"Congratulations Amigo. I hate to break up this celebration, but we better get our hind ends to bed."

"Yeah, Bruce, congratulations from all of us," Richard said and started for his cot.

*　*　*

Chapter 37

Up early the next morning, dressed and ready for inspection, Bruce looked around to see the men in full military dress and ready to meet formation head on. Getting the maneuvers to hell over with was #2 on the list of importance with the race for the chow lines being #1.

Immediately upon the last man to be seated, Commander Wilkins stood up and tapped the table with his knife handle. "Good morning men, I hear we have a new daddy this morning. How do you feel, Lawson… are you ready for battle?"

"Yes Sir, Commander Wilkins, and thanks for letting me have the call."

"You have a persistent young lady there, how could

I resist," Wilkins chuckled and looked around the room. "Alright men, heads up. When you leave here in 20 minutes remember to fill your canteen. Grab 3 MRE's and be ready for your day to run well into the night. What the hell, it might just take all night so you better grab 4 MRE's."

Moans and groans sounded throughout the room. "You enthusiasm gets me here," he slaps his rear. "That is only a hint of what awaits you on the battlefield in Iraq, believe me. Any questions?" He looked around the room. "Yes, Martinez?"

"Commander Sir, we been wondering what was taking so long, we were ready yesterday, hey Amigo's?"

The men shouted in response and waited for further orders. "Very good, your limousine will pick you up in 15 minutes." He answered the men with a salute and walked out.

Bruce turned to Roosevelt and looked into his eyes. "How do you feel, partner?"

"Very good Sarge. I studied the terrain on the map

last night," he said and went on to explain his findings to Bruce, Richard, Longview and the rest of the men. "Us eight men have 16 eyes and if we direct our vision ahead and to our partner's blind side, we should be able to stamp out any man who's a threat to us." He moved around to the other side of Bruce to let the men study his notes.

"This is very good Roosevelt," Richard said and moved away to let the men on his side of the table look at the map.

"I've already seen it," Longview said. "Me and Roosevelt stayed up pretty late working on the maneuvers and what to look for. I know I'm quiet, but I'm like a stick of dynamite when the need arises," Longview laughed. "I just want you to know that Graves."

Richard put his arm around the young man and jostled him around. "Hope to live up to what you expect of me. There's no doubt you will more than meet my expectation."

"Well men, let's go knock em in the butt," Bruce

said and returned his tray and dirty dishes to the drop off tub. He picked up his MRE's and filled his canteens.

The silence on the bus, from the chow hall to the battlefield, was deathlike and continued while positioning the squad and waiting for a signal to move out.

"This is the real deal, Roosevelt, good luck to you."

"Good luck to you Lawson. We'll celebrate tomorrow night at the PX."

"Sounds good."

*   *   *

Chapter 38

Under the weight of full battle rattle his butt was dragging and the rucksack on his back was beginning to paste the inside of his body armor to the sweat on his back. The full ray of the sun was beating down on his head or so it seems and frying his brain while sapping what little strength he had left to play these war games. "Cover me, Roosevelt," he whispered and moved forward. Gunshots erupted from behind and Bruce fell to the hot sand, looking ahead to see the dust rise around the Iraqi when he fell to the ground on top of his gun

"Damn, that had to hurt," Bruce smiled while making a wide search of the area to the front and both sides. He switched back to where he thought the barrel of a gun...Oh Shit!" Snorting like an angry bull and blowing dust puffs in front of his nose, he squeezed the trigger at about the same time Roosevelt stirred the dust at his right shoulder.

"There's the 3 foot sand berm to the right and to the left is the running trench I was telling you about last night, Lawson."

"Keep your eye on the berm and I'll scan the area around and beyond the ditch while we crawl toward it." After three yards or so he stopped to size up the situation. "I don't see a damn thing moving," Bruce said. "Anything along the top edge of the berm or the trenches, head...gun?"

"Nope, nothing, Sir."

"Have you forgotten what I said about the sir word?"

"Sorry Sarge, it slipped out before I could zip my lip."

"I'm gonna crawl forward and when I get to the left of the gully, you shoot anything that moves above the berm and I'll surprise them from the left. Once we claim the trench we can pick off any man above ground and carrying a weapon."

"You got it, Sarge. This damn sweat just won't go away and its stinging hell out of my eyes, how about you?"

"Ignore the pain." Bruce rose to all fours. "I'm moving in!" He fell to his stomach again. "What the hell?"

A helicopter flew low over them, kicking up dust and making visibility impossible. "Why doesn't the stupid bastard get the hell outta here," Bruce's voice was lost to the whirly bird noise. He grabbed his dust mask and cringed at the sand in his eyes.

Once his dust mask was in place, the helicopter moved off down the line for a greeting to the rest of the troop. He caught sight of Richard, who waved and donned his dust mask before the helicopter got to him.

"Son of a bitching fucking bastard," Bruce whispered rather loudly, and tried not the rub the grit around in his eyes.

"Just outside the building to the right Sarge. Do

you see it? Man or woman?"

"Looks like two people, a man hiding behind a woman? Keep your eye on him...shit! A gun! Roll to your right and I'll open fire over her left shoulder." The sand kicked up, leaving a gob of ink between them just as Bruce fired his weapon. "Hope to hell I didn't put a spot on the woman and spoil our perfect score," Bruce laughed at what he prayed wasn't a joke.

"I think we're okay, she's hightailing it back toward the building. I don't see anyone now, but..." Roosevelt stood up and with the SAW to his hip, aimed at three men coming out of the same building and squeezed off more shots than was needed, but what the hell.

"All three of them had guns."

"I know," Roosevelt laughed. "It gave me an adrenalin rush. Is that a good sign?"

"Hell yeah, man, it means you're still alive!" Bruce said and gave his partner a shoulder punch. "Watch the gully while I try to move around to the left."

"There's a jeep coming this way," Roosevelt yelled.

Something fell to the ground and rolled under the front of it. The explosion rolled the jeep and tossed the three passengers into the air. "The jeep is on fire and the men on the ground are too close to the flames. That's one for old Buck," Bruce said and looked around to return the old man's wave before crawling away.

"I see men running this way Sarge, and they look ready to take us out."

"Show em what you can do with that SAW of yours. I'm still trying to get around to the left side of the gully." Bruce searched the area around him and continued to inch toward the berm. Sand kick up around it and Bruce looked around to see Roosevelt with his machine gun still aimed at the berm.

*　*　*

Chapter 39

Nearing the edge of the ravine and dying of thirst, he heard a murmur of voices and with the stench of unwashed bodies, Bruce thought he was going to lose his innards. He worried too, about the distance between him and his partner, but wiped the sweat out of his eyes and stripped a grenade off his belt. He pulled the pin and tossed it into the gully.

After the explosion all was quiet. He belly crawled near the edge of the ravine to find six Iraqis sprawled out and looking very dead. "Oh shit," he sputtered and gagged again.

With the sudden appearance of Iraqi soldiers coming around the corner, Bruce rolled to his back and pulled the pin of another grenade. He tossed it into the ditch and did a double roll away from the blast

of heat that followed. He looked around at the noise

behind him to find Roosevelt with his SAW and bullets

flying over the dead bodies of the last Iraqi rush.

They jumped into the ravine at about the same

time and ran in the direction from which the Iraqis had

come. Four men were around the corner, laughing and

talking in Arabic.

Weary of hands in the air trick, Bruce raised his

weapon but recognition to the shouts of 'Congratula-

tions' he stepped back.

Roosevelt said something in Arabic. The men

returned a few words and both the men and Roosevelt

laughed. "Not to worry Sarge, they're dead."

"Ask them if they have been sleeping on these dirty

mattresses." There was a lack of trust as Bruce watched

and waited while the men and Roosevelt held a short

conversation.

"They slept here for two nights and warned me to

not let our guard down Sarge, because there's a lot more

Iraqis out there with the will to kill all American dogs."

They shook hands with the enemy and jogged a short distance in the manmade trench. "The sweat and sand in my eyes is hurting like hell and beginning to take a lot out of me. Let's stop and rest a minute but keep your eyes on the ledge," Bruce said. "You ready for a sip of water?"

"May as well work up an MRE and have lunch."

"Sounds like a winner to me." Bruce leaned his aching back into the bank. "Sounds like a war going on out there," he said and at the same instant, a grenade fell into the ditch between them. Roosevelt grabbed it and tossed it over the berm and not a second too soon as it exploded shortly after it left his hand.

"Oh shit!" Bruce said and grabbed his partner as he was sliding down the edge of the berm. "Are you hurt?"

"Just a little burn, nothing to worry about," Roosevelt said with a half assed grin. "We could've both been out of the game and this is a hell of spot to lay dead for the duration of the war."

"That was a brave move Roosevelt, but if it had of been the real thing it could have blown your hand off. What the hell made you take a chance like that?"

"I never thought about it Sarge, I just did it."

Feeling something more than partnership, Bruce pulled the young man into his arms and held on tight until the fear was under control.

*   *   *

Chapter 40

After lunch and the incident with the grenade, Bruce balanced his helmet on the butt of his rifle and raised it above the bank, his eye on Roosevelt's expression when he looked over the edge and back down again.

"A jeep is coming in this direction, Sarge. I'll take out the driver, you go for the gunner." Both men fired at the same time. The jeep rocked from side to side before it tossed the gunner to the ground and burst into flames with the driver still inside.

Roosevelt slid down into the ditch. "I think I'm sick, Sarge. I feel dizzy, like the heat inside my helmet is cooking my brain. I'm gonna move to the shady side and lay back against the berm."

Bruce knelt down beside him and held the portable canteen to his lips. "No Sarge, I'm gonna be sick."

"You're a little dehydrated, take a sip and it'll settle you right down." Bruce poured a little water into his palm and put it to Roosevelt's neck. He stopped for a quick glance over the berm and settled in again, alongside his partner in the shade. "It looks a little quiet. Do you feel up to moving down a ways just in case they know where we are?"

"Thanks Lawson, I think I'm coming around. They warned us of dehydration, but it just slipped up on me. I guess my mind was on other things. I thought for sure I was going to pass out on you, scared hell out of me."

"Learning and living this shit is believing. I almost fell out in Kuwait and Richard was just about in the same shape, but thank goodness he brought us both around. We were fresh out of boot camp and the reasoning behind partnering two young punks is beyond me."

"Lucky for me, I had you today," Roosevelt laughs at his lack of experience. "Maybe by the time we're sent to Iraq, I can carry my own weight."

Bruce did a squat shuffle in the ditch and with rifle ready, he rose up for a quick glance and just as his heart fell to his toes, he pulled off three quick rounds. Within seconds, Roosevelt was there at his side, his machine gun ready, but the three Iraqis lay flat of their backs, roasting in the hot sun like three dead pigs.

"Damn Sarge, three yards or so more and they would have been on top of us."

"Do you believe in God?" Bruce asks and looks at Roosevelt for an answer.

"You damn betcha, Lawson," Roosevelt said with his finger pointed to the sky. "Us old country boys learned a long time ago, the need for the man up there."

Bruce made a wide sweep of the terrain. "That rock formation to the left?"

"Yeah, three of them," Roosevelt said and aimed his SAW alongside Bruce's M16. Call it gut feeling or whatever, Roosevelt whirled around and pulled off another two quick rounds.

Bruce cringed, but kept a vigil on the rock while hoping Roosevelt ended the battle for whatever lay behind them.

"God again," Roosevelt laughed and aimed his machine gun toward the target.

Shutting the sounds of rifle shots and explosions out, his eyes never wavered from the rock formation. Three men stepped out of the Iraqi hut to the left. Roosevelt turned his SAW on the men and yelled in Arabic. All six hands reached for the sky.

Bruce felt like he had one eye on the Iraqis and the other on the rock. At about the same time Bruce felt they were clean, Roosevelt yells again and the men fall to the ground.

Three men came out from behind the rock, their guns pumping ink spots in the sand too damn close to be funny. Bruce took out the enemy of three and looked around to see the three prisoners on the ground spring to their feet.   One of them ripped something from his waist and pulled back to throw. Roosevelt pulled off a round from his Saw causing a quarterback fumble and all three men to bury their noses in the hot sand.

Bruce felt the blast from the grenade but not nearly to the extent as the dead Iraqis. The noise going on further down the line was war, but the trench was eerie quiet. Bruce's knees felt so unmanageable at the moment, he just lay against the edge of the berm and tried not to let Roosevelt know how damn scared he was.

"Oh Lordy me!!!" Roosevelt turned and slid down the side of the berm.

"They were blown up by their own grenade." Bruce gave him a knuckle punch to the shoulder. "War is hell."

"We haven't even begun to fight and already I hate it." Bruce looked back at him and let him rant on. "Back home we hunted almost everything there was to hunt and it was fun. We could eat the kill and hang the heads on the wall," his boyish smile won him a man hug from Bruce. "I hadn't noticed but it's getting dark. Let's move down a ways Sarge, and I'll take first guard while you sleep."

Silence fell between them and brought a sideways glance from Bruce. He vowed to keep this tender young man safe and knew at that moment, he would give his own life to save the life of young Vernon T. Roosevelt.

Bruce looked down when he felt Roosevelt squeeze his hand. "Thank you Sarge for being my friend as well as my partner."

"You speak Arabic so good I had to look at you to be sure you were you and not someone from the other side."

"When war in Iraq looked like a sure thing, I took night classes to learn the language," Roosevelt said. "I wanted to be as ready as I could to help win this war."

"Lucky for us," the two men share a chuckle as Bruce brushed aside the larger rocks so he could lay back for a little shuteye.

* * *

Chapter 41

Except for a few stars twinkling in the sky, the night was so dark it was hard for a man to see his own hand in front of his face. The Iraqis were chanting threats in the distance and wondering if the enemy is on a 24-7 week, Bruce donned his night vision glasses and pushed his sleeve away from his watch face. Two hours and he felt like he'd hardly slept at all.

"You awake Sarge?"

"Yeah," Bruce said and crawled over to the berm to have a look around the terrain. "What's all the noise about?"

"Playing with our minds no doubt."

"It'll be daylight in about three hours, why don't you try to get some sleep?" He watched Roosevelt settle down in a fetal position with his head on the rucksack. His mind wavers between his two men friends, and wondered where Richard was spending the night.

Bruce looked out across the terrain and for reasons unknown to him, gut instinct no doubt; he whirled around to find a shadowy figure on the bank above his partner. He squeezed the trigger and the man fell into the ditch across Roosevelt's leg.

Roosevelt rolled to his side and grabbed up his gun. The Iraqi said something, but unable to understand him, Bruce had the man's head in his sights but lowered it when his partner's hand came up. "The man's dead Sarge and feels it a privilege to shake the hand of the best combat soldiers he's ever come up against."

Bruce laughed and shook the man's hand, but kept vigilance on the area surrounding them. He looked around again and chuckled when he caught sight of his purple mark on the man's forehead.

Roosevelt laughed and translated what the man had said to Bruce. "He said not to worry, you already shot his head off."

Bruce chuckled again, but soon tuned out the men's conversation and after covering the terrain above the two men, he looked back around and over the berm. "Don't let the enemy distract you Roosevelt, I hear tell they're good at that."

The sudden lack of conversation behind him brought Bruce around to find Roosevelt and the Iraqi had called it a day. His night vision goggles seemed to be having a bit of a problem or maybe it was just him having trouble seeing through sleep-craved eyes, but the chants were still out there.

*   *   *

Chapter 42

Two hours later, the sunshine was a welcome sight but the heat he could do without. He pulled the bandana from around his neck and wiped the sweat off of his face and out of his eyes, miserable as hell and starving to death.

"How's it going, Sarge?"

"Don't see shit going on out there," he said and turned when the two men leaned into the berm beside him. "Could be we've won the battle," he chuckled and caught the, *I know something you don't know* in the Iraqis expression and was troubled by it. "How about some breakfast?" Bruce said and told Roosevelt to ask his friend if he has breakfast.

The Iraqi pulled out an MRE from his backpack

and smiled at Bruce. "Yes sir, Sergeant."

"Fancy that," Bruce said as he lay against the bank and churned up his breakfast. "The man speaks English." He whirled to the sound of rifle shots and seeing Richard behind the rifle and his heart pounding against his rib cage Bruce tossed what was left of his breakfast aside and brought the barrel of his gun around to the tank advancing toward his friend. Just as he yelled, "damn Buck, let him have it," a grenade fell into the tank and exploded.

Longview was there at Richard's side, shooting at something beyond the tank. More than a dozen men were running toward them with globs of ink flipping sand perks up about three yards in front of Richard and his partner.

Bruce pushed out of his safety zone and looked around to find Roosevelt at his side. Another grenade landed in front of the advancing enemy. Bodies tumbled in all directions, but the attack continued. At about the right distance, Roosevelt fell to the ground beside

Bruce and they began to fire upon the enemy at the same time. Between the four of them and with the help of Buck and his grenade launcher, the Iraqis were losing the battle.

"You scared shit out of me when you climbed out of that ditch."

"It wasn't so bad Roosevelt, I had you there beside me."

Bruce scanned the area from which the Iraqis had come and another look around the over turned tank. "Do you see anything?"

"Nothing Sir."

Bruce reached up for his partner. "Give the ole man a hand up and let's join the other men." He grabbed Richard first off and pulled him in for a shoulder-to-shoulder man hug and turned to young Longview with a handshake.

Buck Jamison and Jim Brown joined them with shoulder punches and handshakes with everyone talking at the same time. Bruce saw Martinez and Brandon jogging toward them and caught a wave from Martinez at about the same time Brandon stopped to pull off a few rounds at the building.

Bruce whirled around and finding nothing but bodies on the ground, he made a wide sweep around the terrain to find his dead Iraqi peeking over the edge of the berm and back around again, to see Longview with his rifle up and ready to fire at the ditch.

"No!" Roosevelt yelled," the man's already dead."

Longview looked doubtful, but lowered his rifle and stepped back.

"I came about that close to getting shot, Amigos," Martinez laughed and held his finger about two inches from his left ear.

"Did you see that direct hit I made with the grenade launcher?" Buck laughed. "Sheer luck, believe me... nothing but sheeeer luck."

"Luck had nothing to do with it Buck," Richard said but stepped back out of the way when Brandon raised his rifle again.

Brandon lowered his weapon and looked to be staring at something unfavorable to him. "Are you men ready to rush that building?"

"Come on men, let's get this shit over with," Bruce said and waved Roosevelt to the far left. Sweeping the vast openness between him and the building with his eyes, he fell to his stomach again, his chin brushing the hot sand when he searched the area from left to right. "What do you think, Partner?"

"I don't think..." Roosevelt started and reached out to touch Bruce. "There's someone in the window, can't tell if it's male or female."

"Yeah, I see it," Bruce said. "Watch for a gun."

"There's a gun! Looks to me like it's aimed in the direction of the other men."

"How far would you say we are?" Bruce asked as he reasoned the distance in his head. Shots sounded and by chance Bruce was looking to the right to see sand kick up in front of Richard. "Take him out, Roosevelt."

Shots rang out again and the sand in front of

Richard and Longview, turned inside out like spewing bubbles of hot pudding.

Roosevelt answered with a riddle of shots from his machine gun and the body fell across the windowsill seconds before the sound of breaking glass reached him.

Buck launched a grenade in the direction of the building and they watched it disappear behind a mound of sand.

"What the hell?" Bruce muttered at about the same time as the grenade exploded. Arms and legs were all they could see from where they were.

"I sure as hell didn't see any bunkers on the map," Roosevelt admitted and rolled his eyes at Bruce. "Could be more, Sarge."

"Landscape looks undisturbed." He swung around to the ditch where he and Roosevelt had spent the night to see heads and guns of three Iraqis. Without thinking he rolled to his side with a grunt and brought his weapon around with rapid-fire.

Roosevelt whirled to the right and swept the bank

with his SAW. "I wonder how many more are in there?"

The sounds of whirly bird motors roused Bruce to the sight of two apache helicopters. "What the hell are they doing here?" he wondered aloud and watched the two missiles streak across the sky to a ditch they couldn't see from where they were and explode. He could see four or five bodies and possibly more, tossed into the air?

"What do you think Sarge, should we follow the berm around behind those buildings?"

"Good idea."

"Oh shit!" Roosevelt said when a streak of paint sliced the air between the two of them. "Son of a bitch, that was close.

"That shot didn't come from the building. This gully must circle the building with the enemy waiting for us around the corner. It's do or die partner, how about it, ready press on?"

"Yes, Sir...Sarge let's get it to hell over with."

Their rifles aimed as they ran for the ditch and

jumped in to slide down the five foot bank with Bruce covering the right and Roosevelt the left. They moved to within the corner of the ditch with hardly a breath sounding between them. What awaited them around the corner was an imaginary of the worst kind and a possible end to their perfect score.

Roosevelt put an arm around Bruce and whispered in his ear. "Before we turn the corner and step out into the open, let's toss a grenade to both sides of the gully ahead."

"What if it's women and children hiding from danger?" Bruce smiled and put a finger to his lips, as he stole a quick glance around the corner. He grinned at the younger man before they rounded the corner to join four women and nine kids.

Roosevelt laughed the laugh of relief and asked the women if they had explosives on them. A little boy, no more than seven years old shook his head and held up the V sign, showing a gap of missing teeth beneath his smile. One of the women turned to point at the blind corner and turned back with prayer hands beneath her chin to plead with Roosevelt.

"Their husbands are around the bend there, and are being forced to fight. They beg us not to shoot their men."

"Ask her how we can tell them apart," Bruce smiled at the children while waiting.

"She says the soldiers will be behind their husbands, ordering them to shoot or die."

They approached the blind corner to find five men waiting for them. Two men in front fell to their knees and Bruce quickly took out the three men left standing. The two men down on their knees with hands above their heads, bowed several times to kiss the ground.

Bruce whirled around to the activity going on behind him. With caution and weapon ready, he moved aside to let the women rush into their husband's arms.

*   *   *

Chapter 43

Bruce fell in behind Roosevelt for a sneaky approach to the blind corner ahead. "What do you think?" he asked.

"The men back there thanked us and said there would be five men waiting around the corner with guns. The four men in front are being forced to fight," Roosevelt said. "I'll peek around and if the soldier is standing in back of the men, I'll give them the finger and you go in shooting."

The finger call was a new one for Bruce and was all he could do to keep from laughing, but what the hell. Roosevelt used the butt of his gun to get down on his stomach for a sneak peek. When the finger came up, Bruce whipped around the corner and fell to his knees.

The four men in front fell to their stomachs leaving the soldier in back to catch the bullet.

A hundred yards or so further down the gully, the sound of gunshots brought six soldiers around the corner ahead. Four fell to their knees and while the two behind were attempting to aim their rifles, Roosevelt sprang into action with his SAW.

The men bowed to the ground several times and stood up with grins on their faces.

Bruce wondered at the significance of a three-bow thank you, but shook hands with the men while leaving his keen eyesight to search them for hidden weapons. "Wonder where we are and what the hell's going on above ground," Bruce mumbled and chuckled about the finger thing. "Tell me about this finger thing we just did."

"When I talked to the first two men they said, *good men waiting for finger sign fall down, leaving bad guys to eat bullet.*"

Bruce placed his helmet on the butt of his rifle and

raised it to just above the bank and waited for a response. "Something's not right up there," he shook his head and looked at Roosevelt. "Let's move about six yards down the ditch and let the barrel of our rifles and fingers on the trigger, lead the way while we take a look."

Roosevelt fell in behind and once ready to make their move, they looked over the berm. Sure as hell and with never knowing from whom the shots had come from, six Iraqis lay in the sand with their rifles nearby.

"That was easy as taking a rattle from a baby, and a whole hell of lot easier than taking one from a rattle-snake." Roosevelt laughed at his own joke. "When we're finished here and we're both still alive and in the PX, let's get drunk."

"Sounds like a winner and I'll buy the beers, but we're not finished here so let's move down a couple of yards more and check out the building," Bruce whispered near Roosevelt's ear. "If you see a hand with a gun in it and its not one of our men, shoot!"

"I'll sure as the hell try to keep you alive for the celebration," Roosevelt said. "You better damn sure keep me alive to enjoy it."

"I will Partner, you can enter that in your promise book." Bruce looked over the berm and felt his heartbeat run away with him. The window, he wondered, is it man or woman? Blobs of ink kicked up the sand to his left and having no idea where the shots came from, he put a bullet in the window just above their head and slid back into the ditch, grabbing Roosevelt's hip pocket to pull him down. Both men lay against the berm for a breather.

Bruce looked at his partner and the too tired to move reflected his woes as well. "Two hours sleep out of twenty four is hard on this old body," he said and let out a groan when he struggled to his knees. "Sure is quiet out there, what do you think?"

Before Roosevelt could answer, a siren broke the silence and Captain Wilkins' voice on the bullhorn was pleasing to the ear. "Cease fire men, the war is over. We have beer and hamburgers waiting for you at the bar-beque pit."

Bruce took the helping hand offered by his young partner to pull him out of the ditch. He straightened the lopsided rucksack on his back and jiggled the battle armor loose from the hairs on his sweaty chest. "Ready?" he said and turned to Roosevelt for an answer.

"Sounds good to me Sarge, I can smell them hamburgers and one has my name on it."

"The dead have risen," Bruce laughed and pointed to the three Iraqis who were brushing dust from their clothing while mopping sweaty foreheads at the same time.

"They're checking one another for ink blobs," Roosevelt chuckled and when he looked around to see he and Bruce were doing the same thing he chuckled again.

Bruce felt something around his leg and looked down to see the little girl they met earlier in the ditch. He picked her up and looked around to find Roosevelt holding the little boy. With a hug and a kiss on her cheek, he lowered her to the ground and stepped away.

With an arm around Roosevelt's waist, he hustled him over to join their comrades, Buck, Richard, Martinez, Brandon, what the hell, all twelve was present and accounted for. They gave each other the once over for ink blobs. "I can still hear that hamburger calling my name," Roosevelt said and turned toward the pit.

Walking across the battlefield and surrounded by a group of Iraqis, Bruce was completely taken aback by the perfect English and said as much to one of the men.

"I was a sergeant in Saddam Hussein's militia Army but had misgivings about Saddam. Two years ago, when I came to this country, I volunteered in the United States Army to spy on the insurgents but was sent here to train these men to fight like Iraqi's."

"Well, what do you know," Bruce sounded completely surprised. "Is that a blob of ink there alongside your shoulder?"

"You mother fuckers knocked out my entire battalion. Maybe now your government will send me abroad and let me do what I do best."

Bruce sat at a picnic table alongside Richard with the two younger men across from them. With everyone talking at the same time, Bruce nursed his beer and took in the smart moves made by his bunkhouse buddies.

"Hell man, no doubt about it, this hombre is ready to fight," Martinez said between bites.

Bruce downed the last of his beer and grabbed another off the waiter's tray. He wanted another hamburger, but three was plenty.

"How the hell did they make my grenades so damn believable?" Buck wonders aloud.

"Had to be rigged," Roosevelt said. "You know, like in the war movies,"

Richard put an arm around Bruce's shoulder. "Why so quiet?"

"Tired, I guess," he said and tried to shake off his worry, but Iraq was weighing heavy on his mind at the moment. "I'm for hitting the shower stall and taking this battle rattle off. See you back at the barracks."

"Want some company?"

"No Roosevelt, stay and enjoy yourself."

* * *

Chapter 44

Bruce opened his laptop and smiled at the list of names and letters waiting to be read. He sat down on his cot and leaned back against the wall while reading the one from pops, his heart swelling with loneliness. "Lord, I miss you Pops, and you too Mom."

Next, came a short one from Billy Joe and surprisingly a short one from Sheila. Selling lots of cars they said and will be glad when I come home. Samantha? Confused as to why she would be writing to him he opened it and found a one-word letter. "Surprise!"

The nut, and how funny, Lana was sending the same thing to Richard. "And now," he murmurs under his breath as he opens Lana's e-mail. "The best is yet to come." His stomach filled with excitement at just the heading.

Hello my darling;

Your daughter said dada today when I showed her
your picture. She helps me get through each day, thank you
sweetheart for giving her to me. Having her around makes
me wonder how I would have passed these miserable lonely
days without you...

He grinned when he came to the part about his
mom helping Lana make new curtains for the kitchen.
That honey of mine can probably work the sewing
machine as well as she works the computer, he thought,
and with fingers working the keyboard and tears in his
eyes, he closed out the final letter and lay back on his
pillow.

"Are you awake Sarge?"

He opened his eyes to find Roosevelt looking down
at him and pushed up on one elbow. "Damn. Must
have fallen asleep and I wanted to clean my rifle."

"Why don't we do it together?"

He swung his feet off the cot and pulling his cleaning supplies out of the closet, he spread the whole works out on the floor alongside Roosevelt.

By the time their rifles were cleaned and put away, most of the men were milling around the barracks while several were cleaning their weapons.

He watched Richard when he opened his laptop and signed in for his e-mail. There was a frown on his face at first and Bruce knew he was wondering why Lana was e-mailing him. He threw back his head and laughed. "Hey bro, our gals are full of tricks," he said and looked around to find Bruce looking back at him.

"Knowing those two, I bet they're saving the best for last."

* * *

Chapter 45

Good morning beautiful world, Bruce smiled his appreciation, and to think all I have to do before the movie tonight is about any damn thing I want as long as I get my packing out of the way, and I sure as hell plan to enjoy every minute of this day. Thinking of his beautiful Lana and baby daughter, he smiled again and aside from the loneliness and a few war game sore spots, he felt surprisingly fit.

Lying there with his head propped up on the pillow and watching the rest of the barracks come to life was like crossing a stream and hoping to reach the other side before the dam breaks. He stretched, adding at least two inches to his 5'11" before swinging his feet out of bed and onto the floor.

He left the barracks and when he returned from his trip to the john, he found Richard standing in the middle of the floor with a smile on his face. "The Commander was just here and believe it or not, we're having a luau tonight Hawaiian style with roasted pig and all the trimmings. After the war movie there will be music and girls in the dance hall."

"Hell, I feel like dancing," Bruce shuffled his feet on the floor and wiggled his hips. "My e-mail from Lana was a confession of sorts and if they can go dancing why the hell not us?"

"I got the same thing from Sam and I'm ready if you are," Richard joined Bruce in a chuckle. "You watch my back and I'll watch yours."

"You're on friend. It's early yet, but think I'll hit the shower before it gets too busy."

Spiffy clean and smelling good, Bruce returned to the barracks and checked his e-mail again to find one from the ole man and a short one from Billy Joe. Other than missing me, the folks are fine and Billy Joe sold nine cars last week. "Way to go, Billy Joe."

His body remained in Ft. Irwin, but his mind took him to Oregon to see Lana, so busy and beautiful, working at her desk. "Boy, I miss you sweetheart," he thought aloud.

Bruce finished his e-mail and feeling the hip bump to his shoulder, turned his nose up to the smell of a handsome young man on the make. "Hey Sarge, might be a good idea if you and Graves go along with me and Longview after the movie tonight, to mix and mingle with the young chicks at the dance hall and maybe keep us young punks out of trouble."

"We're thinking about it," Bruce said. "A two hour nap should be sufficient. You do remember guard duty at 0400 hrs don't you?"

"We can sleep on the plane to Kuwait," Roosevelt said and grinned.

The men left the barracks and long before they reached the chow hall, the smell of a pig barbequing on the spit made his mouth water. Twenty minutes later, he pushed aside an empty plate and rubbed his overstuffed stomach. "That was even better than home cooked, and the apple pie was almost as good as old granny's."

"That's crazy man," Richard said. "I was just recalling good memories of your mother's kitchen and her apple pie."

With tray in hand, Roosevelt caught Bruce at the tray and silverware return. "The movie starts in 45 minutes."

After the movie, the men gathered outside to revel in the acting ability of the leapfrog squad. "Can you believe the reality of those explosions, and what about the stunt men?" Bruce said and looked around for Richard.

"If that had of been us flying through the air and falling to the ground we'd be dead," Richard chuckled. "No doubt about it."

"How do you like the name of the movie Amigo's?" Martinez said with the look of pride about him. "The Fighting Brigade...I like it."

"We did look good out there," Roosevelt said. "And

the enemy died real good."

"Hey Graves, that grenade I launched into that damn tank?" Buck chuckled and landed a knuckle punch to Richard's shoulder. "It sure as hell saved your life because that was one mean looking Iraqi and he was out to squash you and Longview like a couple of bugs."

"Oh hell yeah," Roosevelt joined in. "My heart fell to my big toe and wasn't a damn thing my SAW could do."

"Thanks Buck Jamison, you not only saved their lives but…" Bruce pointed to himself and Roosevelt. "Ours as well hey partner. Maybe after a few beers tonight, I'll give you a full man hug and a kiss of gratitude to the cheek."

"Ye gads Lawson, don't go getting mushy," Buck scrubbed at the imaginary kiss with the back of his hand. "A handshake will do just fine."

"That grenade I tossed into the bunker, the explosion and the men flying through the air looked real enough," Bruce said. "Yep, gotta give it to those stunt men again."

"Hell yeah," Richard said. "What about the one I threw into the bunker at the corner of the building. Sure surprised hell out of me cause I had no idea a bunker was there."

"I thought it was neat, how they caught each of us tossing grenades," Brown joined in. "I didn't know where the hell you men were. It was like me and Buck was on our own."

"I know what the hell you mean Amigos, there was a couple of times I saw the rest of you. Brandon and me were working our territory like Siamese twins, one mind with four arms and four legs. You sure you guys didn't hide out somewhere until the war was over?"

"We saw the camera when it swung around behind Buck and knew somebody was taking pictures," Davidson said. "Don't know how the hell they took pictures of me and Goodwin because when we weren't fighting the fight of our life, I watched for the cameras."

"I came within a half an inch of catching it in the

head," Goodwin joined in.

"Martinez wanted to know if they were sending the injured home," Brandon punched his partner on the shoulder and doubled over with laughter.

"Well, I did almost get hit and the thought of home did cross my mind."

Captain Wilkins slipped into the group and made his presence known. "To answer your question Martinez, we would have put you in the morgue without a barbecue or a movie."

"Thanks to the Holy Man I dodged the bullet," Martinez laughed.

"Well men, the dance hall awaits with decorations, girls and beer," Captain Wilkins said.

"Don't forget guard duty at 0400 hrs. Alright men, you are free to go and don't let me find you in the brig for drunken and disorderly conduct."

The men gave a salute to the departing Captain, let out a yell and tossed their booney hats over their heads.

* * *

Chapter 46

Sitting near the door with Richard and toe tapping to the feel of the music, Bruce was second-guessing the young lady coming in their direction. Am I the image in her eye or is it this guy next to me? He felt flush but smiled his acceptance and took her hand in his.

It hadn't been all that long since he'd held a woman in his arms, but had been a hell of a long time since he'd held a woman this close who wasn't his wife. To his surprise, she fell in step with the sureness of a professional. The tenseness in his shoulders began to relax, letting him enjoy the music and her company. The magic of the moment however, ended much too soon, "You're very smooth on the dance floor," he said and thanked her for the dance.

"You make it easy to be smooth," she smiled and flushed slightly when she pointed to where she had been sitting.

He walked the young woman to her chair and crossed the room to sit down beside Richard and order another beer. "I think I'll head back to the barracks after I drink this and get some beauty sleep before guard duty."

"You sure do know how to dance Sarge," Roosevelt said. "You and your partner looked real good together out there on the dance floor."

"Why don't you young punks go ask these young ladies to dance?"

"Would it make me unfaithful to my girlfriend?"

"Just keep your wits about you and don't let your love tool stray from the harness," Bruce teased and looked up to catch Richard's back sauntering across the floor to bow at the young lady sitting there. She smiled up at him and moved with ease into his waiting arms.

Bruce glimpsed the young lady he had danced with

earlier and turned for the bar. With another beer in hand, he stepped outside to get away from the cigarette smoke for some fresh air. He studied the stars and ignored the feeling of a presence behind him while hoping she would back away.

"Sarge?" Roosevelt called out to him. "Are you alright?"

"I'm fine Roosevelt," Bruce said as relief fell over him. "Needed a breath of fresh air. Look at the sky; have you ever seen this many stars at one time?"

"It is a beautiful night, Sir."

"There you go again."

"How's that, Sir?"

"That title you keep trying to make me wear."

"Sorry Lawson, Sir," Roosevelt said with a hint of laughter in his voice.

"You're a fine young man Vernon, and don't tell anyone I said this, but you are beginning to grow on me and I'm getting used to having you around."

"Thank you Bruce, you're not half bad yourself for a

sergeant."

"Let's go in and dance another round, what do you say?" Bruce turned to find the young lady standing in the doorway and he smiled. "One more and then I must leave for guard duty." After the dance, he thanked the young lady and left the dance hall.

"If you're going to the barracks Sergeant, your limousine awaits?"

Bruce climbed into the back of the jeep. "Hope I have enough money for the fare."

"I'm sure you have nothing to worry about. Don't know if you remember me, but the day you arrived in Ft. Irwin, when was that…four, five weeks ago? I was the one who put out the welcome mat."

"Goodyear, as I recall."

"Yeah. Do you think your stay here will help you in Iraq?"

"Hell man, are you telling me that wasn't the Iraqi desert out there?"

"That real, huh?" Goodyear stopped the jeep in

front of the barracks and let the motor idle. "Well, here you are Lawson and good luck to you."

"Thanks, Goodyear and good luck to you on your next group of recruits."

Bruce set the alarm, lay back on his cot and let his thoughts focus on Lana and the feel of her in his arms. "The young lady tonight had blond hair and was about the same size as you honey," he whispers into the darkness. "Aware of the male hormones kicking in, I shied away from the touch of her body. Oh yes indeedy Sweetheart, I was husband perfect tonight."

*   *   *

Chapter 47

Bruce sprang out of bed to shut off the alarm and he crowded around the corner basin to splash a handful of water to his face and brush his teeth. Roosevelt and the rest of the gang were sitting around and ready for guard duty. "Did you get any sleep?"

"I came in shortly after you so I slept a couple of hours or so," he answered with a grin. "Not nearly enough for a growing boy though."

All twenty-four men stood around in small groups waiting for Sgt. Smith, who arrived shortly after and started two men walking in opposite directions. Every ten minutes thereafter two men were to leave the starting area until twelve men were walking the first perimeter.

Bruce met his first guard with a salute. "Moham-mad," he said.

"Ala," Davidson answered with a salute.

The threats and chants from out of the darkness with only a roll of barbed wire between him and the enemy, was nerve racking to say the least. It was all fun and games, but Bruce however, is aware that anything can happen and is ready to let his ink bullets fly.

It was upon the appearance of guard number three when there was no answer to Bruce's password that he fell to the ground with his rifle ready. "Halt," he called from behind the departing man.

The man whirled around to catch Bruce's ink blotch to the chest. He approached with caution to turn him over and sure as hell, his intuition paid off. He turned to the heavy breathing behind him and found it coming from a man trying to pull his feet free of the barbs in the fence. He sprang to one side, squeezed the trigger while on the move and watched the man roll onto his back. Searching the area around the enemy, he crouched down and waited for a guard to approach from the front or back.

Brandon moved in from behind and stopped. "Mohammed," he called out with a salute.

"Ala," Bruce answered in return with his hand to his brow.

"What the hell happened here?"

"I got me two men," Bruce said and pointed to the man on the ground. "He was pretending to be one of us and this one was trying to come through this roll of barbed wire."

"Holy hell!" Brandon said and moved in to have a look. "You okay, Lawson?"

"Yeah."

"What's up here?" Richard joined the men.

"Lawson picked up on his intuition and shot these two men," Brandon said.

Bruce was starting to worry about his partner. "Say Richard, did you start out after Roosevelt?"

"No, Martinez took off before I did. Longview took

off after Brandon here."

"We've got to look for Martinez," Brandon said. "I can't let anything happen to my partner, why don't you guys continue with your guard duty while I look for my man."

"You're looking at one dumb Mexican," Martinez staggers up to the men. "Remember the Commander telling us if we got shot we'd know it; well I sure as hell knew it because it hurts like hell."

"You're shot?" Brandon said.

"That's what I said," Martinez said. "Sheeit, I thought this damn war was over."

"What seems to be the problem, men?" Sgt. Smith stepped in and looked the men over and laughed when he saw the ink blob on Martinez. "Let this be a lesson to you Martinez, never let your guard down."

"What now, Sgt. Smith?" Martinez said.

"You're dead my man, may as well head to the barracks." Sgt. Smith laughed again. "You just lost your Unit a perfect score. An apology will probably be the first order of the day tomorrow morning."

"Holy Virgin Mary," Martinez said. "I hope you men can forgive me before we go to war with the Iraqis. I promise you, never to let my guard down again."

Guard duty over and their asses dragging behind them, the men returned to the barracks to find Martinez with a grin from ear to ear. "I didn't die," he said. "My blob is here on my armor, look! I'm still alive!"

*   *   *

Chapter 48

More than 500 men were milling around the roadside with most of them worrying with last minute changes to their equipment for easier handling. The first and second half of the leapfrog unit was bunched together around the end of barracks #84 waiting for the covered military transports to arrive. "Do you think all of these men are going to Kuwait?"

Taking a look at the men around them, Richard leans in to Bruce. "Their expression of I'd-rather-be-anywhere-but-here is a carbon copy of yours," Richard chuckles. "Not changing the subject, but I almost fell asleep in my breakfast this morning," he chuckles again.

"I know, but take a look at our partners," Bruce

pointed at the two young men on the ground with their backs to the wall.

"Guess we're holding up pretty well for a couple of oldsters in this young man's army," Richard said. "But then, we didn't play as hard as they did on the dance floor. Did you remember to pack your tape of the fighting brigade?"

"Oh yeah," Bruce said and thinking about the special effects in the film and the feeling of pride in the leapfrog unit brought a smile, however short lived, to his lips. "Damn," he swore and held his back with both hands. "How the hell long do we have to melt in this damn heat? Our transportation vehicles should have been here two hours ago?"

Roosevelt pushed himself up off the ground. "Here they come now, Sarge."

Bruce climbed aboard and squeezed in beside Roosevelt. He looked out the window to see the soldier from Saddam's Army and raised his hand in a salute. Martinez, Brandon, Buck, Brown, Richard and Longview stepped into the bus and sat down somewhere behind. Eight out of our twelve is not bad, but where the hell is the other four?

"Attention men."

He looked up to find Captain Wilkins standing in the aisle at the front of the bus. "Sorry to be late, but we were waiting for orders from headquarters. Your weapons will be returned to you at Camp Wolf, located at the backside of the Kuwait International Airport. It looks pretty much like the rest of the country over there," he smiled and paused for a second or so. "Ugly, barren and dry. However, a 24 hour leave awaits you before you leave for Kuwait."

Bruce ignored the yells and wondered what the hell he's gonna do with 24 damn hours?

"You will report to the waiting area at 1200 hrs and prepare for deployment." He paused at the door and looked at each man. "You're a fine group of soldiers and I feel honored, as your Commanding Officer, to have worked with you here at Ft. Irwin and look forward to more of the same on the battlefield."

Bruce lay back and fell asleep. Almost immediately, or so it seemed, Bruce was awakened by someone shaking his shoulder. "We just pulled into the armory, Sarge, thought you might like to straighten out your legs and get your gear ready to go."

"Thanks partner." Bruce grabbed his gear out from under the seat in front of him and leaned his shoulder into Roosevelt. "What are you going to do with 24 hours?"

"Hadn't thought much about it Sarge, other than where the hell I'm gonna sleep."

"Yeah, me too."

"Look at those people waiting on the tarmac, do you know anybody out there?" The young man smiled again and points out the window. "I see my mother, Sarge. I would like you to meet my two favorite women."

Bruce pushed his rucksack forward to see what his partner was talking about. "Oh my God, oh my God!

The whole damn family is out there, mom, pop, my in-laws and there's my wife with a daughter I get to see for the first time! "

"Hey Bruce," Richard yelled from somewhere behind him. "Look out the damn window man, there's people from home out there and my Samantha's with them."

"Oh my God, Richard, we're gonna have a party tonight." He slid to the edge of his seat to strap on his rucksack and fasten his pouch around his waist. He piled his armored vest, helmet and gas mask on the seat behind him. "Why the hell don't they open the damn doors and let us out of here."

"Calm down men before you have heart failure," the driver called back over his shoulder followed by a hearty laugh. "Your C.O. is on his way," and with that said, he opened the door for Captain Wilkins.

He just stood there with a wide grin on his face. "You can take your equipment with you or leave it here. The bus will be locked and parked near the Armory. I would advise you to take your duffle, find a laundromat and be sure to use the Permethrin chemical as directed on the label. Have a good time men, nobody deserves it more than you. I don't want to see your ugly faces before noon tomorrow."

*   *   *

Chapter 49

Bruce slipped into his rucksack and stepped down off the bus with duffle bag in hand. His knees buckled momentarily until he locked them against the weight before jogging toward his wife and family. He grabbed Lana and squeezed so tight the baby between them began to kick and scream.

"We're hurting Sari, honey." Lana explained with a quick kiss and stepped back to let her mother take the baby. She stepped in again for another hug before backing away to let the rest of the family have a turn.

He pulled his mother gently into his arms and could feel her love. So many years of being her little boy closed in on him, bringing with it tears of joy. "I love you mama, you beautiful lady."

"It's only been a short while honey, but it feels like you've been out of town for a year," she said and kissed him before moving aside to let pops in.

The old man stood there with his hand out, but Bruce threw his arms around the most important man in his life. He yearned for the office and the daily presence of his dad.

"The office is not the same without you around, son."

"I know dad, and I'm not the same without you and the office. My life and love is there with you and Lana."

"We gotta break this up boy, cause you still got more necks to hug."

He looked around for his in-laws and reached out for Lana's mother. "Mom Elkington, one of my favorite women," he pulled her into his arms for a bear hug and reached out with the other arm to embrace his father-in-law. "Pop Elkington, this is an honor to have you here and away from your busy golf schedule. How about after I practice several 18 holes when I get home, you and me get together again, a dollar a hole?"

"You're on Bruce, looking forward to it."

"We reserved the banquet room at Denny's here in Mojave," Pops said. "Here son, take this little wiggle worm before she starts crying."

Bruce pulled the blanket away from the tiny face and grinned at Lana. "She looks like you honey."

Lana cuddled up to the two of them and kissed the baby on the cheek. "She is really looking you over, hon. This is your daddy, Sari."

Bruce held her face up to his and kissed her tiny lips. "Love you Sweet Stuff," he whispers into her ear. "Daddy loves his baby girl."

"Sarge? I want you to meet the two women in my life. Mom, this is my partner, Sgt. Bruce Lawson," Roosevelt said and surprising the hell out of Bruce, he rubs a finger to Sari's chin and she smiles up at him. He takes her into his arms and steps back out of the way.

Mrs. Roosevelt grabbed Bruce around the neck. "Thank you so much for taking my son under your wing, Sgt. Lawson."

"Oh come now, Mrs. Roosevelt, I'm the lucky one here. I'd put my life in the hands of this young sharp shooter any day."

"Yes," she laughed. "Much to my unease his daddy put a water pistol in his hands at age three and from there he graduated every year into something more powerful."

"This is Alice, the girl I intend to marry when I get home," Roosevelt said and nudged her toward Bruce.

"Hello Alice, I'm pleased to meet the lady who brings a smile to my partner, of which is on his face right now." Bruce took his daughter from Roosevelt and waving his family over, he introduced each of them by name and folks, "this is Roosevelt, the young man who has been and will be watching my backside."

"Why don't you and your family join us for lunch," mom invited.

"That would be nice Mrs. Lawson, if it's okay with my women..."

"Thank you that would be nice. I have heard so much about Sgt. Lawson and would like to get to know who will be looking out for my man," Alice said.

Pop Elkingtom picked up one of Bruce's duffel bag and pops reached for one of Roosevelts. "Here son, you have a year of handling this damn thing."

"Two years, Sir," Roosevelt answered.

"Two years?" Pops looked from Roosevelt to Bruce and back again. "Who the hell's gonna watch your back when Bruce comes home?"

"Don't know Sir, guess I'll worry about that when the time comes."

"Come on everybody, our steaks are getting cold," Bruce said and held Sari out to his mother while he and Richard tossed their duffels into the turtle back of the purple Impreza. He reached for Sari again and put her in the car seat between Richard and Sam.

"Sorry for the crowded condition," he said and let Sam buckle her in while he held the door open for his wife to slide in behind the steering wheel. He slammed her door shut and ran around to the passenger side, leaning across the console for a kiss before clicking himself in with the seatbelt. "I love you pretty lady," he said and teased her with a grin. "You gals are spending the night with us horny bastards, right?"

"I can't think of any place I'd rather be, my dear," Lana said and her eyes were teasing him back with the promise of sex and it was sure as hell getting him worked up big time.

"Do you think we can find the time between sex and kisses to hit the Laundromat before we have to report to the airfield?"

"I'm sure Sam and I can handle that, huh Sam?" Lana teases him with that smile again.

"You betcha," Sam answered. "But you guys will have to baby-sit."

"No problem," Richard said when he came up for air, "unless you gals want to wash before you make mad love with your husbands. We haven't been laid for awhile now and I'm already hell fire worked up for a little bed exercise."

"Damn Bruce, do you smell what I smell?" Richard said and jumped out of the backseat as soon as Lana parked the car. "Nothing makes the mouth water like steaks a smoking on a grill. God I'm hungry." He held the door and ushered Bruce and the ladies inside.

With baby in his arms, Bruce pulled out two chairs across from Roosevelt and snuggles into the one next to his mother and pulls Lana down beside him. He kissed the older woman's cheek and smiled across at his partner's mother and girlfriend. Meeting them made keeping their man safe even more important.

After lunch and much hugging, the group began to break up. The folks started to leave, taking Sari and the car seat with them but when she started to cry, Bruce took her back into his arms and felt like his heart was breaking. Rocking from one foot to the other and his lips near her ear, he soothed her with the lullaby his mother sang to him.

"I didn't bring her any diapers, honey," Lana whispered. "We can always buy her some if you want her to stay."

Bruce thought about it, but being alone with his wife and making love to her was making his knees buckle. He placed the warm bundle of joy back into his mother's arms and gave them both a kiss and his mother a tender hug. "I love you mom. Take care of my bundle of joy and Pops too," he said and reached out to pull the old man in for a tight hug. He stepped back after a hug to his in-laws' and waved goodbye.

Bruce turned to Roosevelt and his family with a hug to his mother and Alice and a hand for his partner. "Enjoy your 24 hours partner because we got hard times ahead for sure."

Mrs. Roosevelt stepped up to Bruce again with her hand on his arm. "I'm pleased at having met you Bruce and know now, my son is in good hands."

Bruce pulled her into his arms again. "I'll do the best I can to keep the both of us safe, Mrs. Roosevelt and believe me, your son is one in a million and I'm proud to partner up with him. We make a hell of a pair," he chuckled and jumped into Lana's car. "See you back at the Armory tomorrow," he said and waved at the Roosevelt family from the passenger seat of his wife's subaru.

*   *   *

Chapter 50

Bruce looked across the seat to see a sparkle in the eyes of the most beautiful woman in the world. "So, do we want to make mad passionate love and then wash or wash and then..."

"I vote for passion," Richard called from the back seat.

"I second that," Samantha joined in the banter. "Who the hell wants to wash?"

Bruce became quiet, brought on by the picture of his infant daughter with tears in her eyes and wondered how he could have been so selfish.

"Honey?" Lana looked across at him.

"I need love baby, just lead me to a bed." Making kissing noises between his lips, Bruce leaned across the console for the real thing.

Lana threw her head back and laughed, while every part of her body wanted all that her husband had to offer and it was that laughter that brought about his horny feeling again. He suddenly wanted to give her all that he had to offer and looking down between his legs, it looked like a whole hell of a lot. Shortly after wondering how far they had to go, a smile of appreciation crossed his lips when Lana pulled into the Econo Lodge drive and eased into the parking space for room #14.

Later, after a round of lovemaking and her head on his arm, he inhaled the sweet smell of her over and over again.

"What are you doing, honey?"

"I'm trying to store up enough of my wife's fragrance to carry me through a year of smelly tents and sweaty bodies. I love you so much, and no matter how deep I breathe, I can't get enough of it, especially the scent of a lady who has just been loved."

"How many times do you think it would take to

where you couldn't get it up?"

"Well hell honey, I don't know. We've never tried it before, why?"

"Well...me and Sam are going to screw you guys until you can't get it up, but before we do that, I have a surprise for you."

Bruce lay on the bed with his head propped up on the pillow and watched her walk toward the suitcase in the nude. "My little woman looks just like the dame I had in the bridal suite, except she wasn't running around naked." He sat up with a frown and leaning back on his elbow, watched her slip a DVD into the player. "I don't want to watch a movie honey, I want you...here in my arms."

She pressed play and raced back to the bed. "You want to see this one dear," she smiled and leaned back against the wall with the pillow at her back. "This is when I called you on the telephone, look!...look honey, this is where I'm talking to you on the phone. I could feel Sari's head and made Samantha take video's from where the doctor was so you could see your daughter being born."

Without taking his eyes off of the TV, Bruce swung his feet to the floor and ran around to the foot of the bed to sit down. "I can see her head honey! She has blonde hair?" he glanced around at Lana and back again. Here she comes, push honey, she's almost out!"

"I am pushing, look at my face how red I am. No honey! Don't look at me, keep your eyes on the TV or you'll miss it!"

Bruce wanted to look at his wife, but the baby is out now and the doctor is holding her up to face the camera. When he saw the little girl thing, he looked up to see Lana's lips moving, her head off the pillow and looking down at the doctor. He locked in on Sari again and stays with the camera, watching the doctor place a kicking crying infant on her mother's stomach. "You look so happy honey and with the phone to your mouth and me knowing who you're talking to I know why," he said and when Lana waved at the camera, Bruce waved back from where he sat on the foot of the bed and mouthed the words of love back to her. Remembering his cassette, he rushed across the room and began searching through his rucksack.

Lana swung her feet over the edge of the bed, but when Bruce turned with a cassette in his hand, she grinned. "What's that?"

"A surprise I want you to take it home with you," he said as the player accepted the cassette and he ran around the bed to crawl in beside her. They sat back against the wall with Lana's head on his shoulder and watched the movie of the Fighting Brigade.

She looked up at him with disbelief in her eyes. "Is that really you under all that dirt?"

"Yep, I wanted you to see just how good me and Roosevelt handled the enemy."

"I thought you and Richard would be watching each other's back, but he's so far away."

Bruce retrieved the cassette and left it on top of the television. "We will honey, I promise," he said and crawled back into bed. "It hasn't been all that long since Sari was born, are you well? Did I hurt you tonight?"

"No silly, that was four weeks ago, besides…we still got a lot more loving to do before we sleep, but let's get the laundry out of the way and have dinner first?"

*   *   *

Chapter 51

It was eight the following morning before Bruce woke up and looked around the strange room, lost in his whereabouts, but one look at the lady in bed next to him, he remembered and reached out and pulled her into the folds of his arms. "Hey...hey, pretty lady, it's eight a.m."

Lana grinned up at him. "That was the best night's sleep I've had in a long time," she stretched for the longest time and smiled at him like she knew a secret he didn't.

"Me too lady," Bruce said, wondering at her eye tease. "What?"

"You didn't last as long as I bet you would."

"Bet?"

"Yeah, the one Sam and I made on how much sex would turn you off."

"How many times was I suppose to last, for chris-sakes?"

"At least a dozen."

"Dream on woman," he rolled his eyes and pulled her on top of him for another go around. He put his lips to hers and never wanted to stop. "How many times did Sam say?"

"Eleven," she laughed. "When I said twelve, she wouldn't go any higher."

"How many times did we make love?" he grinned while waiting for her to answer.

"I don't know honey, we fell asleep in the middle of it. How many times do you think?"

"I don't know pretty lady," he looked at her and teasing her again with another go around she pulled out of his arms.

"No honey...let's take a shower and get ready for breakfast."

"You got it," he said and swatted her bare butt. "Must have been fifteen at least."

"Bruce!" She sprang out of bed and looked back at him. "I can't tell Sam that! Our room doesn't even smell like sex, it smells like that stinky yunky junk we put in your rinse water."

"That's better than letting sand fleas lay eggs in my shorts."

"I hate for you to go over there, Sweetheart. Sometime I feel like I'll never see you again and I don't know what to do with the hurt of it."

"Don't worry Sweets, Roosevelt will take excellent care of me."

"You talked a lot about him in your e-mails. It's suddenly like you breathed life into him before my very eyes," she said and headed for the shower. "I'm glad that I met him because now I can picture the two of you together."

Bruce checked the room to make sure everything was ready to go and when Lana stepped out of the shower and turned on the hair dryer, he stepped in. Since last night felt like his wedding night all over again, he started to sing Andy Williams Hawaiian Wedding Song and he remembered... "Hey honey, you did remember to take your birth control pill didn't you?"

"Yes dear, not to worry," she said above the hair blower. "You better get out of there and get ready. Richard and Samantha will be waiting for us."

"Did you call them?"

"Yes dear."

Bruce stepped out of the shower and finding Lana leaning toward the mirror, he rubbed up against her. "Are you sure you wouldn't rather go another round?"

"You should have thought of that while we were still in bed," she said with a turn around and a wiggle against the front of him. "It's too late," she said and picked up her watch to wipe the steam off the face of it. "We have just enough time to eat and get you to the airfield, unless you want to go home with me."

"Don't tempt me baby, don't tempt me," he said

and reached around to pull her close to his naked body. "We'll hurry honey, please…"

"Okay lover boy, you asked for it," she said and leaned over to hold to the bathroom sink and pushing back into him while he worked the front and back at the same time. "Make it good enough to last me a year."

Breathing hard and giving one last hump, he held her tight and with his knees trying to buckle on him, he leaned to the side against the wall while holding Lana in his arms. "I love you sweetheart and thank you for the grand send off. I'm gonna miss hell out of you."

"I miss you already honey, and thank you for the twelfth piece of sex," she said and wet two paper towels. "Here baby, clean yourself up and let's get out of here."

Dressed and ready fifteen minutes later, there was a knock on the door and Bruce rushed to unlock and open it.

"Hey Bruce my buddy, I feel like a brand new man, how about you?" Richard said and followed Samantha into the room. "Our stuff is ready and sitting just inside our door."

"Damn, that stinky gook ruins the smell of sex, you did have sex didn't you?" Samantha said and looked toward the bathroom. "What did you do with your better half?"

"She's in the…here she is now, gorgeous and ready to go," Bruce looked at Lana and the smile on his face was a dead give away to Sam's question.

* * *

Chapter 52

After breakfast and standing in front of the gate to the Armory with a sick feeling in his gut, Bruce turned to his wife and gathered her into his arms. "Do you feel my heart?"

"Yes honey, it's beating the same heartbreak as mine. Thank you my darling husband for all that you have given me, a child, your family and so much unselfish love. It helps me through the waiting and the fear of you never returning to me. I might suffocate on the stink of your bug killer but wish I could crawl into one of your pockets and sneak off with you."

Her laughter was the most beautiful sound in the world. "Wish you could too," he said while feeling more heartache than a man should have to live through.

"Sweetheart?" He put a finger under her chin and turned her lips up to meet his for one last kiss.

He stepped in between the two men who would be filling his days for the next year and feeling no shame for the tears in their eyes, the three of them passed through the gate. Bruce picked up the rest of his equipment and with one backward glance to find Sam and Lana standing with Roosevelt's mother and fiancée, he waved and turned for the Armory. With head bowed, he could hardly breathe through the pain in his throat.

He stopped at the gate to have his ID scanned into the system and turned to find the ladies waiting for one last wave. He kissed his hand and tossed it to Lana of which she caught and put it to her lips. He caught hers and put it in his pocket for later.

Sometime later, however much later Bruce wasn't sure, he looked at his watch and yep, for seven hours now they had been waiting. Hurry up and wait was the military way. He shook his head and looked around to find several men sitting on the tarmac, playing cards and throwing dice. A few others were sitting on their duffel bags or using them as backrests while they either slept the time away or read paperbacks. Probably have to scan our damn cards again before we can board. At about the same time Bruce found where he'd left off in his book, the C.O. ordered Johnson to call formation.

"Alright men, load your gear in these containers," he pointed out two square containers that probably fit in the belly of the plane. "Take your rucksack of personal items with you when you board the plane, but for now sit back and rest awhile before we board."

What the hell you think we been doing for the past twelve hours Johnson, if not resting, Bruce thought and lay back against his rucksack with book in hand until sometime later when he woke up and looked at the time. He shoved his book into the pocket of his rucksack and turned to Richard. "It's daylight, Bro?"

"I know," Richard said and rolled onto his side to face Bruce. "Looks like we're gonna have some breakfast. Johnson is passing out MRE's now."

"Wish I had a phone," Roosevelt said. "My mother and gal are probably sleeping in a motel room somewhere in Fresno."

"Our gals are driving straight through and it has me a little worried," Bruce said, followed by a grunt when he stood up to discard his garbage. "They are both good drivers, but that's a long haul back to Oregon."

*   *   *

Chapter 53

Bruce moved down the aisle and claimed the second set of seats directly behind the division of officer's first class seating. He shoved his rucksack under the seat in front of him and settled back into his seat and looked at his watch again. Shaking his head and letting his feelings be known, he leaned into his partner. "Waiting at the armory for twenty four hours is uncalled for," he caught Roosevelt's look of agreement. "Sure as hell glad we didn't have to wait that long to change planes in Texas. My wife and Samantha are probably near to leaving 205 for Clackamas by now."

In the air and after the plane leveled out, the smiling flight attendants had their carts in the aisles and were taking drink orders. By all appearances, had it not been for the armored vests and gas masks around their legs, it might have been a business trip.

He mixed his CC with water and tapped it against the edge of Roosevelt's glass and looked around to send a smile back to Richard, who sat across the aisle and four seats back. It was good to have a part of home with him.

He downed his second drink and closing one eye while letting the other focus on an old John Wayne movie he was at a loss as to why the army couldn't afford a new movie for their fighting men.

He watched a cloud outside his window for several minutes before he closed his eyes to the curiosity, as to how it was traveling at the same rate of speed as the plane.

It was playing with him, but he kept his eye on the funny cloud. It reached out to him like loving arms and touched his lips like a kiss. It was almost human like and cold, sooo cold. He tried to get away but his head was against something, he couldn't move! So cold, he could feel his teeth chatter from the chill of it. A face formed in front of him, it was Lana. She looked so white and her smile was different somehow and her voice?

"I'm so sorry, my darling husband, but I didn't see him coming. I love you and will wait for you forever." The cloud had her by the hair, pulling her away but her cold arms and lips claimed him again. "Goodbye my darling. I will wait for you. I love you... Looove yooou."

"Lana, don't go," he moans. "What do you mean?"

"Sarge?" He could feel warm hands on him, shaking him. He opened his eyes to find Roosevelt looking back at him, his mouth moving. "You're freezing Sarge," he said. "I'll be right back, see if I can find you a warm blanket."

"Roosevelt? What happened?" The cold held him in a vice grip, his teeth chattered. "Is the air conditioning on me?" The dream came at him again, and Lana? "I'm freezing."

His partner left him alone and returned shortly with a warm blanket. He snuggled the warmth of it around him but was afraid to fall asleep again. The hand on his shoulder slipped away. He looked up to see Sullivan and felt the medic's hand on his chin. "Here Lawson, open your mouth," he said.

Something tightened around his arm. "I'm okay now, just a bad dream," he said around the thermometer in his mouth.

"Let's take your blood pressure, so I can feel as okay as you," Sullivan laughed. "You're starting to get some color back in your face."

Roosevelt returned to his seat and reached out for Bruce. "Feeling better?"

"Yeah, thanks partner."

"Wanna talk about what just happened? How about I warm your blanket again?"

"I'm okay now," Bruce said and went on to explain his dream to Roosevelt, and to Richard, who stood in the aisle looking down at him, apprehension lining his face.

"Why don't you sit in my seat with your good friend? He needs family now and you're about as near to family as he's got here."

"Thanks Roosevelt," Richard said.

"I've just been on a trip into the unknown and it was too damn cold to be hell."

"What do you think it means?"

"When we see the gals again, remind me to give Lana a firm talking to," Bruce said and caught the expression of worry on Richard's face. "You don't think anything is wrong, with the girls I mean?"

"I hope to hell not," Richard said and began shaking his head.

Remembering the dream sent a chill through him again, but he brings the picture of his wife and baby to mind, and smiles. "I'm okay now, Richard."

Roosevelt sat down just as the seat belt light came on and the Captains voice sounded on the intercom. "We will be landing at Rhein-Main Air Base in Germany in about 20 minutes for fuel and a pilot change. We take off for Kuwait in one hour so anyone with a need to stretch his legs, please feel free. The temperature is 62 and rainy. Leave your gear on the plane."

Bruce reached into his pocket and pulled out a five. "Get me a pack of big red, if they don't have it doublemint will do and a big hunk candy bar if they have it here."

"And if they don't?"

"Anything partner. Take Richard with you, he knows what I like." He flipped open his wallet to smile at his two gorgeous females. I love you woman, he thought, but why did you interrupt my sleep to say you're sorry. Sorry about what honey, what did you do?

The unease was so thick Bruce nearly choked on it. He lay back in his seat and closed his eyes for a minute, but the cloud with Lana's face in it hovered over him again. Letting his seat up he looked around to see who had stayed on the plane beside himself and waved at Brown and Buck, both of who were looking back at him while trying to smile away their concern.

* * *

Chapter 54

Bruce watched the activity outside his window while sympathizing with the two man struggle to hold onto the hose. The gas vapors curling around their gloved hands was so much like the cloud in his dream, he felt the chill of it touching his lips again.

Closing his eyes and mind to what was going on around him, Bruce let his seat back and wondered at the time in Germany. Will have to adjust my watch to Kuwaiti time or better yet, he thought with a quiet chuckle, why not just buy another and leave this one on Lana time. He felt someone brush against him and opened his eyes to find Richard, with a look of concern on his face, sitting in Roosevelt's seat. "I'm okay now bro, it was just a dream."

"Was Samantha in your dream?"

"No, it was just a cloud with Lana's face in it. Probably because I was curious about the cloud outside the window moving along with us for a long time before we left it behind."

"Then you're okay with it?"

"Yeah, I'm fine Bro, don't worry."

The two men shared a nervous chuckle and leaving Bruce with a knuckle punch to the shoulder, Richard returned to his seat.

Bruce opened his eyes to the sound of Roosevelt's voice and reached for the gum and candy bar. He felt the plane move and glanced out the window to find the tarmac moving toward the hanger. Looking down at the big hunk on his lap he smiled a thank you at Roosevelt. "My favorite candy bar when I was a boy and always felt I was lucky when I didn't lose a peanut or two during the tug a war with the nougat."

"I got me one too and they are hard on the front teeth," Roosevelt laughed.

Bruce could feel his partner looking at him and waited for what he had to say. "You still don't look so good, Sarge."

"It seemed so real, Roosevelt, but it was just a dream."

"Want to talk about it?"

"Maybe later, after we land," Bruce said, and leaving his partner with a smile, he turned to the window and was surprised to see the barren desert so soon. The striking resemblance of the Kuwaiti desert to the astronaut's moon landing was astonishing.

The ding of the seat belt light brought Bruce around to the window again, to the signs of civilization below. Kuwait, he thought only seconds before the plane made a slight change in altitude. The thud of the landing gear is followed by the familiar rush of adrenalin.

He could see the airport and would breathe a hell of a lot easier when the wheels touched down on the runway but suddenly and unexpected, the plane gained altitude and veered sharply to the right away from the airport. An explosion somewhere between them and the airport rocked the plane.

"What the hell was that?" Several voices made their concern known.

"Must have been a rocket of some kind," Bruce said.

The plane circled around the airport and going down much too fast from a different direction, Bruce closed his eyes and wondered, as he always does when losing altitude, if the pilot is good at what he's doing.

"Do you see Kuwait, Sarge?"

"Yep," he said and leaned back in his seat to let Roosevelt near the window. "Have a look."

Immediately upon a smooth landing on the runway, the men clapped and let out a yell. It was late afternoon when the plane came to a full stop and the ding sounded again. Bruce in his gear and ready to disembark fell in closely behind Roosevelt to follow him out of the plane and into the blast of a hot furnace.

Their first stop is the air-conditioned SUV where two women sat with a hand out and palm up. Bruce dropped his ID into the hand and leaned forward to catch the cool air whistling back at him while reading the orders he held in his hand. She scanned his card into the system and passed it back to him.

He slipped it into his wallet and followed the men into the holding tent, mentioned in their orders. He picked his cot and dropped his gear before stretching out the full length of it with both hands under his head.

*　*　*

Chapter 55

"Lawson?" The voice sounded far away

He opened his eyes to see Sgt. Johnson and swung his feet to the floor. "Yes Sir."

"Please follow me, you're wanted in the CO's office."

He fell in behind Sgt. Johnson out the door and down a ways to a newer and better-looking tent and yep, just as he thought, it was air-conditioned and felt like home. He stepped up to the desk with a salute to Captain Wilkins and waited.

"Sit down, Lawson."

He sat there looking across the desk, awaiting the Captain's orders. The silence and expression on the face looking up at him and the fear of what the man was struggling with was holding him hostage. "Sir?"

"I'm sending you home for a week, two if you feel the need for it."

Pops, he thought, and remembering the dream on the plane, he wanted to walk out of the tent. His heart began to pound against his ribs so hard he could feel it in his throat. "I don't think I want to hear this Sir."

"I'm sorry to have to tell you this Lawson…your wife has been in an accident." The Captain stopped talking and looked down at his hands. "She was killed instantly."

"When do I leave Capt…?" Bruce choked on the words.

"Your gear will be taken care of and orders will be waiting for you when you return. Take only what you need."

"Is there anything further, Sir?"

"Your plane will be fueled and ready to go in one hour. Here is your ticket for the final leg to PDX."

Bruce put the ticket in his pocket and stood up, waiting to be excused.

"I'm sorry Lawson. If you need anything before you leave, let me know," Wilkins stood up with a salute and held out his hand.

Upon an answer to his salute and a touch to his hand, Bruce whirled and left the tent. His throat was so filled with sobs he couldn't breathe. He staggered on rubbery legs and fell to the ground behind the tent. "What the hell am I suppose to do now, honey?" he moaned and in a frenzied moment of uncontrolled feelings, he prayed for God to let him die, to let him be with his wife forever.

"Bruce, what?"

He sprang to his feet and fell into Richard's arms and reached out for Roosevelt to feel his arms around the two of them. "What happened Sarge?"

"Lana's dead!"

"Hell no, oh hell no."

"She is, Richard, killed in an auto accident."

"What about Samantha? They are always together you know."

"The Captain didn't mention Sam. Guess I'll find out everything when I get home. I'm leaving in about an hour on the same plane we came in on. That's what my dream was all about Richard, why she was so cold when she came to tell me goodbye." He broke down again and even more so when Richard and Roosevelt moved in again to wrap their arms around him. "She was crying when she told me how sorry she was and when she promised to wait for me, Oh Lord! It's tearing the heart out of my chest."

"I'm so sorry, Sarge," Roosevelt took his hand and squeezed it.

"Me too, Bro." Richard choked on the tightness in his throat. "Maybe the Captain will let me go with you."

"I'll be alright, just train for me and make me into a killing machine when I return to fight these sons a bitches. They're to blame you know, for taking me away from my wife."

"When will you be back?"

"Two weeks."

"As much waiting around we do, you'll probably get back before we leave here," Roosevelt said and looked to Richard for confirmation.

"That's probably true, but whatever, we'll bring you up to snuff in no time."

"Well, guess I better separate my gear."

"I'll help Sarge. After all, I am your right hand man, remember back at Ft. Irwin? Roosevelt said as he and Richard walked with their arms around Bruce. Me and Richard will take care of your gear."

Bruce stepped into the dusty tent to find the men knew of his misfortune and accepted their condolences without losing control. He pulled out his laptop to check his e-mail. Lana and Sari…he sat down to read the letter again and knew through the pain in his heart of hearts, this letter would see him through the war.

* * *

Chapter 56

Bruce opened his eyes to the ding of the seat belt, and remembering the man hugs from Richard and Roosevelt, he smiled. He remembered too, the handshakes and waves from the best damn bunch of men in the United States Army when he left Kuwait.

With his seat belt cinched around him, he looked out the window to see if he recognized the approach path into PDX and was surprised at the lack of adrenalin rush. Perhaps because he could care less if he lived or died.

He looked around at the passengers who were ignorant to his pain. *My God*, he moaned from within, *my world has fallen apart and nobody seems to care.* Their chitchat and laughter were grinding hell out of his nerves and the struggle from within to hold back the anger in his heart was near to the breaking point.

The plane touched down on the runway and he waited in silence while it taxied to the gate. He looked at the old man seated between him and the old lady in the aisle seat and wondered how long he would have to wait for them to get the hell out of the way?

"I've been wanting to say this for a spell now, but didn't know how. We are proud of you young men offering up your lives as a sacrifice, to me and mama here and all the rest of the world. I know we don't show it like we should, but I love you, Sergeant."

Bruce took the hand offered him and unable to talk, he smiles his thanks.

"I'm so sorry for your pain, and if there was anything I could do to help, I certainly would be happy to do so."

He squeezed the man's hand and looked out the window and back around again. "Thank you Sir, I needed that." He pulled his rucksack from beneath the seat in front of him and when he looked around again, he found the couple in the aisle holding a place for him in front of them. He felt the man squeeze his shoulder before the passengers begin to move forward.

Tears stung his eyes and try as he might to hold them back, tears eased over his lower eye lid to roll down both cheeks. What the hell, if they haven't seen a grown man cry it's about time they did. He began to feel anger again, toward God for taking his wife and leaving him amongst all of these ignorant happy people.

He stepped out of the plane and crowded around the passengers through the walkway to the accordion corner to see inside the waiting room. Pops was standing there, his eyes searching the passengers until they lit on the one man he was looking for. Bruce caught the man's tears of recognition and mom at his side with a hanky over her nose and mouth.

He grabbed Pops and hung on while sobs tore through his throat. He felt mom's arms, bringing the three of them together as one to share in the pain surrounding them. Unaware of the passenger's side-stepping around them, she murmurs softly while the two men cried.

Bruce pulled himself together and looked up to find his in-laws standing to one side with his daughter. "My beautiful Sari, you look just like your mama." He grabbed the three of them and held on tight until Sari began to scream. He held her close and rocked her back and forth while walking in circles. "I love you sweet baby," he whispers in her ear. "Daddy loves his baby girl."

He looked around at Mom and Pop Elkington. "What can I say, what can anybody say to lessen our pain?" he said and fell into the arms that once held his wife. The painful loss of an only daughter to fill their empty arms was ripping what was left of his heart apart.

Bruce turned to the feel of an arm around his waist to find Samantha on the other end of it and her other arm reaching up to his neck. He gave her a full hug, one that was as close to hugging his wife as possible.

"This hurts so bad Bruce. Maybe now that you're home we can soften the loneliness that's eating me up inside."

"Don't know if anything can help, Sam. My life as I knew it is over."

"For both of us, but we'll move forward into a future I'm too blind to see right now."

"Shall we go son?" Pops moved in to put his arm around Bruce and Samantha. "Do you have luggage to pick up?"

"Only what I could carry on my back." He kissed Sari on the cheek. "Let's go home."

"Let me have your backpack." his father-in-law offered.

"Thanks dad, but it's all in place now. I'd probably fall on my face if I take it off." He stepped outside and was surprised to find sunshine in Oregon. "Where's the rain?"

"The weatherman predicted rain," Pops said and led the way to the car. "Perhaps you and Elkington can get in a round of golf before you return to Kuwait."

"We'll see, Pops," he said and turned to find Elkington smiling through the pain in his face. "We'll see."

Pops opened the trunk while Bruce gave the baby to
Samantha and slipped out of his rucksack.

"Here son, you and Sari sit in the front seat and I'll
sit in the back with Samantha."

"Thanks mom, you beautiful lady," he kissed her
cheek before closing the back door. "Talk to me somebody, tell me what happened?"

"You remember me and Lana saying we were going
to drive straight through? That was a long way and
both of us were damn tired when we turned off of 205.
We had the green light at the intersection in Damascus
where you turn one way to Safeway and another into
the parking lot of BiMart. Neither of us saw the man
running the red light from the left until he hit Lana's
door and just kept pushing us sideways until his car
died," Samantha inhaled sharply and dried her eyes.

"I'm so sorry Bruce, I don't think I was asleep but

I might have been. When I looked over at Lana, I knew she was dead. I wanted to roll back the clock and take more time when we stopped at the rest stop so we wouldn't be there when the man had his heart attack."

Bruce looked around to the back seat to see Sam with her hands over her face, her body shaking with sobs and mom trying to console her. "There there honey, we'll talk more after we get home."

*   *   *

Chapter 57

The kitchen aromas met him at the door, tempting his taste buds to no end. He inhales the genuine home-made mouth-watering apple pie smell and oh, how he loved the expression of pleasure on his mother's face.

"How about a slice of pie with a large scoop of ice cream?"

"Oh you temptress you, how can I refuse?"

Halfway to his mouth with a large bite on the spoon, a knock sounded at the door and upon recognizing the voice of his number one salesman, Bruce left the table and hugged his main salesman to his chest.

"We all loved that woman, Bruce, and if you ever need a place to hang out and talk, come on around to my place any time day or night."

"Thanks Billy Joe, I just might take you up on that," Bruce said and led him over to the table. "How about a piece of what met your nose at the door with a scoop of ice cream on it?"

"You bet," Billy Joe said and pulled up at the table. "How you doing, Pops?"

"Hanging in there Billy Joe, just hanging in."

When BJ stood up to leave Bruce stood up and followed him outside. "Would it be rude of me to leave the folks and go with you to the car lot?"

"I'm sure they will understand. You have a hell of a lot of heartache to work through and you should take it one day at a time and do it your way."

"Thanks, BJ."

"No problem."

"I'll wait for you in the car," he grinned and turned toward the green Subaru Outback.

Billy Joe opened the driver's door at exact the same time as Pops opened the back door and crawled inside. "Don't mind me, son, I got work to do."

"That's okay, Pops," Bruce looked around the console into the back seat. "Thought I would take a walk around the lot for a little down time."

"That's fine son, you just go right ahead. Don't pay me no mind."

"I love you, Pops."

"I love you too son and it's killing me inside to see you in so much pain and not be able to help. It's like my hands are tied and watching you suffer like this..."

Aware of the silence in the backseat, Bruce looked around to see the tears and mask of pain on the ole man's face. He reached back with his hand to feel Pops grab it and hold it to his cheek. "Don't even know the right words to say, son. I have always been able to help you through most any problem you ever had, and now... oh Lord God! I don't know what to do."

Billy Joe pulled to the curb and stopped the car. Bruce looked to his left to see the tears running down his cheeks. "Lord Bruce, I know where you dad is coming from because I feel the same damn way."

Bruce squeezed BJ's shoulder and jumped out of the front seat and into the back. He pulled his father to his chest, their bodies shaking with heart wrenching sobs. Arms circled the two of them and he looked up to see BJ.

They reached for handkerchiefs and breaking the silence with nose blowing noise, they shared a chuckle. He was seeing a new side to the men he thought he knew well. "Thanks Pops, BJ, I needed that and will probably have need for it again before I leave for Kuwait."

The men shook hands with Billy Joe as he slid out of the back seat and into the front to bring life to the car again and ease back into the street. Wish it could be that easy to bring life to my wife, he thought and rode to the car lot in the back seat with Pops.

"When you two get ready to leave, I'll be more than happy to taxi you home and it won't cost you a cent."

"Let you know Billy Joe."

"Don't know for sure if the body has been released

but we were told Lana should be ready for viewing today or tomorrow at the latest, maybe the three of us can
go together."

"Don't know Pops, don't know if I'm ready to accept
it for real, but we'll see." Bruce sat with his back rigid
against the back seat. "I know I'm gonna have to sooner
or later. I might just need men like the two of you to
help me through it."

"We're here for you, boss."

"Yes we are son."

Billy Joe pulled the car in his parking space. Pops
left for his office and the salesman of the year spotted a
potential customer and pointed him out to Bruce.

"Go sell a car, BJ. I'm gonna take a walk around
the lot. Can't think of anything better than looking at
beautiful cars to get my mind off things." He smiled
and quickly turned to hide the threat of tears.

*   *   *

Chapter 58

Bruce thought he was cried out and he was, until the threat of a complete breakdown caught his attention. The purple Impreza, with the side bashed in, sat waiting in a lonely corner of the lot for a driver who will never again sit behind the wheel. He tried to stop, to turn and run the other way, but continued on with first one foot and then the other. He moved around to open the passenger's side door and slid into the seat with his head against the head rest. He put a finger to the stains on the inside of the driver's door and wondered? "Help me with this honey, I can't handle a future without you in it."

He caught the movement of a long blond hair out of the corner of his eye, waving at him from the back of the driver's seat. With a thumb and finger grip he pulls ever so gently to free it from the fabric. He put the delicate find into his shirt pocket and buttoned the flap down for safe keeping. Leaning forward to hide his face in the crook of his arms on the dash board, he moans the loss of his beautiful wife, a woman who will forever rest easy on his mind.

"Sorry Bruce, but we didn't know what else to do with it."

"Billy Joe! I didn't see you come up."

"I thought it was well hidden, but guess I was wrong," BJ said as he walked around to the passenger side. "You want us to have the junk man haul it off?"

"Not yet BJ," Bruce said. "Just leave it until I come home."

"You got it boss."

Bruce climbed out of the car and shut the door. "Think I'll check out her office."

"Call my cell when you and pops are ready to leave," BJ said with a hug to Bruce before walking away.

Bruce stopped in the hallway outside Lana's office and cried for her and her love for the purple Impreza. He inhaled deeply, pulled his shoulders back and walked into the office. The chair was partly pulled away from the desk, like she had just left it and was coming right back. He fell into it and looked around, expecting her to walk through the door any minute. Closing his eyes and breathing in the scent of her perfume, he could almost imagine her sitting across the desk from him.

"I'm sorry sweetheart for letting this happen to you."

He jerks back with eyes shut tight. "Lana?"

"Love our baby, take good care of her and she will give you a purpose in life. I love you my darling husband and I want you to know that you were on my mind the day I drew my last breath. We were in the bathroom of the motel again and laughing like we did after we made love in the bathroom. Did you ask Richard how many times they did it that night?"

He reached across the desk, daring to hope for a feel

of her. She wasn't there, but he remained rigid in his seat. "I love you sweetheart."

"Goodbye my darling and please feel free to love and live again   Build a future for our daughter and never let her forget how much her mommy loved her."

His eyes flew open to the sound of her voice at the door. He wanted to run after her, but dropped his head into the fold of his arms on the desk. The pain was like a vice grip around his heart and he prayed for it to stop beating.

He dried his eyes and followed the worn carpet trail to Pop's office and took up the chair across the desk from him. "I was in Lana's office."

"It's just like she left it, son."

"I sat at her desk, breathing in the scent of her perfume. She came to me, Pops. I just sat there with my eyes closed, letting my imagination match her beauty to the voice. It was so real, but when I reached out to touch her..."

"I've heard her footsteps and laughter in the hallway. I sit waiting for her to come into my office but she never did."

"Her ghost was just hanging around. She's gone now Pops, *really gone*."

Pops picked up the phone. "Are you ready to go home?"

"Yep, I need my daughter bad."

Billy Joe pulled up and opened the back door for Pops while Bruce went around to the passenger side.

*   *   *

Chapter 59

"Glad you could come with us, BJ. The funeral home called the office thirty minutes ago to say Lana was ready for viewing," Pops said and followed Bruce inside.

The organ music stopped Bruce at the door, but the power of his love moves him ever so slowly and gently down the aisle to the pretty lady who waited in silence for his arrival. He looks down and felt a moment of disappointment. "The lady in the casket... oh dear God! What have you done with my beautiful Lana?"

He closed his eyes to picture her smile, but feeling his knees give way, he grabbed the edge of the casket. The pain was so heavy in his chest and yet he chuckled, wanting to share with her what almost happened. "I nearly pulled your casket over honey did you know that?" She didn't answer. He was losing touch and could hear himself chuckle again. "How funny it would be sweetheart, if I dumped you out on top of me and we made love in the middle of the floor. Did we ever have sex on the floor?"

"Thank you my darling for coming to me on the plane, but you were so cold." He touched her fingers to find them still cold. Lord God Sweetheart, I'm only half a person without you."

A tear fell on her cheek. "Did you feel that honey?" he asked and reached down with his thumb to wipe it away. "Thought I was all cried out but guess not. I love you my darling, and since you insist on leaving me, there's nothing more I can do, but let you go."

He turned when Pops and BJ put their arms around him, but it was Lana's parents who hugged him. He remembered Lana's hugs and what he used to say to her.

You're the best little hugger that ever hugged from hugsville.
He grabbed them both and tried to return a hug that
would match Pop Elkington's while he choked on the
pain in his throat.

"I'm so sorry folks," Bruce whispered. "She was
mine for such a short time and yours for all the days
of her life. My memories of her are in lifelike color, so
beautiful and yours must be doubly beautiful, from the
time she was a baby until the time she had a baby of her
own. Thank you, if only for a short while, for giving
me your daughter in marriage."

"We love you like a son and wish you could have
had her for as long as we have had each other," mother
Elkington said between sobs. Bruce kissed them both
and backed away to let the grieving parents have lone
time with their only child.

"Are you okay, son?"

"No, I'm not," Bruce said and turned his back on
his in-laws. He felt Pops arms around him and the
struggle with tears were more than he could hold back.

His shoulders shook with more sobs than he could handle, not only his, but pops as well.

Billy Joe held both men and cried as well. "Let's step outside, away from the music."

*   *   *

Chapter 60

The morning after the hardest day of his life, Bruce smiled down into the sleeping face of his daughter. He almost lost it during the final goodbyes to Lana at the cemetery, especially when he saw the plastic with a mound of earth beneath it at her gravesite. For all the days of my life, he thought, Lana will forever be under that pile of dirt! "Oh Lord!"

With Sari asleep in her crib, he felt it safe for him to hit the shower. He returned to the bedroom, changed her diaper and picked her up to follow the smell of bacon.

With Sari in his arms, he was open to the hug and kiss from his mother before taking his place at the table. "Mom, since you will be working in the office until

Pops hires someone," he said and watching her facial expression, continued with what he felt he had to say. "I would like mother and dad Elkington to have Sari until I come home,"

"Thank you son," she smiled her acceptance. "They are in such pain now with losing their only child, Sari will be good for them and I'm sure, Lana would feel the same."

Bruce looked down into the face of his baby daughter and watched her hazel green eyes follow the bite of egg to his mouth. He mashed a tiny bit and put it to her lips but instead of taking the bite into her mouth she smiled and coo'd up to him. Thank you Lana dear for this precious gift, he thought, and I promise to make her into the young lady you can be proud of.

"I love you mom and thanks for your understanding." He turned when the kitchen door closed to find Sam standing there. He pushed away from the table and holding Sari in one arm, put the other around her waist. "Let's take a walk."

"Tell me about you and how you held yourself together when you saw Lana dead after the accident?" Bruce said while they followed the driveway to the sidewalk.

"It was almost more than I could handle, but the police were very kind and treated me with the utmost care and understanding. They took over completely except for the phone calls. I put a call into your CO first and then called the folks to let them know what happened and almost immediately, Pops and Mr. Elkington had the body moved close to home."

Bruce folded her in his arms and held on while they cried. "Was the bastard who ran into you arrested?"

"He suffered a heart attack Bruce and the police said was dead before impact. I try to spend as much time with the Elkington's as I can but it's not the same and I think it makes them miss Lana all the more." Sam leaned into Bruce, her body trembling. "Sometimes, when I'm with them I feel like they're wishing it was me that was killed."

"That's probably the norm, Sam. I don't wish that because I don't wish upon Richard the pain I'm going through. The four of us did have a good wedding, huh?"

"Yep, nobody can take that…?" Sam stopped talking and turned to bury her face in his shoulder again. "I have terrible nightmares Bruce." The tremor in her voice pulled at his heart. "The accident keeps happening over and over again and I keep seeing Lana's face with her eyes open…like she's looking at me."

"Come on Sam," Bruce said. "Let's go back to the house." Once they were seated comfortably in the porch swing with the baby in his lap, he could feel Sam's eyes on him.

"Tell me about Richard and how he's holding up over there. Is his partner a good man? Talk to me Bruce, tell me."

Bruce grinned when he thought about the men in Kuwait, especially his young partner and Richard. "The training in Ft. Irwin was hot and the terrain comes pretty damn close to looking like Kuwait but not as hot. To answer your question Sam, Longview will work like hell to keep Richard safe and Richard will do the same for him. He misses the hell out of you and wanted to come with me."

"I'm glad, but you still have the kill or be killed waiting for you guys. Keep him safe for me Bruce, please...if it's in your power to do so."

"I'll give my own life to keep him safe and if something should happen to me, I want you and Richard to play a part in Sari's life. I can't think of anyone I'd rather see raise her than you two."

"I'm thinking about working for Pops. He asked me but I'm not as smart as Lana. No job was ever too big for Lana to tackle."

Samantha's remark was so on the mark, and remembering Lana's first day on the job brought a grin to his face.

"To sit straight faced at the grave site and pretend a calm I didn't feel was hardest day in my life Sam and when the minister tossed a handful of dirt on the casket, it was like a knife to my chest."

"I know what you mean," Samantha said and laughed. "I'm sorry Bruce, I didn't mean to laugh, but I was just thinking about when she came home after meeting you."

"Yep," Bruce remembers that first day with a chuckle. "Her beauty damn near knocked my pants off."

"She fell crazy in love with you that day."

"What a waste," he murmurs and turns to Samantha, taking her hand in his. "I'll be leaving in a couple of days and I want to spend one of the days with Lana's folks and I'm taking Sari over to stay with them until I come home."

"I'm glad, Bruce. They have been wondering about that now that Lana's gone."

Lana is gone, he moans silently. I will never see her smile, never kiss her lips and that woman sure knew how to kiss, and the hug...Oh my God how she could hug me in all the right places. "Heaven help me Sam,

I don't know if I can make it without her," he cried out and caught Samantha's recognition to the pain he was feeling.

"I'm gonna take you to stay with Grandma Elkington, sweetheart and Auntie Sam will come to see you lots," Bruce said to the little bundle in his lap. She smiled up at him like she understood what he said. "Now is just as good a time as any to go talk with the Elkington's." He stood up and reached out to Sam. "How about it, come with us?"

*　*　*

Chapter 61

Bruce knocked on the door and braced himself for the hug that was sure to come his way. He relinquished his body to the arms of his mother-in-law with baby Sari caught in the middle. "You must be the one who taught Lana the knack of hugging."

"No, oh no, it was her dad who taught the both of us. Maybe by the time Sari grows up he'll teach her the art?"

He heard the question in her statement and began before either of them offered him a chair. "I would like for you and dad Elkington to take over the care of Sari while I'm away."

"Did you hear that, dad?"

Bruce turned in the direction Ernestine was looking.

"What do you say, dad?"

"I'm too choked up to say anything right now."
He cleared his throat and grabbed his son in law. "It's
like the answer to our prayers, son. You damn betcha,
mama and me will tend our granddaughter, might give
us reason to face each new day with laughter."

"I would like nothing better, except for Samantha
here, I want her to be a part of Sari's life." He turned to
Sam to find her all smiles.

"Friends just keep bringing us food and if you
would like, have your folks join us for dinner tonight,"
Mom Elkington invited. "Are you hungry now? My
neighbor next door brought in a big pan of spareribs
and a dish of cheese and macaroni."

"I am a cheese and macaroni man and I never scoff
at barbecued ribs," Bruce smiled his appreciation and
took up the vacant seat left for him between his in-laws.

"Here honey, give me the baby so you can eat,"
mother Elkington lay Sari on her lap and motioned Sam
into the seat next to her. "Glad you came over, gives me

and dad a chance to get something off our minds. Do you want to tell him dad?"

"I'll tell him, honey." he paused for a short while.

Bruce sat there waiting, his heart aching for two men who loved the same woman and wondered at what the older man was working up the courage to say.

"When you married our daughter, we took you into this family as a son. Losing our daughter has nearly drained us of the will to go on, but with you and Sari to stand in for her, it will give us a purpose to move forward with our family."

Bruce touched foreheads with his father-in-law. "You got it dad," he leaned to the other side and kissed Ernestine on the cheek. "And you too, mother."

"I know eventually you will date other women, perhaps marry one day and when you do we will accept her as a daughter and however many more children you have will be our very own grandchildren," dad said.

"This is the best macaroni and cheese I've had in a long time. Your neighbor you say, is she single?" Bruce said, bringing a laugh out of everyone.

"She's single, son," Dad laughed again. "But I don't think you'd be interested in an 87 year old woman."

"That settles that," Bruce said with a soft knuckle punch to the older man's shoulder. "She'd probably think I'm too young for her."

*   *   *

Chapter 62

Bruce pulled up alongside BJ's Outback but before he could turn off the ignition, Sam was out of the car and in the backseat working the harness from around Sari. He slammed his car door and walked around the back to find her blowing kisses around Sari's giggles.

With an arm firmly around her waist, he urged her toward pops office where they stopped in the doorway and waited for the old man to look up.

A slow grin started small and quickly spread from ear to ear across the ole man's face as he slammed his chair against the wall and rushed around the desk. "Come in," he called and pushed Sam toward the only chair in the office and cleared a corner of the desk for Bruce.

"Do you think Sam and I can come in to work tomorrow?"

"Hell yeah," Pops said and put a hand to his mouth. "Sorry Sam, but I guess you may as well get used to it since you'll be working here. When do you want to start?" Pops smiled at the two of them. "Now would be a good time for me. Sari can stay here with me in the playpen while you teach this young lady everything you know."

"What do you say, Bruce? Now that you're home, it might be a good time?"

A moment of panic at the thought of spending time in his wife's office swept through him, but taking a deep breath and letting it out slowly, he introduced Sam to her new office. Lana's perfume teasing his nose was almost like she was looking over them.

Bruce looked at his watch to see he had completely lost track of time and pushed away from the desk. "Wow! Sam, it's 6 o'clock and dinner at the Elkington's is for seven."

"Hey you two," Pops stood in the doorway with a sleeping Sari in his arms. "Me and the little girl here is ready to go."

Samantha took the baby and started for the door. "I'll race you to the car," she laughed and quickly had Sari buckled up in the back seat. With a hand fluff to her hair she looked across the seat at Bruce. "Do I look okay?"

Bruce looked at one side, made her turn so he could see the other side.

"What?" She ran her fingers through her hair again.

He had never noticed before how Sam's action in similar situation was a lot like Lana's. A quick glance into the rearview mirror found Sari sound asleep. "You look beautiful Sam, except for that little..." he reached over and touched her ear. "Pull the visor down and look."

She looked from side to side and wrinkled her nose at him. "I forgot how ornery you are at times, Bruce Lawson."

He could feel Samantha's eyes on him and looked across to see the missing her husband loneliness in her eyes. "I wish he were here too, Sam."

"We are two very lonely people, huh?"

"That we are Sam, oh yes indeed, that we are." He grinned across at her and felt good at having her in his corner.

*   *   *

Chapter 63

The loading announcement came way too soon and brought Bruce out of the arms of his mother-in-law. He stepped back with a chuckle and brushed at a teardrop on her shoulder. "Sorry about that."

She stood on tiptoe to kiss him on the cheek. "Don't worry about it son, might just hang it in the closet for look now and then to remind me of the son I have in Iraq."

"I love you folks."

Dad Elkington pulled him in for a man hug. "Mama and me love you too, son."

He reached out for his mother and rocked from one side to the other with her in his arms. "Love you mom," he whispers in her ear. "Help Pops until I get back."

"I will son, I will."

"Pops held the baby out to Samantha and stepped into his sons outstretched arms. "Wish this homecoming could have been under happier circumstances son, but it has been good having you home, especially in the office."

Bruce reached out to pull Samantha in for a hug and stepped back with his bundle of joy in his arms. He kissed her tiny cheeks and watched her smile up at him. "Daddy's gonna miss the next precious months of your life. You will be a regular little grown up lady in a year."

"Watch over my man Bruce, keep him safe," she wept. "I love him so much."

Bruce held the baby out to his mother. "I'll do my best Sam, and come back here will you? I know Richard's waiting for this, so give me the kind of hug you want me to take back to him." Finding it far more than he bargained for, he backed away with a smile. "Watch over each other while I'm away."

Bruce looked around to see Pops nod his head and back to Samantha for another hug and kisses to his daughter's cheek before he quickly turned away. When he entered the loading ramp it felt like the weight of the whole damn world had hitched a ride in his rucksack. He looked back over his shoulder for one last wave before turning the corner and felt his heart crumble at what he was leaving behind and anger at God for not saving his wife.

Finding it hard to breathe through the tears in his throat, he shoved his rucksack of cleaned clothes, under the passenger seat in front of him. He fell into his seat and turned to the window to hide the presence of tears from the other passengers.

Hardly aware of take off, his unseeing eyes focused on the window while his thoughts wondered from the family he left behind to the unit of men waiting for him in Kuwait. He settled back into his seat and closed his eyes to the memory of emotional pain in Richard and Roosevelt's eyes when he left Kuwait.

A hand closed over his and pulling it into her lap, he thought it might be Lana, but held his eyes closed tight, waiting for her to speak.

"I am so sorry for your pain young man, and if there was something I could do to ease the pain, I certainly would."

Bruce opened his eyes to the elderly lady seated next to him. "Thank you," he said and placed his spare hand over hers. She in turn placed her free hand over the two of his. She closed her eyes and her lips moved in silent prayer. He let the warmth surround him, replacing the pain and anger in his heart with a feeling quite new to him.

Her husband placed his two hands over the four hands in his wife's lap. "This woman has a direct line to God and when she is through with him, young man, he will see you through the hard times ahead."

"Bruce took in the distinguished looking gentleman with gray hair, who made him think of Pop Elkington, and flushed slightly when he realized his hands were still in his wife's lap. "Thank you...?"

"Granny to you young man. I've been granny for a good many years now and this old fart here is Gramps."

Bruce kissed her cheek and shook hands with gramps. He tells them about Lana's death and pulls out the pictures of his wife and daughter.

"Oh my goodness," granny cooed. "You will always have your wife around because this little darling looks just like her mama. Look Gramps."

Gramps smiles in spite of a sadness in his steel blue eyes, and Bruce wondered? "Yeah, she does and it was hard to leave her so soon after the funeral," he put the pictures away. "I'll be back in a year and we should have good times getting acquainted."

"Yes you will, young man," granny looked at him as if she could foresee the future. "You most certainly will."

For reasons unknown to him, Bruce knew at that very moment, he would make it through this war. The thought of seeing Roosevelt and Richard soon brought a twinge of excitement and he asked her to pray for their safety as well.

She closed her eyes and prayed for the two men and for reasons unknown to Bruce, she turned to him with tears in her eyes. She put his hand to her lips and said another prayer.

When Granny finished her prayers, he shoved the little pillow under his head, and remembered the two of them with a smile before he lay back and closed his eyes. Unsure as to what had awakened him, he looked around to find granny and gramps both sound asleep.

He lay back again and just as he did, a baby begins to cry. Sari, he thought and tried to make out to whom the soft voice belonged. It wasn't Lana, no...not her voice.

"You have to put your seat up, young man. We are getting ready to land."

He looked around at granny and back again to the window to see the airport ahead.

"We've come to visit our daughter and attend her

husband's funeral."

"I'm so sorry granny, gramps," he said. "Funerals are tough."

"Yes, I imagine so young man," Gramps said. "Our daughter is still in shock. His body probably came in on the plane that will take you to Kuwait."

When the plane came to a stop and the seat belt light went out, Gramps shuffled out of his seat and made room in the aisle for granny and Bruce. He dropped his rucksack on the seat to help the older man with their carry on.

Inside the airport and after meeting the daughter, Bruce excused himself to find a book for the rest of his flight. He pulled out his cell phone to fulfill an urgency to leave the sound of his voice with his daughter.

* * *

Chapter 64

The wheels left the runway, the landing gear closed with a final thump, and turning from the window once McCord Air Force Base disappeared beneath the clouds, Bruce turned to see the young man in uniform sitting next to him. Almost immediately upon leveling off, the seat belt light went off and Bruce looked around to see the hostess pushing the drink cart down the aisle. His tray down and ready, he reached for the can of 7up and a shot bottle of Canadian Mist. He quickly mixed the two together and downs more than half before coming up for air.

Suffering the food aroma teasing his taste buds, Bruce is near to drowning in his own saliva and is restless in his eagerness for the stewardess to park her cart next to his row of seats. He downed the rest of his drink while waiting for his dinner and a cup of coffee.

The cleanup ladies came through and with his tray up again, he pushed back to flip through to the second page of his paperback and scans the preface. "Oh yes, I remember now," he mumbles, "the Stone Barrington series by Stuart Woods."

Well into the story, he looked from his watch to the young man on his right. "I'm Sgt. Bruce Lawson by the way. You think that snoring will follow us all the way to Kuwait?"

"Sgt. James Webb here and to answer your question, looks like his buddy is ready to grab him around the neck."

"If I fall asleep and make that noise, wake me to hell up before somebody gets a strangle hold on me," Bruce said and positioned the paperback under his nose again to pick up where he'd left off.

"Same here," Webb said as he looked around and down the aisle. "I know the guy, but not well enough to say anything."

Bruce opened his eyes, surprised he had fallen asleep and the plane was on the ground. He leans forward to look out the window and murmurs his surprise. "Germany?"

"Yep and we're just about ready to take off for Kuwait."

"I'll be damned."

"You dropped this and I'm about third of the way through it. I remember reading about this Stone fellow before." Webb put a bag of caramels in Bruce's lap. "Here, take a handful."

"Big Hunk candy bars have been a favorite of mine since I was a kid," Bruce chuckles. "But caramels are good."

"Abracadabra and look what the man of magic has pulled out of his hat," Webb said and flashed two Big Hunk candy bars in Bruce's face.

Bruce shares a chuckle with the young man. "How the hell did you know?" he asked in amazement. "Did I talk in my sleep?"

"It's my favorite," Webb laughed. "I bought two just in case you wanted one."

"Miracles never cease." His mouth watering for that first chewy bite, he pulls the sticky wrapping back part way. "Not many people know how good these things are?"

"Does that make us unique or what?" Webb looked rather smug with himself. "If you finish that book before we reach our destination, I'll take it off your hands."

"If I fall asleep again, be my guest," Bruce leafed through the pages looking for his place, but accepted Webb's help when he fingered the page. "Thanks friend."

"Anytime," Webb said and crammed the last of his candy bar between his teeth. "Damn, this is good."

Bruce laughed in agreement and turned to his novel again. He reads fast, but sure of reaching their destination before reaching the last page he glanced at Webb to find him not paying attention and leafed through to the beginning of the last ten chapters.

Webb reached for the novel with a smile of sorts. "That was fast."

"I cheated a little but the ending was still the same."

"Thanks Lawson. Where you stationed in Kuwait?"

"That's a surprise waiting to happen. Maybe we'll meet up at the same camp."

"I don't know why the army hurries us around like cattle only to make us wait and never let us know where we're going other than to fight in Iraq."

"Do you think all troops go through the same shit?"

"Don't know Lawson, but I've been going nowhere now for two weeks."

"My unit is in Kuwait now and I'm wondering how the hell the army plans to connect me with my men." Bruce stripped the paper off of two caramels and put both in his mouth at once. He looked out the window to see the same barren desert he'd seen a week or so ago.

The airport below has a firm grip on his attention

and a tremor of anxiety is using the nap of his neck for a playground. The portrait of his unit flashed before him, his friend and partner so close and yet so far and he is worried too, as to just how far away they are.

With eyes shut tight to the loss of altitude, he settled back to await the contact of tires upon runway and let the rush of adrenalin have its way with him. Worries hounded him again, about the location of his unit and admittedly so, a sense of insecurity.

Giving Webb a handshake and thank you for the candy bar, he shuffled out into the aisle to shrug into his rucksack and wait, for what felt like forever before the men in front began to move. Once outside, he faced the blast of desert heat with a shake of his head.

Dusk was closing in fast, but luck hitched a ride on his shoulder, making him fourth in a line of 500 plus men. The approach to the SUV Station was slow. The same young lady of a week ago scanned his ID into the system. It was just as he remembered from last time, the cold air from the air conditioning whistling through the four-inch opening in the window and him stealing a cold blow before he turned away.

"Sgt. Bruce Lawson?"

"Yes ma'am."

"You will leave immediately on the bus and the gentleman to your left is here to accompany you to your unit at Camp Udairi."

"Thank you ma'am," Bruce said and looked around to find Roosevelt with a half ass grin looking back at him. He reached for his ID card, slipped it into his wallet and pulls the young man in for a handshake and a shoulder bump.

"Glad to see you partner, yes sir, but how the hell... Did the Captain send you?"

"The guys had a lot to do with it," Roosevelt said, his eyes darting in all directions. "We better get a move on before we miss the bus."

"You're not AWOL, tell me you're not AWOL."

"Okay, I'm not AWOL."

"You are! Damn let's get the hell out of here."

"I was afraid you might get lost in the cracks."

Bruce wanted to grab the young man and run with him, but shoulder-to-shoulder in a half assed military march, he pretended a self-confidence he sure as hell didn't feel.

"Here's the mini bus and when they say mini Sarge, you can believe it."

Bruce slid in next to the window, looked all around and back again at his partner. "How the hell did you do it?"

"Nobody knows much around here, let alone where the men are. We're more or less free to roam as we please once the morning formation is over, so..."

"Don't talk so loud."

"The men's decision to go in all directions this morning was voluntary and it was the only thing we could come up with to give me the time needed to pick you up."

"What the hell do we do if Capt. Wilkins sends Johnson after me and finds you here without orders?

How in hells name did you know my arrival time?"

"Samantha sent Richard an e-mail and it was him that got us all together to plot the whole thing. He wanted to come, but like I told him, I don't have any stripes to strip."

Bruce put his rucksack on the floor between his knees and took the battle rattle Roosevelt held out to him. Space was cramped but he managed enough room to slip his arms into it and strap the gas mask to his leg. He pulled the neckerchief from around his neck to mop up the sweat. "Whew partner, I think my radiator is boiling over."

"Give it a day or two and it won't feel so bad. Better drink some water so you can sweat some more," Roosevelt chuckled. "That's how our air conditioning works here on the desert."

*   *   *

Chapter 65

The Kuwaiti driver settled into the driver's seat, eyes on the rearview mirror and said something. Roosevelt reached across Bruce to pull down the window shade. "Don't know if this is to keep us from seeing out or the outside seeing in. We were in a holding tent at Camp Wolf for a week," Roosevelt said. "This driver is just as short and looks like the same man who drove us to Camp Udairi a couple days ago."

Along into the second hour, the sand began to move in waves across the tracks of the US Army Humvee escort, its taillights almost nonexistent from ten yards away. The lights of the mini bus approaching from the right, apparently lost control and disappeared in the darkness. The driver slapped his steering wheel, said something and left the smart ass behind.

"Is it much further?"

"Oh...probably another hour or so, unless we're forced off the road," Roosevelt said and whirled around to the right. "Oh shit! Here comes another crazy on the your side this time."

Bruce looked through the crack between the window and the shade to see headlights, just as the crazy driver scraped the side of the bus. The driver laughed and banged his hand on the steering wheel.

Bruce stared through the windshield and whispers in Roosevelt's ear when they were within inches of the humvee. "Tho' we travel in the valley of Kuwait, I will feel no evil when we ram the bumper in front, for thine is with me oh Lord."

"Where did that come from?"

"Hell I don't know," Bruce said with a shrug of his shoulders. "It's better than saying this guy is scaring shit out of me."

A mini bus from behind rammed them hard, sending them sliding into a sand bank, but the driver was quick to maneuver back into the road. Bruce looked back just as the driver who had rammed them, pulled back into the road and looked ready to try it again, but evidently changed his mind and slowed to a safe distance behind.

"Don't worry Sarge, this is Kuwait at its finest, so sit back and enjoy the entertainment."

"Was it this dark?"

"Hell yeah and just for kicks we had a dust storm."

Bruce lost sight of the taillights ahead and wondered if they had lost the humvee. He could feel Roosevelt watching him but dared not take his eyes off the road. The driver let out a yell in Arabic and stepped out of the bus. Bruce had no idea what was taking place and as far as he was concerned and sure as hell, they were lost.

"He said the American Bastards left us in the dust," Roosevelt said. "Don't worry about it Sarge, same shit they pulled on us. Look at the dance and curl of sand drifts in the road up ahead, fascinating huh, almost like the sand is alive and crawling across the road?"

The driver climbed back into the bus and moved forward to the sudden sight of taillights. It was ten maybe fifteen minutes later when lights began to appear through the distant haze.

"Is that home up ahead?"

"Yep, up there somewhere."

The driver pulled up to the tent with the flap up and stopped. He slapped the steering wheel and clapped his hands with a shout in Arabic. The door opened and the men headed toward the tent.

"Don't know how in hell the men know where to go." Roosevelt said. "We just picked the first tent we came to and we're still there." He waited for Bruce and led the way to the barracks. "Better get a move on Sarge before they realize we're not a part of this group."

Bruce wondered if his partner was lost, but followed without question in and around several tents until he recognized the young man's strategy. Roosevelt opened the door to tent #84 and rushed Bruce inside to meet the mob waiting for him.

It was after the hugs and handshakes of men he knew and some he didn't, plus an extra from both Roosevelt and Richard before he noticed more signatures than he could count, on a 2X2 foot card on his corner cot. *'We are so sorry for your loss, Sergeant Bruce Lawson and if the need for understanding and companionship arises, you can count us in.'* He struggled with the near to surface tears and focused on the men as he mouthed a thank you to each one.

* * *

Chapter 66

Shortly after 0600 formation the men gathered around Bruce talking at the same time, but Roosevelt's voice and a nudge toward the chow hall was loud and clear. "How about after a breakfast that will blow your mind, we give you the grand tour of Camp Udairi?"

Martinez shuffled up to the left of Bruce to wash his hands. "A thirty minute wait for breakfast is a gift from the heavens mi amigo."

Shortly after, with tray in hand, Bruce did as the men ahead of him and held his tray toward the servers. Pancakes? He could hardly believe his eyes when three slices of bacon slid from the spatula to keep company with scrambled eggs and country fried potatoes?

With a cup of coffee in hand, he sat down between

Roosevelt and Richard and forked a bite of egg. "Don't tell me you guys have been eating this good every morning."

"Some mornings we have ham or sausage. Probably should have warned you before you started eating, but," Richard said with a chuckle, "just pretend the grit between your teeth is salt and not sand."

"I'll remember that," Bruce said and looked around the mess hall to see Webb sitting two tables over. He told Richard and Roosevelt about meeting him on the plane. "There was this old couple in flight to McCord Air Force Base to be with their daughter when she claimed the body of her husband. He was killed in Iraq."

"I sure hope to holy hell that don't happen to one of us," Martinez said with a shake of his head. "No sir amigos, I don't want to see you hombres with your guts hanging out."

"Please Alberto, we're eating here," Buck said. "Besides, me and my grenade launcher ain't gonna let it happen."

"You're a good man Buck, but how about us good men getting the hell out of here and show Lawson the sights," the silent one said and grinning from ear to ear, he led the way to the tray return.

Bruce looked at the surprise in Richard's face and shrugged off a surprise of his own at Longview's sudden outburst. With Roosevelt on one side and Richard on the other, Bruce was taking in what Camp Udairi had to offer. The desert outpost look about it made him think of a movie scene with acres and acres of flat barren land around it. "How far are we from Iraq?"

"Don't know how the hell far away Iraq is from here," Brown said. "But Camp Udairi is located northeast of Kuwait City,"

Bruce recalled Richard's email, the one about the stars in Kuwait and how they appear so close you can almost reach out and touch them. He would check it out tonight and the dust, oh yes indeed just like he said, damn stuff is everywhere and in everything.

Whew it's hot, he thought and wiped at the sweat in his eyes with the back of his fist. "The army must've got a real sweet deal on tents," he said and looked around as if trying to measure them. They look to be about the same size."

"10 by 20 yards and can house 50 cots," Roosevelt said.

We figure 35 square feet for each man to call home. We have 48 men in our tent, 24 per leapfrog team," Richard said. "I'm just beginning to half ass recognize our team of 24."

A breeze came up and the smell of the honey wagon pumping out the portable toilets brings the Glendoveer Golf Course to mind. "Hey Richard, this smell reminds me of when we went golfing and I sliced my tee shot to within inches of the porta pottie on the 5th fairway? Was a damn good tee shot and perfect timing for a piss break."

Wiping the perspiration out of his eyes with the corner of his brown neckerchief, Bruce sipped at the hydration system Roosevelt had given him. "Must be in the triple digits," he said while watching the two men in a jeep whip up their rifles to shoot at desert targets. "What the hell are those men doing?"

"Training," Richard said. "Drive by shooting."

Bruce looked around to see Buck and the other men looking up. He looked up to see what looked like the gray outer limits was closing in on them.

"The wind is getting strong, better get back to the..." before Buck could yell out the warning, the sand began to whirl and curl. Garbage can lids and lawn chairs were cart wheeling in all directions along with anything else not tied down.

"This is the second one since we've been here, Lawson," Brandon said as he pushed a towel up against the door to keep the dust out.

Sounds like all hell was breaking loose outside and a tent full of men with sweat glands working overtime, Bruce was smothering down. I'm gonna die for sure if I don't get a breath of fresh air soon, he thought and fell back across the cot to cover his face with a pillow. The humidity in here feels like mom's hothouse back home.

"Hey amigos I hope to hell our tent don't fly away," Martinez said above the roar and the tent flaps snapping at the three-foot wallboard.

*   *   *

Chapter 67

Bruce felt someone sit on the edge of his cot and pushed aside his pillow to find Richard looking down at him. "What's up Bro?"

"Do you feel like talking about home, the funeral? Sam?"

"She was shaken up Richard and rightfully so, they were best of friends and you know how that feels. Sam thinks everyone had rather she died instead of Lana."

"Yeah, that's what she said in her email. I heard from her every day while you were gone," Richard said and momentarily hesitant he went on. "She told me about the funeral and how sad it was to see you suffer and her unable to console you."

"It was bad Richard, not only for me and Samantha. My in-laws lost their only child," Bruce cleared his throat of tears.

"I thought I was going to die when the plane took off from here without me. I knew in my heart of hearts, you and Sam needed me."

"We did Richard, yes we did, but Sam was great and promised to stay close to my daughter and Lana's parents."

"She e-mailed me your flight schedule. I wanted to be there for you when..."

"I know. Roosevelt told me how you and the men planned the whole thing. Chrissakes Richard. Hope to hell it never comes to it, but the whole unit can be court-martialed."

"They were aware of that and maintained a willing-ness to participate in spite of it."

Bruce grabbed his best friend's hand and pulled him down for a quick chest hug. "I'm sorry Richard, but I was so wrapped up in the pain of losing Lana I was hardly aware of what was going on around me. My people were at the airport and it was...like Lana's cloud hovered around us, allowing each of us to feed off the other."

"I sit at my computer here, feeding off the information Sam sent me, but the need to be at your side made me feel isolated, like I was being held prisoner by the army."

"It was the hardest days of my life, the ending to a beautiful chapter...there is nothing so final as losing a loved one in death."

"Hey, you hombres," Martinez yelled and turned his ear toward the door. "What do you don't hear?"

The wind had stopped and the tent flaps were calm. Bruce opened the door and looked out to see Sgt. Johnson headed their way. His knees started to tremble, but he held to the door and stepped to one side to let the man in.

"Sorry for your loss, Lawson, but glad to have you back and just in time for a little work out." He turned to the other men and ordered them to dress for battle, rifle, water and MRE's. "As soon as you're dressed and ready, meet me outside in 20 minutes."

Immediately upon stepping outside, Drill Sgt. Johnson ordered formation. Two rows with twelve men in each row, partner alongside partner. "Expect pop up creep targets along the way whereas some of them will be the enemy and others will be family with children. There will be Improvised Explosive Devices. Are there any questions before we get started?" Sgt. Johnson asked and upon the silence that followed, he waved the men forward for a jog to the training track.

Bruce spotted two soldiers up ahead, one on each side of the line passing out clips of ammunition. "Good thing we cleaned our rifles last night," he whispers in Roosevelt's ear.

"Alright men, remember...your weapon is an extension of your arm. Keep your finger to the side of your trigger until you're ready for the kill. I don't want anyone claiming fault in an accidental shooting. If I didn't have faith, I'd be running behind instead of in front," he said and the men joined him in a chuckle.

"Thirty minutes into the run, the front two men will peel to the left for a head count and fall in behind the last two men. We repeat the drill every two minutes thereafter until every man has made a head count. Remember to keep your eyes and ears open for the unexpected. Let's spread out men and leave room between you for maneuvers,. The GPS has been set and you know what to do with it. Two miles in we stop for a 20 minute rest to let our counter parts leap for the lead. Are you ready men?" Johnson yelled.

"Yes Sir, Sgt. Johnson," the men called out and as usual, Martinez could be heard above all the rest.

Twenty minutes into the run, Bruce leaned in toward Roosevelt and wiped the sweat out of his eyes. "Are you sure we haven't died and gone to hell?"

"Don't know Sarge, but to the left I think I saw a puff of dust from the dust devil."

Bruce looked up and saw the pop ups at about the same time Roosevelt did. He threw aside his rucksack and fell to his knees. His chin just above the sand berm and rifle aimed, he pulled off two quick rounds. Save the civilians and kill the enemy, he repeated the warning under his breath, and make sure of the target before you squeeze the trigger. "Holy shit Roosevelt, children out there!"

Bruce grabbed up his rucksack and looked around to find Roosevelt at his side. Shots sounded somewhere in the rear and the two men were quick to follow Johnson's lead. They fell to the ground for a quick survey of the terrain ahead and behind.

"Damn Sarge, I'm so hot and tired I don't know if I have the stamina to last until the 20 minute rest period," Roosevelt said when they stopped again and fell to the hot sand.

Bruce looked into the young man's eyes. "Suck on your straw Roosevelt. Take off your helmet and use it to shade your head for ten seconds or so."

* * *

Chapter 68

Two miles into the run, they set up a 4-man tent and crawled inside. The humidity from sweaty bodies was like sitting in a sauna but had the direct sun beat by a mile.

"What I'd give for a couple of beers right now," Sgt. Johnson said.

Bruce licked his lips and chuckled at the thought. "This MRE would go down a hell of a lot better with a cold can of Coors light."

"We have a surprise for later."

"Cold drinks and beautiful women?"

"Nothing that elaborate, Roosevelt. Didn't I hear somewhere that you have a beautiful young lady waiting for you?"

"That's right, Sgt. Johnson Sir."

"Sorry Lawson, I wasn't thinking," Johnson apologized. "Just how the hell did you find your Unit? I inquired at the assignment window and was told you had been picked up."

"Yes Sir, it was enough to boggle the mind when I stepped off the plane into a crowd of new recruits. A fat chance anyone can find me in this crowd, I thought to myself, but once my ID was scanned into the system, the woman pointed me in the right direction."

Bruce could feel the sting of Sgt. Johnson's stare and felt his ears flush, a sure giveaway to the lie he just told and to his drill sergeant, no less. He fought the urge to see if Roosevelt looked as scared as he felt. "I want to thank you sir, for the smooth transition."

"We'll check into that later."

Bruce realized he was still in the hot seat and looked away at about the same time the leapfrog counter parts mouthed the password and hustled around the tents. He covered his face to the dust they kicked up and followed Roosevelt outside for a look around and to stare at the retreating unit. "It'll be dark soon and the GPS is all that will keep us on track," he whispered to Roosevelt.

Sgt. Johnson crawled out of the tent to straighten the kinks out of his back and did a complete turnaround, taking in the nearby territory. "It will be dark soon," he said and pointed to the right. "Holy shit! You men ever see camels up close?"

Bruce looked around at the camels and fell to his stomach. He motioned the men to get down. "Saw something out there to the left of the camels."

"Could be the herder," Sgt. Sullivan said.

"They herd Camels?" Roosevelt appeared surprised.

"Better believe it, Arabs use Camels as a form of transportation," Sullivan said.

"Are they in Iraq or Kuwait?" Roosevelt looked a bit disorientated.

"Kuwait," Sgt. Johnson said. "Iraq is 15 miles from the Northern section of the range. Probably come within thirty miles of it before we turn back." He went back to packing up the rest of his gear. "A couple miles of daylight left before our final leap. We'll take a thirty-minute rest at that time before heading back."

Shortly after sunset, the stars did indeed appear close enough to touch but did little to light their way home. "It's looking pretty dark out there."

"It is Lawson and we're dependent on the GPS now. As each man breaks off for a head count your replacement must be shown our location before leaving him in charge," Johnson said. "Any questions before we head out?"

"No Sir," Roosevelt said.

"Lawson?"

"None that I can think of Sir."

They fell into quick step jog and were on their way again. The weather was much cooler, almost chilly. Other than tired, Bruce felt capable of jogging another four hours. It was still mind boggling as to how far into the darkness he could see with his night vision goggles.

Johnson and Sullivan peeled off to the left leaving the location on the GPS with Bruce.

Near the two-minute deadline, he checked their position on the GPS. "Time," Bruce said and turned for a quick GPS instruction before a hand off to Brown and Buck. He motioned Roosevelt to the left for a rest and head count.

Hours later or so it seemed, they passed the last two men counting heads and welcomed the last rest stop before returning to camp. "Thank you God!" Roosevelt moaned.

"Let's erect the pup tents and have a bite. Who the hell knows, after a rest we may feel like a couple more miles before we turn back?" Johnson chuckled. "Close your mouth Roosevelt before the night bugs home in on it."

Bruce crawled into the tent and lay on his back for five minutes or so before making dinner. "Damn I'm tired."

"I'll make desert and you make the main course, a

feast fit for a king."

"Good idea Roosevelt," Johnson said and turned to his partner, the medic. "How about it Sullivan? I'll do the stew and you do the chocolate pudding."

The four men sat there with one eye on the time and a bite or so of food left on their plate when Bruce caught Sgt. Johnson looking at him. Desperate with the need to escape more questions as to how he got from the airport to Camp Udairi, Bruce stood up and started for the door. "Think I'll step outside and have a look around."

Damn, he thought, how the hell do I dodge the bullet again? Think Lawson. Yeah, that's it, I'll just act as confused as Johnson.

He tried it out for the sound of sincerity. *You got me Sgt. Johnson, but I want to thank you again for cutting me out of the herd and seeing that I made it here in one piece.* Hell yeah, that sounds good. Just make it short and to the point, Bruce thought and sauntered away from camp to take a leak.

Johnson pushed a button on the GPS to feed in the location for the trip back to camp and called formation. It was the promise of a party in Sgt. Johnson's tent and a cold can of Bud lite that helped pass the four mile jog back to camp.

*   *   *

Chapter 69

It was early yet, not quite dawn, and already the tent felt like a bake oven. Bruce was in dire need of an energy boost and with temperatures rising, the thought of humping a rucksack was way more than he could bear. He rolled to his back and swung around to sit on the edge of the cot and wished to hell he was home. After a shave, his face washed, his teeth brushed and in full dress, he still felt hot but somewhat better.

"Up to a jump start for the chow hall?" Richard said. "Shouldn't be much of a line this time of day."

Reluctant to leave and feeling disgruntled, Bruce fell in behind the others. "There's a hell of a lot of sand between here and there," he said but continued to put one foot in front of the other, in spite of the sun filling

his boonie hat with steam. "Wonder what's playing at .
the theater we'll miss tonight while on maneuvers?"

"A Few Good Men with Tom Cruise and Demi
Moore," Roosevelt said. "A relatively new movie, I
think."

"Eh Si, the line is not so long," Martinez said and
stepped in behind the last man.

As luck would have it, they shuffled through the
empty washroom unscathed. Bruce tossed his paper
towel in the trashcan and joined the line with tray in
hand and his plate out to catch his spaghetti, salad and
garlic bread.

He joined the men at the table and crowded in
between Brown and Richard across from their three
partners, Buck, Roosevelt and Longview. He looked
around, grinned at the sight of Webb and returns his
wave.

"Who's that?" Richard asked.

"Sgt. James Webb, the young man on the plane I
was telling you about. The man who likes Big Hunk

candy bars."

"Hey!" Roosevelt turned his nose up for a sniff. "You guys smell anything?"

"Bruce sniffed. "Yeah, I do...smells like smoke but where the hell's it coming from?"

"Fire!" Someone yelled. "Fire!"

Bruce grabbed his rucksack, shoved Roosevelt and Longview in front him and followed Richard outside.

They joined the crowd of onlookers outside to watch the blaze, but suddenly stepped back when the wind came up, whipping the flames in all directions and through nearby tents. The men with heavy equipment were working against time, trying to reach the diesel and propane tanks before the unthinkable happened.

An hour or so later, the fire out and excitement over, they stopped at the fast food area for a cafe latte. "Si, something warm inside make you cool outside, eh amigo's."

"So they say," Longview shared a chuckle with Martinez.

Bruce stepped into the barracks to unpack his rucksack and repack it with only what he thought he would need for the three-day desert maneuvers. He rolled up his sleeping bag, laid out the facemask, night vision goggles, netting and what else?

He closed his eyes and tried to imagine what the desert would be like at night, but his vision was interrupted when Richard sat down beside him. "Hey friend, glad you're here?" Bruce said. "Did I give you what Sam sent back with me?"

"No?" Eyes aglow and looking for whatever Bruce was talking about, Richard waited.

"Come a little closer." Bruce grinned when Richard moved in as close as he could without sitting on his lap. "A little closer, Bro."

"What the hell are you trying to do here, Bruce?"

"Lean in toward me a little," Bruce said and grabbed Richard for a full kiss on the lips before he could pull away.

"You mean Sam kissed you?"

"No, not me...you!"

"Oh hell."

"That woman is madly in love with you man. She's really good with Sari too," Bruce smiled when he thought of his daughter. "You may as well make up your mind to give her a baby when you get home."

"That's the first thing on my, to do list."

*   *   *

Chapter 70

"Heads up men," Sgt. Johnson called from the doorway. "For the next three days your ass, as well as mine and Sullivan's, will belong to the Special Forces." His chuckle left a lot to the imagination. "Save room for me and my partner in the first truck."

Bruce strapped the gas mask to his leg and wiggled into his rucksack. With sleeping bag under his arm and rifle in hand, he tossed his gear into the second troop carrier and climbed aboard to give a hand to the men behind until all eight were in the truck. The excitement on his partner's face well surpassed the feel of anxiety in his gut.

Immediately upon reaching their destination, the men jumped out of the trucks for a look around at the vast nothingness of the Kuwaiti desert. No sign of civilization for miles around except for the generator producing electricity to feed a couple of big lights and several port-a-potties. That's it! No buildings, trailers, fences and no berms for protection, absolutely nothing, not even a shower.

Two supply trucks pulled up with tents, cases of bottled water and MRE's. The first order of the day was to unload the truck and set up camp. Taking one last look at the raw premises and newborn tent city, Bruce joined the formation with a shrug.

"Are you ready?" Mackey yelled.

"Yes Sir."

"I didn't hear you."

"Yes Sir, Lieutenant Sir," the men shouts of harmony sounded even better than when they practiced.

"My name is Lt. Mackey with Special Forces and for the next three days I will be your worst nightmare. Before completion of the next three days of torture, every man here will wish he'd never met me. Let's see how fast you maneuver the back of a moving truck," he flashed a sadistic smile and turned to the men at the head of the line. "The first eight men will catch the first truck and once the last man is on board, you will then jump out and fall to your bellies in the dust. If you don't remember anything else, remember this. Speed is of the utmost importance behind enemy lines."

Bruce smiled his pleasure at finding him and his eight-man group last in line. "Watch and learn Roosevelt so we can look reeeal good out there."

"It's a hell of a lot harder Lawson," Sullivan said. "Than it looks from back here."

The first five men did a fairly decent climb into the truck, but the sixth, losing his balance held fast to the bumper. "Take care of that man," Mackey yelled. "He might just be the man who will save your life." The men in the truck grabbed his hands and two men pushing from behind, heaved him into the back. The last two men struggle to cover the ground between them and the moving truck.

The second group of men learned from the first and gave each man a hand up. There was two hours of in and out of moving trucks before Lt. Mackey called for a rest.

Roosevelt sat down with one arm cradled in the other. "Damn, Sarge, I banged hell out of my elbow," he made a fist and flexed his elbow. "Still works."

"You can bet my mama's little Mexican baby is sure as hell gonna be a banged up hombre," Martinez said and fell down alongside his partner, Brandon.

Bruce sat quietly while listening to the grunts and groans around him and thinking there was very little about his body that didn't hurt.

"Why so quiet?"

"Resting, Richard. Just resting."

"Okay men, liven up. Let's try an hour of crawling on your bellies," Lt. Mackey yelled.

Five minutes into the exercise, Bruce crawled alongside Richard. "This damn hard pack of Kuwaiti sand is rubbing my stomach raw and the armor slipping around is playing holy hell with the hairs on my chest!"

"Know what you mean," Richard moaned. "Thought it would be soft like you see on TV, you know...like what the camels kick up when they walk across the desert."

"On your belly, Martinez!" Mackey yelled. "You men up ahead, stop talking and save your breath, you may need it down the line."

"It's hot, Sir," Martinez said.

"Better hot than getting your butt shot off."

"Yes Sir, Lieutenant Sir."

"Who feels like a fifteen minute jog after lunch?"

"Si, Lt. Mackey Sir, anything to get this Mexican belly out of the hot sand."

Bruce joined the laughter and climbed into the back of the truck to get out of the sun and work up his MRE for lunch.

"How much would you pay for a can of beer, gentlemen?" Sgt Johnson had no more than sounded the words when wallets came out and offers were being made. "Put your money away and I'll see what I can round up."

"So it's not a Coors lite, but what the hell," Bruce said. "Hey you young farts listen up and pay attention to this old fart, you better include Sgt. Johnson in your prayers at night cause you'll never, in this whole United States Army, find another Drill Sergeant who will treat you to a beer after a hot day at work believe me. Damn, this is good," he smacked his lips and gave Johnson the high sign. "Thanks Sgt Johnson Sir, I'll remember you in my will."

He looked around to find Lt. Mackey with a beer in his hand and a grin on his face. Not a bad fellow when he's not yelling orders, Bruce thought and raised his beer in a salute.

"Hey, me too Amigo," Martinez said. "You better pray this hombre don't die before he makes his millions."

Holding a small portion of heaven in his hand, Bruce sipped at his beer and thanked God for a drill

Sergeant like Johnson. "The drawback in one can of beer," Bruce said and looked at Richard who looked as bad if not worse than he felt. "The alcohol content is almost, but not quite enough to kill the muscle pain in a work worn body."

"One more of these," Roosevelt said and rolled his eyes at the can of beer in his hand. "And I could feel like a newly made over man."

* * *

Chapter 71

The sound of Mackey's voice brought an echo of the earlier moans and groans. Bruce jumped out the back to find gun trucks lined up in front of the covered transport.

"I want two rows, partner alongside partner," Mackey yelled. "The old men will man the wheel for the first round of drive by shooting while the younger gents take on the guns."

Bruce and Roosevelt pulled third start and settled into position on their gun truck to wait. He turned the key and listened to the motor hum while watching the first two teams move out. A quick glance around back caught Richard and Longview ready and waiting with Brandon and Martinez behind them. Brown and Buck were just ahead and looking pretty good.

Bruce neared the target and slowed at Roosevelt's first round of shooting. He kept his mind on his driving and not on the killing machine in back of him. He made a U behind Brown and Buck and could hear Roosevelt changing positions.

Once they had returned to where they started, Roosevelt slid in behind the wheel and Bruce took over the gun seat. "Okay partner, I'm ready when you are," he called down to his driver and positioned his grip much the same as Roosevelt. With the machine gun aimed at the target, he blasted it sure as hell! A quick change of position at the U enabled him to shoot from the opposite side. Thinking this the easiest maneuver thus far, he grinned and watched Richard and his partner pull up behind them.

"Splendid job, men," Mackey called out to his twenty-four-man team and stepped aside to relinquish the reigns to the Lieutenant in charge of the second 24 man leapfrog unit.

Bruce sat down beside Roosevelt and realized during the excitement, he'd forgotten how damn hot it was. He removed his helmet, wiped his forehead and gargles a mouthful of water before he spits it out and takes another to quench his thirst.

"Well, gentlemen," Mackey said and waved Johnson and Sullivan over as his models. "Dusk is closing in fast and we have one last maneuver before we call it a day."

The two men fell to their knees with the aid of their rifle stock and tossing their rucksack aside, fell to their stomachs and fired two shots into the target

Bruce knew without a doubt from past experience at Ft. Irwin, it would be midnight before he could match the speed in which these two highly trained men found the target. He felt a renewed respect for both Johnson and Sullivan.

"Don't tell me that medics are required to learn this shit," Martinez looked around as if he spoke for the entire unit and turned his eyes on Sullivan in disbelief.

Looking pleased at being singled out, Sullivan

chuckled. "Martinez, you would be surprised at how us medicine men are mistreated."

"Whew," Martinez shook his head. "May as well get with it amigos, our man Mackey ain't going away til we do."

There was a chill in the air and night was coming at them fast. Bruce hugged himself and looked up at a helicopter flying around the perimeter. "That white truck out there, is it Iraqis?" He called out to no one in particular and raised his binoculars to find what looked like two men in back of the pickup with binoculars looking back at him. Both men grabbed for a hand hold when the driver spun around and started back in the direction they had come.

"Not to worry, Lawson," Mackey said. "Those humvee gun trucks are out there to keep them at bay, not only that but the men up there are here for the same reason. The only things you have to worry about around here are scorpions, kangaroo rats, snakes, bugs, mice and camel spiders."

"Camel Spiders?" Martinez jumped up, looked around and brushed at the imaginary spiders on his rear end.

"Huge, Martinez and the scorpions are looking for a place to call home, like sharing your sleeping bag, oh yeah. Remember to fill your shoes with paper or put them in bed with you." Mackey looked away, pretending an interest elsewhere other than the fear in Martinez' eyes. "Good night men and sleep tight. Got another hard day ahead of us."

Bruce pushed up off the ground with a groan. Every muscle in his body was sore and the memory of the latest maneuver, how the first attempt near tore him apart, left him feeling old and out of shape.

Feeling around inside his open sleeping bag for uninvited guest and finding none, he crawled in and zipped the sides tight around his neck, careful not to catch his chin hairs in the zipper. Aside from the wild-life scampering around in the dark, the night was calm, cold and the ground damn uncomfortable.

He could hear himself starting to snore softly when something furry with a cold nose touched his ear. He opened his eyes to see two little beady ones in the semi-darkness. He pushed it away, thinking it was a kangaroo rat and slid down into his sleeping bag.

"I've learned a lot out here Sarge, and making sure you kill a man is a hell of a lot harder than hunting for game."

Bruce pulled his head out of the sleeping bag and looked in the direction of his partner's voice. Just as he was about to cover his head he looked again in the direction of where the voice was coming from?

"Usually one good shot will take an animal down, but if you don't kill a man with the first shot, there's a chance he'll get the last shot," Roosevelt said. "I'll shut up so you can get some sleep. Goodnight Sarge."

"Goodnight Roosevelt."

* * *

Chapter 72

Aching from head to toe, Bruce opened his eyes to the sound of his worst nightmare, Mackey outside yelling rise and shine orders. It was still starlight out and too damn cold for a workout. He sat still for a moment while spiders and scorpions crossed his mind.

"Good morning men," Mackey greeted with a half assed grin. "At the end of the day, you will have one left for a repeat performance of each maneuver before the final curtain call," he chuckled. "You have 30 minutes for breakfast so hop to it."

His body bruised and his spirit broken, doubt was playing with his mind again. What if I fail to comply with what is expected of me during maneuvers today, what then? Sgt. Johnson, stepped out of the tent, his face lined with pain and his movements slow. Bruce grins.

"How do you feel, Lawson?" Longview asked.

"Like I have one foot in the grave."

"Your friend tried to get up and had to crawl around on all fours before he could push up on two feet."

Bruce looked around to find Richard trying to straighten the kinks out of his back. "Give me another two days of this and I'll be too damn sore to fight this damn war."

"Know what you mean Richard, but Johnson says we will have two days to mend."

"Line up men and let the games begin." Mackey said. "Maneuvers will be the same, but with a slight change. You will not jump out of the truck until after it turns onto its side. You will then escape the flaming truck and for those of you who are injured, the responsibility falls on the healthy to see that each man is saved and accounted for." He looked around as if to make sure each man had his eyes open.

"The same will happen during the maneuvers on your gun truck. As it is turning over, both of you are to jump free and run for cover, because the enemy will be trying to take you out. Make sure your partner is on his feet, if he's down, pick him up and carry him to safety."

"I know this sounds hard, but saving your men will be the utmost thought in your mind and I want you to get the feel of it today. I want it to be as easy as aiming your rifle and pulling the trigger. How about it, Sgt. Johnson you and Sullivan ready?"

The two men stepped in front of the eight men who would be leading off with them. Bruce looked across at Roosevelt and mouthed a good luck.

He felt a fist to his shoulder and looked around to find Richard and Longview next in line with Martinez and Brandon behind them. Buck and Brown brought up the rear.

The truck started out slowly with Johnson and Sullivan grabbing the tailgate and using the bumper to step up into the truck. Bruce and Roosevelt reached for the tailgate and were helped by the first two men and half assed pushed up by the men in back and continued until all ten men were seated inside. The hind end of the truck suddenly swerved first to one side and then the other and before the men could prepare for what was to come, it rolled onto its side. The Special Force men began to yell. "The truck is on fire, get out...!"

Bruce jumped out and looked back to see Sullivan lying on his side, his eyes closed. He rushed back into the flaming truck and with the help of his partner and Johnson; they pulled the unconscious man to safety.

Sullivan stood up with a smile and looked at Bruce and Roosevelt. "I sure as hell agree with Mackey, I'll go to war with you men anytime."

"Damn, Sullivan." Roosevelt said. "You sure as the hell had me fooled. I thought you were hurt bad." He looked around to see the truck on its wheels again and the flames out. "Was it my imagination or were those flames hot or not?"

Bruce looked around at the other men waiting their

turn to find expressions of amazement and disbelief. He settled down beside Roosevelt and caught up in the excitement, sat back to enjoy the trial run of the second group to find the fiery crash was indeed mind boggling.

Mackey looked at the men to feel them out about their take on maneuvers thus far. "Tomorrow will be a repeat of everything you have learned thus far and now for the last maneuver of the day before we turn in."

Bruce waited for the Special Force drivers to park the special equipped gun trucks and climbed aboard with Roosevelt. They settled back into their seats to watch Johnson and Sullivan give them a trial run. "What do you think Sarge? Do we have it in us to jump and roll before the damn vehicle rolls on top of us?"

"Hell yeah. Be ready to jump when the lever comes down to tip us over?" Bruce looked around and up at Roosevelt atop the gunners seat. "You have further to jump than I do partner, so pretend you're jumping down the ravine to pick up your kill."

Bruce turned the starter and eased forward, slowly at first and just as he pressed harder on the gas pedal, it sounded like a blowout and the ground was coming at them fast. Bruce jumped and rolled, looking around to see Roosevelt hit the ground with an even smoother roll than his. They grabbed and held to each other, as they ran from the blazing gun truck.

*   *   *

Chapter 73

Sometime before daybreak and grimacing from painful bruises, Bruce played around with the question of sickbay. The agony of moving what felt like broken bones and dislocated body parts, and while massaging a muscle cramp in his calf he bit down hard on his lip. He swiped his tongue across his lower lip and sure as hell, he'd drawn the taste of blood.

He rolled to his side with a groan, pulling the blanket over his head to muffle the men's laughter and their take on the three-day maneuvers. Remembering the similarity of his shower last night, a chuckle nearly slipped out when Martinez brought up his shower woes.

"Hell yeah amigo's, no shit. I sudsed up three fuckin' times before I got clean."

Sudden awareness to the quiet, Bruce stole a quick peek from beneath the covers to find the room empty except for three men plus Richard still in bed. He took a brisk ten-count exercise of knees to chest and not yet ready to face the day, fluffed his pillow and crammed it under his head.

He suddenly remembered his neglect and reluctantly tossed his blanket aside to clean his weapon and saw Richard up and working the kinks out of his back. "Nothing like a hard day on the job, hey bro?"

Richard returned a half ass look through slits beneath his eyelashes. "Shouldn't be much of a line at the dining room, feel like breakfast?"

"Oh yes indeedy." Bruce said and pushed such thoughts as weapon cleaning aside.

Buck and Brandon joined the twosome in the dining hall where very little conversation passed between them. After breakfast and into the heat, silence continued to hover about until Bruce stopped at the Moral Welfare Recreation area. He turned to the three old farts with a show of muscles. "Who's game for a little workout in the gym?"

"What the shit," Buck said. "May be good for what ails me."

Back in the barracks after a vigorous round of exercise and feeling somewhat better, they found the young men stretched out in the middle of the floor with the smell of cleaning fluid in the air. Bruce grabbed his weapon and eased down very slowly alongside Roosevelt. He tore down his M16 and giving Roosevelt a wink, placed the parts within easy reach for him to clean. "A clean rifle could mean the difference between life and death, eh partner."

Roosevelt polished his rifle to bring up a clear reflection of his face on the barrel. "Better believe it Sarge," he said and wrapped it in a towel. "Need any help?"

"Never refuse a helping hand," Bruce said with a fist bump to the young man's shoulder. "I'll clean while you inspect and reassemble. You're the best little polisher that ever polished from polishville so I'll leave the spit and shine to you."

"You got it," Roosevelt returned the shoulder bump with a hesitant grin on his face. "Do you think my lady will give me a baby as beautiful as your little one?"

"Roosevelt! You didn't?"

"I did," Roosevelt looked at Bruce with a sheepish grin. "Alice wanted a baby so bad and hell..."

"But your mama?" Bruce looked at him with a frown. "How?"

"We grabbed our chance when mama was in the shower."

Bruce thought about his young partner's predicament and grinned at the thought of him becoming a father. "How about we celebrate over a Hazelnut Latté at the cafe?"

"A shame there isn't something stronger," Roosevelt wiggles his eyebrows. " How about a cheeseburger and fries to go with it?" Roosevelt said.

"Where the hell can we get a cheeseburger?"

"At Burger King my friend," Longview joined in.

Bruce walked over and looked down at Richard and Longview to see how far along they were. "Are you two about finished fooling around with your toys?"

"Soon as I wipe it down," Richard said. "Is Samantha gonna be okay?"

"Yes, Richard. She helped me big time through Lana's funeral." Bruce smiled when the memory of Sam crossed his mind, how they had laughed and cried together. "You got yourself a special kind of woman there Richard, almost as special as I had."

"We were two lucky men on our wedding day." The sparkle in Richard's eyes was telling more than words ever could.

"Damn," Bruce said with a shake of his head. "That seems so long ago."

"Hell, it feels like a long time since Sam raped the hell out of me at the Econo Lodge," Richard threw back his head and laughed. "Did you know she and Lana had a bet on which of us could get it up the most times?"

It wasn't until Roosevelt and Longview fell into a fit of laughter that Bruce realized the two young lads had been listening. He hadn't blushed in a very long time, but couldn't deny the sudden facial burn.

"Hey punks, we're not too old to have a little bedtime fun."

"Oh no Graves, what's so funny is what I told Longview about my girl. She did the same thing to me, tried to give me enough to last for two years. Now that's a hell of a lotta loving going on between the sheets."

"Yeah, is it okay if I tell em the outcome?"

"Sure Longview, go ahead. Lawson knows already."

"Well...Roosevelt gave his girl enough to keep her busy for two years, his baby."

"Congratulation Roosevelt," Richard said. "I should have given Sam as much."

"Don't worry about it Richard, Sam's got her hands full with Sari." Bruce could picture the two of them together. "My daughter will help her through the pain of losing Lana."

He closed his eyes and smiled on the memory of the last three days at home. Visions of his daughter danced in his head and Sam, her first day on the job working in Lana's office, he smiled again. She's not as smart as Lana, but Pops will be proud of her. May take her a little longer to learn the business, but she's got the smarts and she'll make it.

"Formation at 0600," Richard said. "Reading between the lines of Johnson's speech, we may be leaving here soon."

* * *

Chapter 74

The pounding at the door came as no surprise because every so often, Johnson had a smart ass way of waking the men an hour before formation. Bruce swung his feet off the cot and waited while Buck opened the door and held it. A second or so of hearing nothing and seeing less, he could feel the blood rush from his head to the tips of his toes. The unit could be in deep dung if the Captain found out how I got from the airport to Camp Udairi.

Three Special Force men from yesterday's maneuvers pushed into the room. "Before you men leave for Iraq and can be in full dress by1700 hrs, we would like to award you with a lobster feast before you leave Iraq."

"We will be ready Sir, Lt. Mackey," Martinez said

with a salute.

The men rallied together at 0600 and stood to attention when Sgt. Johnson suddenly rushed around the corner out of breath. "Attention men! Sorry I'm late, but double-checked our orders against the wild rumors. Please disregard whatever you might have heard. I now have in my hands, orders signed and sealed by Captain Wilkins. Sgt. Lawson, please step forward."

"Yes Sir, Sgt. Johnson."

"See that all 48 men of the leap frog unit receive a copy. We will be leaving for Iraq within the week. That will be all, Squad dismissed."

Bruce stood in the doorway making sure each man received a copy of the orders. He eased down onto his cot to go over the document a second time. "Well men, I vote we have breakfast and see if we can find this Milvan they're talking about."

"I second it, mi amigo," Martinez said.

Returning to the barracks after breakfast, Bruce cleaned out his locker and dumped the contents of his rucksack on the cot. He pulled his duffle of dirty clothes nearby and added a few dirty items to be washed later in the day.

"We let our appreciation be known in church and in prayer for the many gifts and supplies we received in abundance from volunteers and now my amiable amigos, we must leave some of them behind," Martinez said.

Buck scratched his head and looked at his stash on the bed. "Amen to that, Alberto."

Bruce and his partner stood looking down at the stash they had collected while here in Kuwait. 16 packages of baby wipes, 12 bars of soap and 10 tubes of toothpaste. He pulled 3 bars of Irish Spring, 4 tubes of Crest to go with his 2 toothbrushes to his end of the cot and stepped back with 3 sticks of deodorant in his hand. "Deodorant in this country is losing the war on sweat."

"Yeah Sarge, but we got it cheap so we may as well use it and pretend it makes us smell good," Roosevelt said. "Sixteen packages of baby wipes, "8 for you and 8 for me. Do you think we'll need this many?"

Bruce sat down for a rest and pulls Roosevelt down with him. "Your guess is as good as mine, but water might be hard to come by in Iraq, much the same as it was on maneuvers."

With most of the packing out of the way, Bruce thought about the comforts of home, suds you can make while taking a shower in soft water. Thick shag carpets to cuddle my toes and my soft king size bed! Just the thought of Lana not sharing his king size bed filled him with hot rage. He wanted to splatter the blood of the man responsible for his wife's accident and had the fucker not of died of a heart attack…

"You can say that again, Sarge."

Bruce searched his mind for what he might have said and wanted to ask Roosevelt why he could say it again, but shrugs off the thought.

"Hey Bruce," Richard said. "I'm waiting until the last minute to pack my laptop."

"Sounds like a winner, Bro. What are you doing about clothing?"

"Don't know until after we hit the laundry room."

Bruce turned back to his cot and thought about the ins and outs of clothing. "Will we have inspections on the battlefield you think?"

"If we crawl around in the sand like we did on maneuvers, who the hell's gonna be the wiser if we change pants or not," Roosevelt said.

Makes sense, he thought. The supply truck should be close behind with water, MRE's, ammunition. "3 each of neckerchiefs, handkerchiefs, tee shirts, shorts and 1 pair of pants should be plenty," Bruce said.

"And 3 pairs of socks, please..." Longview said.

"Oh hell yeah," Richard said. "God forbid we forget clean socks."

"Stinky feet?" Bruce wonders aloud. "My feet don't stink!"

* * *

Chapter 75

Now's a good time to answer Pops email, he thought, and if by chance we don't leave right away, I can always send another before the milvan drop. First he opened the one from Samantha and laughed out loud. "I have an email from my daughter Richard, and she's only 8 weeks old."

"Yeah, Sam say's she sent you one."

He smiles at how good she is at baby talk but could feel the sting of tears in his eyes by the time he finished reading the letter.

Dear Dada:

I love you dada and miss you. Wish you were here with me right now, but it's okay cause Grandma and Grandpa Elkington are spoiling me to death, oh...and oh yeah, mama Sam is too. Please daddy, come home soon cause I miss you sooo much and I have a XX and a OO waiting for you.

Auntie Sam wants to say something to you.

Bye bye Dada, I love you,

Hi friend:

How are you doing? I love my job at the office and just in case you don't feel the love of your family around here, this is to let you know just how much you are missed and loved, it's more than I can spread my arms.

I absolutely adore your daughter and wish I had one of my own.

Love you friend,

Sam

He wiped at the tears with the back of his hand. Thank you Samantha, you rascal, he thought and decided to answer as if he was writing to Sari.

My dearest daughter:

You boootiful, boootiful baby girl. Dada loves you so much and misses you sooo much it hurts my heart and

makes me cry. Be good my darling and don't give Aunty
Sam a bad time. Hug grandpa and grandma Elkington
for me and give them all the love I have after you take
what you want...

Love you Sari,

Dada

Dear Samantha, my dear friend;

Thanks Sam for keeping me in touch with everything
going on at home, just hang in there and it won't be long
until your husband is home and giving you a baby just like
Sari.

I look forward to hearing from you again.

Love you two ladies

Dada...Bruce

He sent a quick e-mail to Billy Joe and a lengthy
one to Pops, with a suggestion that he gives Samantha a
raise, and pressed send.

Bruce locked his laptop case and slipped it into his
duffle bag on top of what he wouldn't be taking with
him. "No way am I missing dinner tonight," he said

to no one in particular. "Could be our last good meal before we return home and if rumor has it right, lobster and steak are on the menu."

"My mama's little Mexican boy is ready to get the shit outta here," Martinez said. "If they move our departure back, it means the same old shit all over again."

"Let's go eat now and worry about it later," Richard said and waited by the door. "If we hurry we might get there before the line gets too long."

Thirty minutes later and leaving the washroom with clean hands, they stepped into the dining hall for dinner. "Hey, look at this place," Bruce said. "I think it looks better than it did before the fire." He held his plate out to let Mr. Lobster settle down on it and pushed his steak to one side with his fork to make room for a baked potato. Chunks of blue cheese in the salad dressing were missing...but what the hell.

Bruce joined Richard at the urn for a cup of coffee and followed him across the floor to settle in alongside Roosevelt. He dipped a bite of lobster in melted butter, put it on his tongue and sucked on the full lobster flavor. "Damn, this is to die for."

"Yeah, and it don't cost us no $25.00 a tail thanks to Mackey," Martinez said and rolled his eyes at the bite on his fork.

Roosevelt leaned forward to look down the table at Martinez. "I don't know about that Alberto, ole Mackey worked us pretty damn hard for this lobster."

"Si, that he did, amigo."

∗   ∗   ∗

Chapter 76

Tomorrow was weighing heavy on his mind when Bruce stepped into the shower and turned his face up to catch the spray. Come in at the right time of night when the water is neither too hot nor too cold is almost like home, he thought, but with men waiting in line there was never enough time to enjoy.

When Mr. Lobster suddenly began having a hoe-down in his gut, Bruce left the shower in a hurry. He toweled off with a half ass dry job and pulling his pants up as he ran, his foot became tangled with the hem of his britches leg and nearly threw him, but he reached the port-a-potty not a minute too soon. "Whew," he mutters to himself, "the smell in here is enough to knock a man over."

Someone bumped into the front of his port-a-pot. A quick glance at the door to see if it was locked, Bruce heard the person slam into the next potty.

"Sweet mother above have mercy on this poor Mexican boy. Oh hell...damn!" he groaned and let fly with a noise similar to what Bruce had made.

"Is that you, Martinez?"

"Si, amigo. I think my dinner has declared war on this poor Mexican."

"Me too," Bruce said. "Maybe we better go back to eating MRE's."

"Si Lawson. How can anything so delicious stink like sheeit?"

"Got me says the poor white boy," Bruce said and felt good when Martinez laughed.

"Gas! Gas! Gas!" the warning sounded just outside the door. He wonders if it's a trick, but strips the gas mask from his leg and covers his nose and mouth. Martinez was making noises in the next potty again.

"Oh sheeit," Martinez moaned.

"You got your gas mask, Alberto?"

"Si amigo. It smells so sheeity in here I don't know if I got a sniff of gas or not."

When the all clear sounded, Bruce stepped outside to wait for Martinez. "Sure glad that bellyache hit me here and not in the desert," Martinez chuckled.

Roosevelt came out of the potty next door and sounded out of breath. "I pulled my pants down so fast I got my gas masked tangled up somehow and never did get it loose. Held my breath the whole damn time."

Martinez threw back his head and laughed. "Hey Hombre, did you get the sheeits?"

"Hell amigo," Roosevelt said. "For a while there, with the way your potty humped and bumped against mine, I thought you were making out with some over-sexed drop-dead lady. It's a wonder you didn't turn us both over."

Bruce joined Roosevelt in a bent over belly laugh as the thought of Martinez turning the potty's over had crossed his mind as well.

Laughter followed the three men all the way to the barracks. "I won't say nothing to nobody if you guys don't," Roosevelt said.

Bruce glimpsed the expression of pain on Richard's face and sat down beside him. "Just a word from a man in the know. The best medicine to kill the pain is a potty break."

"You gotta have a stomach like me." Buck said and rubbing his stomach reminded Bruce of Lana when she did the same love rub on a belly full of baby.

"Did anybody see Brandon?" Buck asked. "He was outa here so fast, I thought the tent was on fire."

"Nope, but somebody did go into the potty on the end when we came out," Roosevelt said while looking at Bruce for confirmation.

Bruce hadn't seen anybody, but if Roosevelt said he did, that was good enough for him and he answered with a nod. "There's still a lot of daylight out there and this may be our last night here before we leave for Iraq," Bruce said and looked around to see if the men were paying him any mind. "I was just thinking that maybe we should go to the range and see if we still got what it takes."

Six men volunteered, but Richard still looked doubtful about his condition. "I would like to go, but..." he looked toward the door. "Let me go to the thunder room."

The bus pulled up before Richard returned from the john and momentarily hesitant leave or stay, Bruce jumped for the step and joined the other men on the bus. They stepped into the weapons tent, once the bus stopped and sidled up to the counter where each of them received a 30 round clip.

Bruce looked around for the target and edged up to the firing line. He snapped the clip into his rifle and waited until all six men were in place.

He lowered his trigger finger when Sgt. Pascall rushed out of the weapons tent yelling. Bruce looked to where Pascall was pointing to find Bedouins driving their seven camels single file across the range.

"Hey Sarge! A camel for each of us," Roosevelt said. My daddy and me never bagged us a camel before."

"Do you have a hunting license, Amigo?"

"Probably not hunting season on camels anyway," Richard said.

"What are they doing out there Sgt. Pascall, looking for greener pastures," Martinez shouted.

Bruce looked down the line, surprised to find his friend with rifle and ammunition and waiting for the camels to clear the field. "Hey Bro, glad to have you amongst the living, how do you feel?"

"Lord Bruce, it's been a long time since I had a bellyache like that."

"Rich guys like me eat lobster every other day at home," Longview laughed.

Bruce looked at the young man, wondering at just how much of this rich shit he keeps dishing out to believe. The laugh says no, but what the hell. He looked across the range to find the camels safely out of range.

* * *

Chapter 77

A quick knock sounded at the door just before it opened to honor them with the presence of a high-ranking guest. The men quickly sprang to attention with a 48-man salute. Johnson cleared his throat and struggles to hold a straight face. "Attention men, the Captain James Wilkins would like a word with you." He stepped back with a salute. "Sir?"

Another 48-man salute and the men settled down to wait and listen to what the Captain had to say. Wilkins covered the 1st and 2nd Battalion with a fleeting glance and a smile for each man. "Thank you Sgt. Johnson. Gentlemen...Rumors of your ability and willingness to fight this war have crossed my desk. Glad to have you aboard."

Captain Wilkins looked toward the door and back again. "The first twenty-four men of our leapfrog unit will load up tonight at 2100 hrs in three armored transports. Our second twenty-four unit will follow thirty minutes later. They will carry us 90 miles inside Iraq and from there we will travel to Najaf on foot. The question of fact or fiction has been settled; we are indeed going to war," the captain looked at the door again and the men followed his gaze. Sgt. Sullivan stepped into the room and all eyes turn to him and the weapons in his arms.

"I agree with the recommendations I received from Colonel Weir at Ft. Irwin," Wilkins said and reached for the first weapon. "Private Roosevelt, step forward please."

"Yes Sir Captain Wilkins, Sir."

"Have a feel of your new weapon, a U.S. M249 Squad Automatic Weapon, better known in the military as a SAW...Your new SAW, Pvt. Eldon Roosevelt."

"Thank you Captain, Sir," the young man smiled

and looked it over like a child with a brand new toy. "I will care for it as I would my right arm, Sir."

"Yes, I am sure you will." Captain Wilkins shook Roosevelt's hand and turned to his notes. "Sergeant Kevin Kemp, please step forward."

"Yes Sir, Captain Wilkins."

"You as well as Roosevelt received an excellent report. Your new Saw weighs 15.16 lbs unloaded. A little more weight, but after our range practice and trial run, you will know if it's too much for you. Private Buck Jamison, please step forward."

"Yes Sir, Captain Wilkins."

"This is the M16 A1 rifle with a M203 40mm grenade launcher. You made perfect launches out of a 100 at Ft. Irwin. How do you feel about the role of Grenade Man?"

Buck threw back his head with a hearty laugh. "Grenade Man, huh? I like it, yeah...I like it real good. Thanks for the confidence Captain Wilkins. I'll try not to be a disappointment to the troop and my partner."

"I have here your written orders for the day and well into the night. After your visit to the dining room, please read them over carefully," Captain Wilkins said and motioned the men immediately to his left over to join him "Gentlemen, I would like you to meet Drill Sgt. Jess Osburn and Medic. Sgt. Loren Green. They will lead the 2nd half of our team in the war zone. I will leave Sgt. Osburn to distribute firearms to his men. Formation in one hour."

*   *   *

Chapter 78

Shortly after breakfast and a trip to the crapper, Bruce settled back on his bunk to read the orders for today and into the night. The border crossing tonight brought a change in heart rate. The day has come, he thought and looked around to find Roosevelt looking back at him. "Are you ready to try out that new weapon?"

"Guess I better learn to use it good, Sarge."

The approach of Richard came not as surprise. "Don't know if I'm scared of the unknown or not liking the idea of touching down on enemy soil," he said and sat down beside Bruce. "Are you ready for roll call?"

"As ready as possible," Bruce laughed, "but may as well get it over with and hit the rifle range. My partner is anxious to see what he can do with his new SAW."

"Good morning men," Sgt. Johnson called out and looked around with a smirk on his face. "The partner of the name I call will settle in at his side to form a two line formation."

Bruce was the first name called and he looked around just as Roosevelt moved in to stand beside him. He listens for Richard's name to find him four sets back.

"This is your permanent formation, here and on the battle field. The mini buses are here to take us to the firing range."

Bruce and Roosevelt were among the first four men out of twelve to board the first bus and claim the first seat to the right of the aisle. Roosevelt laid his SAW on Bruce's lap. "Damn good looking weapon you got here," Bruce said as he pulled it up and aimed through the windshield. "You'll be able to save our butts for damn sure, partner."

"Yeah," Roosevelt grinned. "Sure glad they're letting us get some practice in before we take off tonight."

Standing in a long line outside the weapons facility during the hottest time of the day, Bruce looked out across the desert to where the ripple of a mirage began messing with his mind. He wiped the sweat out of his eyes and turned from the devilish temptation of cool water to the war materializing before his eyes. There were three Apache helicopters in flight and several others waiting nearby. Looking through his field glasses, Bruce is able to make out the Abrams tanks but was too far away to make out what was going on. "What the hell, Sgt. Johnson?"

"Those Abrams tanks and Bradley Fighting Vehicles will cross the border in about thirty minutes and upon our helicopter leaving us off in the desert tonight, we will locate and follow their tracks. Sgt. Johnson lowered his field glasses. "Look! See those helicopters taking off now?" he said and turned back to the activity going on around the airport.

Roosevelt raised his field glasses to his eyes. "Yes Sir."

"Those Apache helicopters equipped with scudd

missiles are heading out to replace the ones that took off earlier. There go the transport helicopters carrying the 182nd infantry troops. They will parachute near the combat zone sometime tonight. We probably should remember them in our prayers!"

Captain Wilkins motioned Sgt. Johnson and Sgt. Sullivan into the weapons room to return later, laden down with ammunition. Bruce carried his two thirty round clips and a link of his partners artillery to the first stall set up with a target. He watched Roosevelt claim the one next to him, his SAW in hand and two links of artillery shells draped across his shoulder.

A loud explosion sounded nearby, followed by air raid sirens. Thinking it should have been the other way around, Bruce grabbed a link of Roosevelt's artillery and pulled him to the nearest shelter. The smartest move the army ever made, he thought, posting shelter location maps in the barracks.

"Gas! Gas! Gas!" someone outside the shelter yelled.

Bruce slapped on his gas mask and looked around to

find the other men doing the same. They were packed together like a can sardines and the warning '*a rifle is the extension of our arms*' drilled into them by Sgt. Edwards at Ft. Irwin came to mind. He took notice of the men's trigger fingers and felt immediately at ease.

Thinking of all the things that could go wrong in a tent full of armed men, the all clear sirens failed to give much relief as another explosion shook the shelter. The unbearable heat was wearing him down and the sweat, seeping into the corner of his eyes was stinging like hell. His gas mask was starting to fog up big time and just as he started to take it off for a breath of fresh air, some bastard outside was yelling again.

"Gas! Gas! Gas!"

"Enough to give you nightmares," he whispered to where Roosevelt's ear should be and returned the smile he thought his partner might've given.

When the all clear sounded again, the men returned to finalize their weapons training. He finished his final clip and stepped back with Roosevelt. "What do you think?"

"We'll know more after the leapfrog trial run Sarge."

"Did you notice how the men were holding their rifles inside the shelter?"

"Other than to make sure we were together, I was too damn scared to notice anyone else," Roosevelt chuckled.

Bruce felt a fist bump to his shoulder and looked around. "How's it going Bro?"

"Two 30 round clips and don't think I missed the target one time," Richard said with a chuckle and looked around at Roosevelt. "That's worth bragging about because I didn't have an old man to teach me about guns."

Roosevelt laughed at Richard's remark and moved around to stand beside his friend, Longview. "How'd you do, Eldon?"

"Surprisingly well for a rich boy."

Bruce laughed at the remark but curiosity about Eldon's riches were getting the better of him, he opened his mouth but swallowed the question and raced for the breakfast bus.

* * *

Chapter 79

Huddled together on the track after breakfast while waiting for Johnson to call Leapfrog formation, Roosevelt fell back in line to exchange weapons with Buck for a look at each other's new toy. "Hell man," Roosevelt said. "That's a hell of a lot lighter than my mine."

"Yeah, but we don't know the weight of Buck's grenades," Brown said.

"Probably won't be as heavy as Roosevelt's ammo, but then I guess you'll be carrying ammunition as well," Bruce said. "If they have this much confidence in you Buck, you may get some of them stripes back."

"Don't know about that Lawson, but I do feel indebted to fulfill their confidence in me."

"I have confidence in my partner here," Brown said

with a knuckle punch to Buck's shoulder.

"Thanks, Jim."

An hour or so later and after repeated advanced warnings of what could happen on the two mile run, Bruce could almost imagine the accidental discharge of weapons behind him.

A half-mile into the run, Capt. Wilkins, Sgt. Johnson and Sgt. Sullivan peeled off to the left for a head-count. Bruce counted 60 right foot jog steps twice and peeled to the left to stand with Roosevelt for a head count and a high sign to Richard when he jogged passed. They peeled in behind Johnson and Sullivan, but all they could see of Capt. Wilkins was the hind end of his jeep going in the opposite direction.

Upon the finale of the two hour run, and from where they sat at the edge of the barbed wire atop a 3 foot sand berm, Bruce and Richard pulled up their field glasses and watched the activity going on around the airfield while they waited further orders from Sgt. Johnson.

The driver parked his jeep and Wilkins climbed out. He approached the men with his smile of approval. "Well men, feel like another round?" he asked and laughed at the lack of volunteers. "Sgt. Johnson and I are proud of your performance today and look forward to fighting alongside you in Iraq. Spend time with your new group and get acquainted, who knows, one of them could be your Guardian Angel."

"The best group I ever trained with," Sgt. Johnson said and came down the line shaking hands with each man, followed by Captain Wilkins.

"Three light weight helicopters will carry us 90 miles inside the enemy terrain and drop us off to locate and follow a set of tracks left by the Abrams tanks. Our mission is to take and hold Najaf until further orders. Do you want to dismiss them, Sgt. Johnson?" Upon a shake of his head, Captain Wilkins dismissed the group.

Longview sidled up to Roosevelt. "How about we go to the café for a bite of dinner?"

Bruce looked across at Richard with a shrug of his

shoulders. "Sounds good to me."

Jim Brown stepped up beside Bruce. "How about me and Buck joining you? From rumors I've heard, looks like us six along with Brandon and Martinez will be taking off in the first helicopter tonight with Sgt. Sullivan."

Dinner trays in the drop off and upon leaving the chow hall, the six men corner Brandon and Martinez outside the door for a chat. "No shieeet amigos, we eight men a team?"

"Well, Edminston, Wilson, Davidson and Goodwin will make up our fighting dozen, but us eight will be joining Sgt. Sullivan on the first helicopter tonight," Brown explained.

"We're off for a jog to the barracks," Bruce called back as he grabbed Brown and fell in step with the other four men.

"We'll see you two later," Brown said and waved with a hand free from Bruce's grip.

Breathing hard when he slammed into the barracks,

Bruce dropped to the side of his cot for a rest and to let his mind touch on chores left to do before tonight. He looked up to find Roosevelt looking down at him.

"Are you worried, Sarge?"

"No, well a little," he admitted. "I was just putting a timer on the next four hours," he said and went on to explain. "Shower, 30 minutes, laundromat for a final wash and rinse in the permethrin treatment, 90 minutes, E-mail and put laptop in its case to pack in the duffel, 30 minutes, Pack what goes in my rucksack, 45 minutes, nap, 45 minutes."

"Oh yeah, mustn't forget the nap," Roosevelt laughed as he rolled up his dirty laundry in the sleeping bag and filled his pockets with toiletries. "I'm ready if you are."

"The water is great Roosevelt, come on in," Bruce said while attacking his body with a bar of soap. "Oh for the bliss of an extra 20 minutes in here would be pure heaven." He grinned back over his shoulder at the men waiting in line and grabbed up his towel.

They hit the laundromat next and filled three machines, two for sleeping bags and one for clothes. They sat on the bench to clean their battle rattle by hand. Bruce pulled a fiver out of his billfold. "Here partner, run over to the refreshment stand and bring us back a Pepsi,"

"Put your money away Sarge, my treat." Roosevelt picked up his weapon and left.

Bruce lay back against the seat and closed his eyes, hopefully for a little nap before the return of his partner. The smell of baby powder tickled his nose but when he opened his eyes the laundry room was empty. Sari is here, he thought, I can smell her as sure as I did back home. "Thank you God," he mumbles just a Roosevelt walked in.

"Sorry to take so long Sarge, but I think every soldier in camp had the same idea."

Bruce put the cold can to his lips and noticed the washers had stopped. He filled three dryers and had no more than sit down when he felt a fist bump to his shoulder. "Hey Bro, we just emptied three washers and you better grab em before someone else comes in."

"Come on," Roosevelt said when Longview finished loading the washers. "These two ole farts look like they need a picker upper and some alone time."

Richard backed away from helping Longview with the laundry to where Bruce stood waiting to give him a hug. "I love you bro," he said and for some unknown reason, shied back from the feel of apprehension and crossed his arms to ward off the chill of it. "It's cold in here, why don't we go outside for a minute."

*　*　*

Chapter 80

Bruce looked up to see the two young men coming their way with a paper bag in hand. "Waiting around is worse than going to war," he mumbled and wondered what the young partners had in the bag.

"Once we're on the helicopter," Longview said and waved the aroma under the nose of his partner so he could enjoy a whiff. "This is the last chance we have to eat something that smells so good as this."

"Hot dogs!" Richard grabbed the bag and ran inside with it.

Longview hurried the wash to the dryer and grabbed his hot dog from out of the bag. "Do you guys have much left to do?" he asked around a mouthful of bun and weenie.

"Not a hell of a lot," Roosevelt said as he dug into the pile of clothing and came out with two pairs of shorts identical in size and color. "Good thing our names are on our clothing," he said and held them up for Bruce to see.

"Sure hope our duffels make it to where we're going before we do." Bruce stuffed the last bite in his mouth and rolled it around on his tongue for the taste buds to savor before removing the sleeping bags from the dryer. He laid the first rolled sleeping bag to one side. "The tighter the better," he said and went down on his knees to roll the second one. Anxious to open his e-mail, he and Roosevelt left with a wave to Richard and Longview and hitched a ride to the barracks.

Laughing at the pictures on his laptop, Bruce read the letter from Samantha and looked up to find Roosevelt, who had come over to stand behind him. "Have you ever seen a baby this cute before?" The pride with which Bruce turned on his partner, what else could he possibly say, but no. He turned back to the half read letter from Sam.

I know today is the last day I can get an e-mail to you, so I took all of these pictures of Sari...and that's me in some of them, ha ha. I asked her what she was going to do when you came home. "Hug dada," she said

"This is from Richard's wife," Bruce said with a glance over his shoulder to see Roosevelt still standing there. "She claims my daughter said she's going to hug dada when I get home and the little twerp isn't big enough to be talking."

The Elkington's told me about Lana being a good hugger and I'm looking forward to getting one of those from you when you come home. Well, dear friend, I want to send this now to make sure you'll get it before you leave. I will write again, so when you get your laptop up and working, Sari and I will be there looking back at you. I love my job and Pops likes my work as well, he gave me a $2.00 an hour raise!" Be careful please and watch over my man.

We love you dada and dear friend,
Samantha and Sari

"Yeah Sam, Pops is pleased with your work and you deserve all of $2.00," he whispered to the signature on Sam's letter. He quickly opened and answered the emails from Pops, Billy Joe and Sheila.

*   *   *

Chapter 81

Silence fell among the leapfrog team as they settled in near the airfield to await further orders and watch Captain Wilkins approach with a salute, to which all twenty-four of them returned the honor. "Well men," he chuckled. "Are you ready for your sing along shuffle?"

"Yes sir, Captain Wilkins."

"I didn't hear you."

"Yes sir, Captain Wilkins," their voices were strong and convincing even to themselves.

"We were born with a fear of the unknown and carry it around with us every day of our lives, but we mustn't allow ourselves to let it affect the way we operate. Once we are on Iraqi soil and locate the tracks made by the artillery brigade, you will adhere to the leapfrog drill. Our final twenty-four-man unit will let down in the Iraqi sandbox in thirty minutes," he chuckled. "Sgt. Johnson, please. Wouldn't want to miss our flight would we?"

"All right men, listen up for quick step jog," Johnson yelled. "We're the meanest fighting machine."

"We're the meanest fighting machine."

'We're gonna kick your ass tis true," Johnson sang.

"We're gonna kick your ass tis true," they repeated in the same sing along voice.

"Cause we're the meanest fighting machine," they sang together, Johnson's voice included, until they stood alongside the three lightweight passenger helicopters.

Bruce was the first to board and gave a hand up to his partner. A broad grin claimed his face when Richard and Longview climbed aboard to sit across from him. Brown, Buck, Brandon and Martinez completed the eight-man team. We are like family, he thought, and realizing the possibility of one or more of them injured or killed brought a feeling of turmoil in his stomach, or was it the sudden drop of the helicopter?

The pilots hovered above the desert just long enough to leave off the twenty-four men plus officers and lift off again with a wide sweep, leaving them alone in the eerie silence of darkness and the chilling fear of the enemy nearby.

Bruce threw off his rucksack, fell to his belly and looked around to find Roosevelt at his side. Unlike two days ago when there was a full moon it took awhile to adjust to the total darkness as he scanned the terrain with his night vision glasses.

"We have practiced this more times than I have toes and fingers but this is the real gut deal and is damn scary," Bruce said to whoever might be listening. "Even to a tough guy like me," he chuckles.

Sgt. Johnson and Captain Wilkins crawled around to join Sgt. Sullivan. "See anything Sergeant?"

"Not a thing Sir," Sullivan answers. "So far all is going as planned."

Johnson leaned in close. "What do you think, Captain?"

"Pass the word to load up and move out."

Whispers of readiness was passed down the line and with knees locked against the weight of his load, Bruce joined the jog. Other than heavy breathing and battle rattle, it was quiet. There was a hell of a lot more action back at Camp Udairi during trial run exercises.

*   *   *

Chapter 82

After the usual butt swatting and shoulder punching with fellow leapfrog comrades, they made a second and final leap before digging in for dinner and a couple of hour's shuteye.

"All right men," Captain Wilkins said. "After dinner, the younger men take first watch."

Bruce tossed his rucksack to the sand and pulled out his sleeping bag. He rolled it out and motioned Roosevelt to sit with him while working up their MRE's. "I'll do the stew and you the dessert," he said and looked for signs of fatigue. "Think you can handle guard duty?"

"Yeah, it's better than trying to stay awake after only an hour of sleep under my belt."

Sgt. Johnson moved over to sit between Bruce and Buck. "See something, men?"

"Nothing Sir, just a feeling I have that something's out there waiting to happen," Buck said, as he worked up his dinner.

"I'm surprised," Bruce pushed up onto his elbow, a frown on his face that only he was aware of. "Two hours in Iraq and no sign of the enemy."

"This area is one of the more sparsely populated section of Southern Iraq and is the very reason we are here." Captain Wilkins squeezed in amongst the men. "We didn't expect any serious Iraqi opposition for the first 100 to 200 miles."

With little more than two hours of darkness left Johnson's command barely more than a whisper came loud and clear to Bruce. "Belly down."

Waving his weapon both left and right, Bruce scanned the area through the riflescope. "Nothing, Sgt. Johnson."

"To the left Lawson, what do you see?"

"Not sure Sir, a reflection of some sort?"

"Yeah, I see it," Roosevelt whispered while feeling not quite awake.

"Keep your eye on it," Wilkins said. "When I give the word, sweep the area with your SAW and roll to your right. You Lawson, roll left with us and make ready to return fire."

"Yes Sir, Captain."

Almost before Bruce had a chance to let the order register, Roosevelt let the bullets fly with a wide sweep and rolled to the right. Feeling scared, hyped up or whatever the hell you want to call it, Bruce rolled to the left and brought his rifle sights up. His finger, caressing the weapon near the trigger was daring the enemy to make a move.

Brown and Buck came around from the back and settled in between Johnson and the Captain, his grenade launcher aimed and ready.

The excitement over, and rucksacks packed and ready, Bruce shrugged into his and fell in behind the three leaders. The front-runners wheeled to the left for a rest and a head count. Bruce gave Roosevelt a shoulder punch to let him know they were now leading the unit and to make sure his alert antenna was plugged in and working.

It was near their turn for a rest and head count when Bruce saw something off to the right. "Belly," he whispered to Roosevelt and the men in back of him, to find Buck and Jim on the sand nearby. "To the right, men...don't know how in the hell we missed them or they missed us, but I'm sure someone is out there."

He swept the area with his scope and whispered the location to his partner, who passed it down the line and aimed his SAW while awaiting orders. Buck's grenade launcher was primed and ready. He felt Johnson wiggle in beside him. "What do you think Johnson; shall we shoot and wait or wait and shoot?"

Johnson swung his riflescope around to the nest of Iraqi's. It was like a standoff, men with itchy fingers and ready to squeeze. "Why don't we show them just how tough we are?"

"Spread out men and give the suckers a taste of what we have for them," Bruce said and left Buck with his grenade launcher to take out the bunker and Roosevelt to sweep for strays.

After three minutes or so of one-sided firepower, Bruce shook his head. "Something is not right here, Sgt. Johnson." He whirled around to see if someone was sneaking up from behind, nothing but partial moonlight and sandy terrain. "What do you think?"

"Belly crawl a short distance ahead while I crawl back to the Captain," Sgt. Johnson whispered. "Brown, you and Buck take the lead and don't forget your rest and head count later, just remember to keep your eyes on the tracks in the sand and the GPS. Come on Lawson, you and Roosevelt follow me."

"Yes Sir, Sergeant," Brown said as he began to crawl forward alongside Buck.

On their bellies at the edge of the tracks and after finding all men accounted for, Bruce, Roosevelt and

Johnson fell in behind Sgt. Sullivan and the Captain.

"Don't know, Captain, but I'm with Lawson. Something smells bad."

Captain Wilkins put the radio to his mouth and talks into it. The one-sided conversation led Bruce to believe, the caravan up ahead was in trouble.

*   *   *

Chapter 83

The desert sunrise on day two held the men hostage and nothing much to show for it. Better than getting shot at I suppose, Bruce thought and turned to the Captain. "What the hell happened to our supply convoy?"

Captain Wilkins motioned him and Johnson a safe distance from the others. "They took a wrong turn at the crossing in back of us."

Curious as to how long the captain had known about this, Bruce frowns, "Sgt. Estes?"

"Nobody's heard from them, Lawson."

Remembering Estes, his ability to grin and accept the complaints on his cooking with a middle finger salute above his head, brings a sick feeling to his gut.

"A replacement is on the way," Captain Wilkins

smile was far from encouraging. "We will just have to make do with what we have."

"Someone should enlighten the men Captain, warn them to use their water sparingly."

"I know Lawson," Wilkins shook his head and looked at Sgt. Johnson?

The men took in the warning and probably felt as Bruce did, the water they had wasted may rear up to bite them in the butt later.

By late afternoon and near exhaustion, the pace had slowed to a half ass jog. Bruce leaned into his partner with a whisper. "No one has fallen by the wayside yet."

"Remember how I felt sick at my stomach when we were in the ravine?" Roosevelt said between gasps. "I think I'm feeling that way again."

"Wrap your lips around your drinking tube and hold your helmet above your head." Bruce said remembering how fast dehydration takes command when you least expect it.

Fatigue set in, making it hard for Bruce to remember how many head counts let alone how many rests they had taken, when the Captain, Johnson and Sullivan rolled to the left for a head count. Anxious for timeout, he began to double his 60-count right foot jog. "Okay partner, our turn for a rest." They peeled off at about the same time as the first three fell in behind the end of the line.

Well into the night, Bruce and his partner were near the middle of the pack when he was sure he heard something behind them. "Hear anything?"

Roosevelt turned his head first one way the then the other. "Not sure. I hear a motor I think but I don't hear a damn thing now."

Bruce jogged up between Captain Wilkins and Johnson. "Thought I heard something Sir, but it fades in and out so I can't be sure."

"Yeah, we heard it too," said Johnson. "Could be our supply truck."

Captain Wilkins ordered Sgt. Johnson to stop the men, and put the radio to his ear. "Ho, yeah think we hear you," he looked around while talking and down again at the GPS. "Looks like we will have dinner tonight," he smiled and gave the maintenance team our location. "The cook, Sgt. Luke Rankin and his helper Corp. Joseph Fleming, says dinner should be ready in about fifteen minutes."

It seemed more like an hour before Bruce sat down beside Roosevelt with a bowl of stew and cornbread.

"Hey Sarge," Roosevelt coughed and tried to clear his throat. "I think I just ate a friggin miniature grass-hopper."

"What the heeell Amigo," Martinez laughed. "Was the little hombre eating your stew?"

"Something like that Martinez," Roosevelt chuckled and cleared his throat again. "I sure as hell let the little critters know, stealing my food is a death sentence."

"Hey Sgt. Luke," Buck said. "Best damn stew I eeever tasted, I kid you not."

"Sgt. Luke is going to hang around with us through-out the tour and see to it we have a kitchen in Najaf," the Captain announced. "He says to stay away from his food or he'll take a butcher knife after you and I for one don't feel up to eating soldier roast."

Martinez threw back his head in a fit of laughter. "Hey Amigo's, wonder what soldier stew would taste like."

"Don't care to find out, Amigo," Roosevelt said.

"Oh si, senior," Martinez chuckles again. "We can always stand at the door and beg."

"That might get you a dog biscuit," Luke said.

Bruce held his hand above his eyes and squinted up at Luke. "My name is Bruce Lawson and this is Vernon Roosevelt, my fine young partner, the sharpshooter."

"Hmmm, I suppose I could be forced to sneak you a bite now and then," Luke said. "But don't count on it."

"I got a pretty good partner myself," Jim Brown spoke up. "Old Buck is our grenade man and he's really handy with his weapon."

"Twist my arm please, but aim your heavy artillery at the enemy," Luke said and joined the chuckle.

* * *

Chapter 84

Just before daybreak, while taking a two-hour rest stop Bruce caught a bright flash of light out of the corner of his eye. Watching the horizon to the Northeast of them he saw yet another one even larger than the first, rise from the desert like a huge ball of fire. The sound of an explosion followed immediately to rumble across the sky like a roll of thunder.

With eyes focused on whatever the hell was taking place ahead, Bruce turned his good ear toward the sky and listened to what sounded like a swarm of bees homing in on a tree at the Sah-Hah-Lee golf course back home, but the faint whoosh of rotary blades proved to be a swarm of helicopters?

There was no mistaking the intermittent flashes and

sounds of explosion of large guns finding their targets to know there was a war going on.

"We must be making better time than the convoy of fighting machines ahead," Captain Wilkins said. "They should have rolled through Najaf yesterday."

"What does that mean for us?" Sgt. Johnson stole the question from Bruce, leaving him with his mouth hanging open.

"We may have to improvise as we go," the Captain said. "Stay alert men, we may have a run on stray Iraqis coming our way."

The night all too suddenly introduced the men to a barren desert eastern sunrise. A heat wave from hell, Bruce thought and crawled into the four-man pup tent for shade and to enjoy a breakfast of scrambled eggs and bacon.

"There's more coffee here if anyone's interested," Luke announced and Bruce smiled...

Captain Wilkins put his radio away and looking around to find the men's hands free of empty plates, he brought the rest period to an abrupt end. "Time to gear up men," he chuckled. "Are you ready to show the Iraqis how damn good we really are?"

"Yes Sir, Captain Wilkins," the men answered.

After a quick cleanup and rucksacks on their shoulders they were on the move again. Bruce looked around to see the second twenty-four-man leapfrog fall in behind, making them forty-eight men strong. He turned to Roosevelt with a shoulder punch. "Hell yeah," he said. "This is Ft. Irwin all over again partner, and I'm ready to hit it head-on."

"You know, I thought for sure I'd be scared when the real thing came along," Roosevelt said. "but I'm not and furthermore, I'll never be more ready to fight than I am right now."

"Be alert men and be smart," Captain Wilkins warns. "Don't give the enemy a chance to play with your head, if in doubt, shoot to kill!" He ordered Sgt. Johnson back down the line to pick out six men to guard the lunch wagon and supply truck.

Up close to the fighting machines and leaning into

the berm, Bruce watched the Bradley's big guns hitting their targets. "And I thought the war games in Ft. Irwin were down and dirty."

"We haven't had a lot of sleep so shuffle crawl down the line and warn the men to stay alert and keep their butts down. Tell Sgt. Osborn to relate the orders to his men."

The Captain leaned in close to Bruce's ear. "How do you see it, Lawson?"

"Looks like the big machines are working big time on the area with the camouflage netting over it," he laughed and looked at the men around him. "Sure hope they leave one of the buildings intact for a barracks tonight."

"Look to the left, between those two buildings," Roosevelt said and Bruce turned to see what he was talking about. "Are those children on a school playground?"

"Probably making us see one thing so as to take our minds off another. Remember those fox holes at Ft.

Irwin, the one's we failed to see?"

Brown and Buck crowded in beside Roosevelt. "There's a hell of a lot more noise here than in Ft. Irwin," Brown said.

Bruce looked around and wondering about the four-foot berm, he sidled up next to the Captain. "How did the men construct this berm while under the watchful eye of the enemy?"

"Heavy duty road crews used the road grader while under the protection of Apache Helicopters," he said and turned to Sgt. Johnson, who no more than settled in again before Wilkins ordered him back down the line. "Tell the men to hold their fire, and memorize everything they see to mind."

"Yes Sir, Captain."

"And Sgt, might be a good idea if one partner sleeps while the other stands guard and trade off after an hour or so,"

"Yes sir, Captain, anything else?"

* * *

Chapter 85

Awakened by the silence and momentarily unsure as to where he was, Bruce looked around and down at the sleeping man beside him, to the rapid movement beneath his eyelids. Must be dreaming about war machines and gun toting Iraqis, he thought and smiled when the Captain suddenly opened his eyes. "The big guns are gone, Captain,"

Wilkins pulled up beside Bruce to look over the berm. Men and women were walking around and looking at the damage made upon their fine city. They were holding what looked like handkerchiefs to their mouth while some of the soldiers patrolled the grounds with weapons and gas masks? "Captain?"

"Don't worry about it Lawson," Wilkins said and

looked at the men around him. "What do you think Johnson?"

Johnson stole a peek over the berm. "Don't know, Captain. I bet five to one they know we're here and just bidding their time?"

"Wouldn't be surprised," Wilkins said and waved his arm between him and the men. "Spread the men out but keep the berm between them and the Iraqis?"

"Sounds good Captain. I'll crawl back and let them know. The fifteen to the back can't see much of what's going on."

"Bring them back and settle them in around the edge of that camouflage area," Wilkins said. "It could be hiding the cause of our being here."

"Right away, Sir," Johnson said and turned with a salute to shuffle away.

"The heavy machinery before us made a thorough search of the area Sir, and if they found weapons of mass destruction, wouldn't they still be here?" Bruce said and turned to his partner. "To the left there, the building near the school yard," he pointed. "The window?"

"Yeah Sarge, I see it."

"They know of our presence, Captain and just waiting for us to get brave enough to show ourselves."

"Don't make a move Lawson, wait until Johnson has his men in place," Wilkins said and brought up his binoculars for a quick peek in the direction of the building. "Looks like soldiers alright but if you take notice, each window has what looks like hostages in front of the armed men."

Bruce took up the binoculars for another look. "Right Captain."

Waiting until the very last minute Wilkins gave a thumb up to start maneuvers. He pointed at Bruce for window one, Roosevelt two, Jim Brown three, Buck the alert signal, Richard four and Longview five. That covered all five windows and the men were quick to rally. Their scopes up for visibility and upon Wilkins signal each man covered his window and fired their weapons.

Bruce saw the hostage in his window fall to the right

just before he ducked down. He made two steps to the right, as did the other men and swung his rifle around to find the look of terror on the face of a little girl. He ducked down without firing a shot.

The Captain placed his hand to Bruce's shoulder. "What happened, Lawson?"

"There's a little girl at the window and a man kneeling beside her with his gun resting on the window ledge. Two men with guns are standing to the back of her. I'll get all three of the stinking bastards Captain, don't worry about it."

The men shifted again and when Wilkins gave two thumbs up, Bruce brought his rifle up and about the same time he squeezed off three quick rounds the sand kicked up on the bank between him and the Captain.

"Did you get the cowardly bastards?"

"Yes Sir, Captain," Bruce answered and leaned back against the berm.

"The little girl?"

"Don't know Sir," he whispered with a sinking sensation in his stomach. "But the three men will never use her as a shield again." With gun ready, he peeked over the berm to find his window empty. Not completely satisfied, he stole another quick look to find the little girl waving her hand. Bruce slid down the berm with a smile on his face. "I got em Captain and the little girl is okay."

*   *   *

Chapter 86

Under siege of Iraq's famous dust storm and sealed in behind the berm for two days, Bruce was well aware of the bullets kicking up blobs of sand down on their heads from above. Finding his vision from behind the fogged up dust mask nil to none, he pulled it off for a quick swipe with his handkerchief. He blinked several times to wash the grit out of his eyes, but it was like using a windshield wiper with no fluid.

"Don't know if I can take much more of this Sarge." Roosevelt's complaint from behind his dust mask was muffled and hard to understand. "My eyes are so damn gritty I can hardly see, and breathing this damn stuff is gonna give us emphysema."

They shared a brief chuckle as Bruce pushed out

from under the sand covered canvas. "Anything happen while I was asleep?"

"Nothing since the jeep headed our way was stopped by the grenade man. Other than that, everything is okay as far as I can see, and that ain't very damn far."

Bruce looked around to see the Captain push out from under his tarp of sand. "A man must be out of his head to fight for this God forsaken country," he coughed and brushed at the sand on his chest.

"Don't know Captain, but I see what looks like an Eastern sunrise coming our way," Bruce said, looking from the clear skies back down to Wilkins.

"Let's get our butt in gear and give the good citizens of Najaf a helping hand to the road of freedom," the Captain said with a warning wave down the line.

Bruce shook the sand out of his hair and removed his dust mask. A bullet hit the sand behind him to ding across the top of his helmet.

"What the shit!" Roosevelt yelled and swung his

SAW around with a spray of bullets to stop the three men who were primed and ready for another shot.

"What the hell?" Bruce muttered and looked at the scratch across the top of his helmet. "Whew, that was too damn close."

"Don't know about you men, but two days behind this sand berm and eating dust is about to come to an end," Buck said and looked over the edge. "Another jeep!"

Bruce looked over and sure as hell, not only was there a jeep headed their way, but the taxi with a passenger? With rifle up and ready, they watched it to see the driver and young lad with a V sign when they drove by.

The jeep exploded with a blast that tossed all three passengers in the air and the jeep on its side. "Not to worry, Captain," Buck said. "The two passengers both had guns and their aim was in our direction."

"The windows are clear so what's your take on the situation?" Wilkins asked.

Bruce looked around for Johnson but finding him nowhere around, he turned to fill Wilkins in on the area above the berm, but found him in a squat run in the opposite direction.

Bruce received the shoulder bump as friendly and looked around to find Richard behind him. "Don't forget about the creep targets," Richard said and for a moment there, the eye contact between the two men said more than words ever could. "How the hell long are we gonna stay crouched behind this damn berm?"

"Creep targets in Ft. Irwin was a hell of a lot easier to spot there than here with the real thing walking around," Longview said.

"It's good you guys bringing that up because I for one haven't been looking for IED's or creep targets," Bruce chuckled and pointed. "See that building to the left?"

"Yeah Lawson," Brown said. "What do you have in mind?"

"Let's move down the berm a ways and make a run for it." He looked at the men to find them looking back at him.

"Good idea Lawson" Buck said. "Can probably see

more of the landscape from there, like bunkers I can launch a grenade into."

"Let's just do something Amigo's, this fuckin the dog is wearing this Mexican soldier down and before you know it, I'm gonna be too damn scared to make a move."

They kicked through the door to find the room empty. "What the hell?" Bruce said and looked out the window. "Hey! The kids are not on the playground?"

"Maybe recess is over, Lawson," Martinez said and fell to his knees.

Bruce searched the room for suspicious IED's and finding none, he fell down beside Martinez. "See anything?"

"In the alley way mi Amigo, see them?"

Buck crawled over for a look. "Too close to the school for a grenade."

The men rushed to the windows at the sound of gunshots. "Our men are moving in blind! Hey Roosevelt, how the hell many men can you take out with that SAW?" Bruce yelled and opened the door a crack to see men in a bunker near the building. "For chrissake Buck, get the hell over here and take a look. That bunker, the men can't see it from where they are."

Buck fell to the floor with his weapon and let go with the first grenade and had another in with added distance to let fly. It was a direct hit with the first grenade and a warning to the men as to what lay ahead.

Bruce turned to the sound of breaking glass to find Roosevelt with his SAW aimed for the men in the alley way. He fell down beside his partner to take out more men who were back in the windows hiding behind hostages again.

Buck took out another bunker, "Holy shit!"

Buck's tone of voice brought Bruce around to see the Iraqi fighting machines between two buildings. His brain reeling with helpless frustration, he let out a yell. "Son of a bitch! The men are open targets for what the hell's coming at them!"

* * *

Chapter 87

Bruce heard the hum of motors overhead and the question of good guys or bad guys came to mind just seconds before the enemy's fighting machines exploded. "Good guys!" he roared with laughter and saw two bunkers near the alleyway between the buildings explode. "What the hell, did you guys see them damn bunkers?"

Bullets were spraying the windows across the way. Bruce couldn't be sure if his bullet hit the target, but let out a yell when his man fell across the windowsill.

"Sumbitch," Buck said and looked at his upper arm. "That's about as close I want to come to getting hit."

Bruce started for him but found Sullivan there with his little black bag. "You're a very lucky man Buck, a little band-aid should do the trick."

"How the hell did you know I was injured?"

"I'm here with orders from the Captain. He says good job men but wants you to scout the outer premises and the schoolhouse." Sullivan covered the men in his search for injuries and finding none, he started for the door. "Oh yeah, don't let your guard down," he chuckled. "The Captain says to save the little children."

They waited, but instead of giving the order, Sullivan left the room. "All right men," Bruce said. "We will move out under cover, two at a time,"

"We'll go first," Brandon volunteered.

"Oh Si, says my brave partner without asking his underling Mexican slave."

The men moved in a squat shuffle to and around the south side of the schoolhouse to settle in beneath the windows. The children's voices rang out in song and except for the language barrier it sounded friendly, Bruce thought, but one never knows what may be waiting for them inside.

Bruce pointed southward, bringing the men's attention around to a pair of vapor clouds touching ground and heading their way. With his face up to the downpour, he caught a handful of water to wash the sand out of his eyelashes.

"Hey Amigos, too bad we don't have soap, eh. If it wasn't for the school kids, I might just take off my britches and wash this dirty body reeel good." His hands out for more water, Martinez looked up at the sky…"What the sheeit?"

The rain stopped and the men held back the threat of laughter while watching the steam rise from their wet clothing. "So much for a quickie," Bruce said, as he started for the corner of the building in a squat shuffle. "Come on men, let's go check on the little ones."

The rocket fire was heavy, but at a disadvantage in their crouched position outside the school building it was impossible to tell from what direction it came or what the hell it hit. The worry of enemy or friendly fire was put on the back burner as Bruce rushed around the building and kicked the door open. The men were caught in the doorway by an onslaught of children and Arabic squeals. He held fast to the teacher's expression, but stepped aside to let Roosevelt take over.

The Iraqi laced his fingers behind his head and turned his back. Roosevelt shouted again and the man fell to the floor on his belly. Both fascinated and proud of his partner, Bruce felt it even more so when Roosevelt reached under the desk and helped the teacher to his feet.

"Hey amigo, how the hell did you know the teacher was under the desk?"

"That's what the children were squealing about."

They searched the room thoroughly for IED's before leaving the teacher in charge of his pupils.

"What the hell do we do with the prisoner?" Martinez asked.

"Take him with us."

"Oh Si, Lawson, but I don't prisoner sit."

Each classroom was a repeat of the first, except for the small hand in Bruce's palm. He looked down into the smiling face of the little hostage in the window?

Finding the room free of explosives, Bruce knelt down for a second and held the frail youngster in his arms. He kissed her cheek and left the room, taking with him a picture of Sari in just such a situation and wondered if a soldier would be around to protect her?

After an explanation to Roosevelt in letting the prisoners go, he stood to one side while his partner told the prisoners they were free to go. The Iraqi's bowed three times, and with a wave of the V sign they turned and hurried away.

"Why don't we check out the building we used for target practice," Richard said and pointed to the door. "See how many Iraqis we slaughtered."

Edminston and Wilson stepped around the corner and just as they did, Bruce pulled his rifle up to his hip.

"Son of a bitch, guys!" He could feel his facial nerves twitch at the thought of friendly fire in their gut. "You scared shit out of me."

"The Captain wants to see all of you right away," Wilson said.

*　　*　　*

Chapter 88

"**W**ould you look at that?" Brown said and moved around for a better look. "Can you believe the disguise? The walls look enough like the desert you could slam into it without ever seeing it."

"What the hell?" Roosevelt yelled.

The fighting eight whirled around to find one lone Iraqi soldier, his gun pointed at them for another shot. Richard stopped the man with one shot, while at the same time another bullet struck the sand near Brandon's left foot.

Bruce raised his rifle and caught the shooter just as he peeked around the corner for another shot. "What the hell's with these bastards?" He said and rushed to the building for a quickpeek around the corner. There lay his little hostage on the ground. "Cover me." He ran zig zag and knelt down to find her still alive and talking.

"She said she was trying to warn you about the prisoners," Roosevelt said.

Bruce picked her up into his arms and carried her to the side of the building. The fear in her eyes pulled at his heart and then a sigh so soft, like a whisper in his ear before she went limp in his arms. He looked up to see the circle of backs protecting him and the little girl.

Roosevelt stepped in to take her out of his arms and gently stretched her out next to the wall. "Come on Sarge there's nothing more we can do for her."

His heart ached for the little girl's parents, the devastating loss of a child. He wanted to feel Sari in his arms, to feel her laugh in his face, to breathe in the sweet smell of her breath.

The sound of helicopters brought Bruce around to see four of them coming in from the east over the Euphrates River. Their whistling missiles aimed toward the area behind the building where the little girl lay.

Within seconds after the explosions he felt the ground shake and saw black smoke rise toward the sky. All hell suddenly broke loose, people running out from behind the buildings, some with their clothes on fire and screaming for help. Bruce wanted to help but the fight was on. Armed Iraqi soldiers came at them from all directions.

Buck fell to the ground, his grenade launcher aimed between the buildings. Roosevelt fell to Buck's left and took out a wide sweep of Iraqis with his SAW. Bruce stood behind his partner with Richard and Longview, all rifles firing simultaneously.

"Dumb bastard's didn't know what the hell they were up against, hey Amigo's," Martinez yelled and joined the group for handshakes all around.

While looking each other over for signs of fresh blood, the fear of death touched each of them with a sound of hysteria in their laughter.

Bruce fell down to a squat and rocked back on his

heels, his eyes closed and hands over his ears to shut out the screams and the smell of burnt bodies. He looked up at the sound of Captain Wilkins' voice.

"Good job men. Rumor has it, Iraqi soldiers are using the Historic Mosque as a covert base of operation," he said and pointed to the Iraqi at his side. "This is Mahhad Shaha and has agreed to show us the way."

Bruce shook his head to clear the sight and screams around him and checked his clip to find it nearly full and couldn't remember reloading it.

"Are you men superstitious?" The captain looked at all twelve of them one at a time.

"About what Captain Wilkins, Sir?" Martinez looked bewildered.

"We're talking about an invasion here with you twelve men and I make thirteen."

"Oh Si, Captain Sir, one never knows when we might have the need for first aid."

The men shared a chuckle and agreed with the Captain, when he called Sullivan over to join the team.

Along the way to where they had never been before, Bruce glanced into a bunker of dead Iraqis to see a dirty mangle of mattress pieces and blankets. The smell of blood, dirty bodies and spent gunpowder was overpowering.

He put a handkerchief to his nose and looked in again to find their arsenal consisted of a few hand grenades, an old rocket launcher that probably didn't work and a couple dozen clips for the assault rifles. Six corpses lay in the ditch, some with gas masks still on what hardly looked like heads at all.

"Do you think these men were afraid of a gas attack?" Bruce asked and looked to the Captain for an answer.

"Perhaps the weapons of mass destruction are buried around here," Captain Wilkins suggested and waved Sullivan over to stand in front of Brandon.

"Come on Captain," Brandon said, his face flush. "It's only a little blood blister and before you assholes ask, I don't know how the hell I did it."

The Iraqi guide said something in Arabic and motioned the Captain to follow. "Arms ready men," he said and walked off alongside his guide.

After a brief conversation between the Captain and his guide, Roosevelt turned with a whispered translation of the conversation. "He wants four men to stand guard at the side door around the corner." He nudged Bruce over to Richard and Longview. "Shall we volunteer?"

Bruce searched the faces around him with a shrug. "May as well."

"Fine with us," Richard said with a questioning look at Longview.

The four men had no more than taken up guard outside the door when the little children, all chattering at once, suddenly appear from out of nowhere. Their faces lit up like a ray of sunshine when Roosevelt said something to them and they began jumping up and down in front of him. As suddenly as they appeared they were gone again.

"One of the little girls told me not to trust that man standing over there," Roosevelt said. "Does he look like he's standing guard in front of that building?"

Bruce wasn't too worried as long as the man's barrel was pointed to the ground, but leaned into Roosevelt with a whisper. "Keep your eye on him while I talk to the other men, just make sure you get the first shot."

He found the other men in agreement and returned to Roosevelt with their suggestion. "He may be drawing us away from something else. Keep your eyes on him while I have a look around the corner and if he makes any sudden move with that gun, let him have it."

Call it intuition or whatever but when Bruce fell to the ground bullets peppered the building where his head had been. He looked in the direction from which the shots had come and saw the man with his weapon up and ready to shoot again but Roosevelt's bullets tore into his chest and knocked him to the ground. After a keen search of the area, he looked back at the man guarding the door and detected a slight movement of the man and his weapon.

Roosevelt fired first while Bruce, Richard and Longview took out the other five men coming around the corner with weapons up and threatening.

There was a noise in the building in back of them and just moments before the door opened.   Bruce gave a quick nod to Roosevelt, who turned his SAW on the door while the other three men searched the area for more snipers.

"At ease Roosevelt," Wilkins eyed the weapon and grinned. "What the hell's...?"

The Captain started but fell to a squat behind the four men, pulling his Iraqi guide down with him. Roosevelt searched the area while telling the Captain what had taken place.

"We didn't find a damn Iraqi inside the Mosque," Wilkins said and looked around at his guide. "Mahhad says it was a set up."

Roosevelt raised his Saw and yelled when seven Iraq-is stepped out of the shadows. They put their hands on top of their heads and began walking toward him. He yelled again and they fell to their stomachs.

Richard fired his weapon into the shadows from where the men had come. Bruce looked up to see nothing and wondering if Richard's nerves were acting up, a man suddenly staggers out of the shadows and falls to the ground.

Bruce looked down at the men on the ground and yelled when he saw one of them going for something in his pocket, but it was Roosevelt's orders the man heard and withdrew a handgun with a finger and thumb grip to the barrel and tossed it toward them.

At about the same time, two ambulances with the Red Crescent symbol whipped in to park between the fighting eight and the men on the ground. Bruce is suddenly bathed in an uneasy sweat and keeping an eye on the medic, he saw the Iraqis leaving the ambulance from the other side. He raised his hand and yelled a warning.

Roosevelt and Longview fell to the ground with

Bruce, Richard and Brown kneeling behind sending a spray of lead when the men came around the front of the ambulance. Within five seconds, the battle was over and the medics were still alive to tend the injured.

"Shit," Brown cursed and held up his arm. "It's just a scratch but gushing like the blow of a new oil well."

"Hell man," Martinez joshed. "For a black man you sure do bleed red."

"Don't get smart young feller, just grab the towel off my belt." Brown laughed.

Bruce pulled Brown's handkerchief out of his hind pocket and wiped the sweat off of his forehead, while Martinez wrapped the towel around his arm.

Brown backed up to the wall and slid down into a sitting position. "Just give me a minute and I'll be okay."

Sullivan moved in to bandage his arm and put it in a sling. "Once you calm down you're gonna be in a lot of hurt," he warned. "Do you want that pain shot now or later?"

"I'll take it later," Brown grimaced. "Just in case you hadn't noticed Sullivan, we're in the middle of a war here." With the help of his good arm around Buck's shoulder, he struggled to his feet and pushed away from the wall. "Thanks pardner I needed that."

*   *   *

Chapter 89

Brown sat with his bandaged arm in the cradle of his good one and looking like he might be near to passing out, Bruce knelt down and reached out with his finger to rub the swollen thumb of the injured. "How you feeling?"

"Not bad Lawson," he laughed. "Sullivan gave me another shot. Don't think I'll be able to handle guard duty. Don't feel much like eating either so you guys go on ahead."

Bruce and Buck left Brown to mend and grabbed a dinner at the diner and settled in around the table with the rest of the men.

A series of explosions sounded while they were having dinner and all eyes turned to the Captain. "Not to worry, those sounds are coming from the north east along the Tigris River."

Bruce turned to his unit as to where they wanted to spend the night. "Brandon and Brown are injured," he said and looked across the table to the younger men. "Since Davidson, Edminston, Richard and I have an age advantage, how about you young fellows take first watch?"

"I'm too uptight to sleep anyway," Roosevelt laughed. "How about it, Alberto?"

"We don't have no date tonight Amigo, so might just as well protect these old farts."

"How about we clean the glass out of that first building and spread our sleeping bags in the floor?" Richard said. "Dusk is closing in fast and we better get the hell on it."

Bruce gave up the impossible task of cleaning without a broom and hoped for the best. He spread out his sleeping bag and succumbed to the cries of his body. Sometime in the night, he was awakened by the sound of mortar shells, but fluffed his pillow and was near sleep again when he caught the sound of Roosevelt's voice.

"Psst. Sarge?"

"Yeah."

"All hell is breaking loose out here."

"Until you hear from the men on guard duty, don't worry about it," Captain Wilkins said. "In exactly two hours and fifty two minutes you will be taking their place and that's going to be a hell of a hard duty stretch with no sleep."

"Yes Sir, Captain, but I am on duty," Roosevelt said and backed out of the room pulling the door shut behind him.

Surprised to find Wilkins amongst them, Bruce rose to an elbow to find the sound of his voice coming from the center of the room and curiosity was getting the better of him. The floor was already filled with sleeping bags, so how the hell did he maneuver around in the dark no less, without waking anyone, let alone finding enough space for his sleeping bag?

He fluffed his pillow again, his mind playing with the worry of how easy it would be for the enemy to sneak in and surprise them while they sleep, but closed his eyes to the warning and soon fell into a deep slumber.

*   *   *

Chapter 90

Bruce put his night vision goggles on and looked around again to what he saw two minutes ago and marvels at the difference, almost like turning a switch and ole, a near daylight suddenly appears in the room.

"Hey in here," Roosevelt calls out to the sleeping men. "Time for you old farts to hit the road and make room for us tired young men."

Bruce pocketed his night goggles and let out a groan in the direction of Roosevelt's voice. Dressed in full gear and ready for battle, he stepped out into the darkness with his mighty M16 over his shoulder.

With the exception of explosions in the distance, the exchange of password between the men went without mishap. As the night turned into a desert sunrise, he shoved his night vision glasses into his pocket and turned to the slamming of a door to see Roosevelt walking in his direction. "Hey there," he called out to the young man. "Good morning."

"Morning Sarge," he said and taking in the area around him, commented on the surprise at finding everything so peacefully quiet and hot hot hot.

"Except for a few broken windows, empty bunkers and bodies cleared away, it doesn't look so much like a war zone," Bruce laughed but shook his head when the waste of lives in yesterday's slaughter came to mind.

Roosevelt joined in the chuckle. "Yeah, the body snatchers came through early last night right after you went to bed."

Richard stepped around the corner with his nose in the air and smiled his pleasure. "You guys smell what I smell?" he chuckled. "Let's get the lead out of our ass and find what else the cook has made for our breakfast besides bacon?"

The four men stepped into the dining hall and were

pleasantly surprised to find tables and chairs waiting for them. "Sgt. Luke my man," Bruce greeted and gave a soft whistle at each spoonful of food Luke put on his plate. "Did you and the corporal work all night?"

"Oh no, we had as much damn sleep as the rest of you."

Bruce sat down at the first table and spooned a bite of scrambled egg into his mouth. He looked up to find Sgt. Luke looking back at him and held up a thumb and finger okay.

After breakfast, the men stepped out into the sunlight and Bruce looked around. "Who's manning the guard post today?"

Looks like Edminston, Wilson, Goodwin and Davidson." Roosevelt said. "The men need a stop sign printed in Arabic, so guess I better take care of that."

"Don't know about you Richard," Bruce said. "But I'm ready for a little R&R."

Richard gave Bruce a knuckle punch. "Think I'll goof off for an hour or so,"

"Love you Bro, watch your back, huh?" Bruce said and moments later, after a goodnight to his daughter, he was stretched out on his sleeping bag sound asleep and snoring.

* * *

Chapter 91

"**H**ey Sarge," Roosevelt yelled from the doorway. "Sarge come quick! We got a mess out here and Richard is in bad shape!"

Still half asleep, Bruce rolled out of his sleeping bag and pulled on his clothes. Fear squeezed him so tight he was finding it hard to breath. He fell in behind Roosevelt across the compound, his feet sliding in and out of his untied shoes. Bruce fell to the ground beside Longview and reached for the unrecognizable mangled body of his best friend and cradled him to his chest. Unashamed of the guttural moans ripping his heart out, he rocked him back and forth as if he were a baby.

"I told him not to go," Longview moaned.

Bruce reached out and pulled young Longview to

his side. He wanted to say something, but what the hell was there to say. Richard is dead! Aware of Roosevelt's knee at his back and toe under his knee, he wanted to respond to the expression of sympathy, but couldn't let go of the man he dearly loved.

Sgt. Sullivan and the Captain pushed through the group of men, who had gathered around the accident scene.

"They're dead, Captain," Roosevelt said, and with the help of Sullivan, they pulled Bruce out from under Richard and away from the accident scene.

"Nooo! No, please no," he agonized over the realization of never talking with his friend again. He turned, pulling the men around with him for one last look at a disaster that would forever be etched in his memory.

Bruce was aware of Roosevelt sitting close and leaning into his shoulder. Sleep was far from his mind at the moment when he looked around to the feel of a needle in his shoulder and a warming sensation. "I hate needles," he murmurs and turned to find Roosevelt with a wet washcloth and was vaguely aware of him washing the blood off of his arms and clothing.

"I hate needles," he moans again and leaned forward with his face in his hands, choking on the painful sobs that were tearing his body apart. "Richard, Oh Lord God dear friend..."

"What happened out there?" Captain Wilkins asked.

"Me and Richard joined the four men at the check-point when it looked like they were having problems with a taxi driver," Roosevelt said. "I pointed to the stop sign I had printed in Arabic, but the man kept asking someone to help get his taxi started."

"Goodwin said he knew something about cars and went out to help. Richard wasn't on duty, but him, Edministon and Wilson followed Goodwin and..." Longview dropped his head momentarily.

"Me and a couple of the other guys were trying to get them to come back," Longview continued. "All of a sudden, it was like the whole damn world blew apart in our faces. The taxi driver and all four men were caught in the middle of the blast. I hope to God, I am never around to see anything like that ever again."

"Come with us, Longview," Captain Wilkins said. "Help us make out a report."

＊　＊　＊

Chapter 92

Sometime later, when Bruce thought he was alone, he opened his eyes to the realization of never seeing his friend again. "Lana's death is still so painfully raw and now this...how do I live with the emptiness and longing for the people I will never see or hug again?" He sat up and hugged his knees to his chest. "I just want to touch him," he choked on pain in his throat and closed his eyes against the tears. "I gotta go to Richard's funer.." he choked on the word and yearns for yesterday when Richard was alive!

"How about a cup of coffee?"

"Roosevelt!" He dried his eyes and looked around to find his partner with two cups. He shook his shoulders, trying to shake off the image of Richard's mangled body. A shudder ran through him and he couldn't help but cry out. "Oh Lord Roosevelt!" He reached for the cup of coffee and touched the hot rim to his lips.

The young man with tears in his eyes put a hand to Bruce's shoulder. "Wish there was something I could do to make this not so bad."

"I know Roosevelt," Bruce said and smoothed out the foot of his sleeping bag. "Here, sit with me. You're the only present and good thing I have going for me right now."

"You've been asleep for over fourty-eight hours nonstop, Sarge. Bet we could get Sgt. Luke to fix something real good for breakfast."

"I don't remember taking my clothes off."

"Me and Sullivan did that and I washed them. Here put em on and let's go eat."

"Thanks partner." Bruce swung his feet around and into the pants Roosevelt held out to him. "I probably should eat something, but not sure if I can."

"I know how you feel, and how hard it is to swallow when your throat is constricted with tears." Roosevelt became suddenly quiet and Bruce realized he had slipped back to the painful memory of losing his father.

He thought about Lana and moaned with the added agony of Richard's death, and Sam...I must return the moral support she gave me. "I have to go home with Richard."

"He's gone," Roosevelt said and squat down to tie Bruce's shoes. "They took him away early this morning."

He swallowed his disappointment. "Have they notified his wife yet?"

"Don't know Sarge."

"I must send her an e-mail. Sam would want to hear about this from me."

"Saturday afternoon we had more problems," Roosevelt said and turned a sad eye look on Bruce. "Buck, Brown, Brandon and Martinez ordered a van to stop at the checkpoint."

"No Roosevelt! Don't tell me, I don't want to hear it."

"Oh no, the men are okay Sarge, but with everyone spooked and when it didn't stop after five warning shots...there were 13 women and children and all but four were killed."

"There's so much hate in my gut right now," Bruce said. "I don't know if I can be trusted with a gun in my hands."

Luke's willingness to scrape up a late breakfast for Bruce and a cup of coffee for Roosevelt came as no surprise. "How about a pancake to go with that egg, Lawson?"

"Thanks Luke, but I don't feel much like eating."

When Luke stepped up with coffee pot in hand and poured each of them a refill, Bruce formed his lips into a smile of thanks. "What about the other three men?" Luke said and sat down beside Bruce.

"They're all gone," Roosevelt took a sip of his coffee. "Sgt. Johnson collected some of the men's belongings and we had their memorial this morning."

With a sharp intake of breath, Bruce remembered

the last man hug from Richard. "Why the hell didn't I make him take a nap? Why the hell did I think I needed a nap instead of going with him?" Bruce said. "I promised Samantha I would keep him alive for her and I failed, Roosevelt. Oh Lord God, I failed my friend and I failed Sam!"

"Don't torture yourself like this, Lawson," Luke said and put a hand to Bruce's shoulder.

"There was nothing you could have done, other than going with him and getting your head blown off," Roosevelt said. "We tried, but none of them would listen."

"We should probably go to church and pray for the rest of us." Bruce said and looked around to see what caught Roosevelt and Luke's attention.

Sullivan, with a cup of coffee in hand, pulled out a chair and sit down across from them. "This is Monday, Lawson, we held church yesterday," he said. "You lost near to three days in the sack after that second shot I gave you."

"I have to e-mail Richard's wife to let her know."

"She is probably being notified as we speak. Lt. Colonel Markham was to pay her a visit sometime this morning," Sgt. Sullivan said. "Our computer room is up and running and I'm sure she is probably worried and waiting to hear from you."

*   *   *

Chapter 93

Bruce sat down at the computer and leaned back for a minute or so while he tried to remember the e-mail she had sent him when Lana was killed.

Dearest friend of mine;

What can I say to lessen our pain, dear lady? I wanted to go home with him, but the medic gave me a shot that knocked me out for 3 days. By the time I woke up, all four men had been sent home. I'm sending an e-mail to pops.

He is waiting with my hugs for you, so pretend his arms are mine. Lana's father is a good hugger, let him give you a few. I am there with you Sam, in mind and spirit, just close your eyes and pretend my arms are around you and put yours around me, cause I really need it right now. Oh Lord God, Sam! I can feel your pain because the pain of losing Lana is still fresh, like a disease inside, gnawing and won't let go. They say time heals all wounds but I feel there will always be two gaping holes in my heart. If this letter brings tears to your eyes that's okay, because my tears are in it as well. You will never know how much I'm hurting for you and myself right now and how I need your arms around me and mine around you. God Sam, why? We lose your friend and my wife and now, without enough time to get over the grieving we lose my friend and your husband. The pain is almost unbearable and not being with you, makes it doubly so.

   Love you gal,

   Bye Sam

   Your friend forever,

   Bruce

He pressed send and checked his e-mail to find one from pops and one from Sam. He opened the one from Sam and it nearly killed him, knowing the news of Richard's death hadn't reached her yet and when it does it will bring her down in body and soul to the depths of heart rendering agony that comes with losing the true love of your life. He left the computer room with tears in his eyes and an ache in his heart for the woman, Richard left behind.

Bruce slipped into the room and finding it empty he lay down on his sleeping bag and buried his face into the pillow to soften the sound of his heart breaking. "If only I could turn back the clock," he moans while turning the dry side of the pillow up. "It's too damn late to save Richard," he moans softly before closing his eyes to the demons and ghastly pictures of Richard's face.

He rose to his elbow, surprised he'd fallen asleep, and looked around to find the men laying out their sleeping bags. "What the hell time is it?"

"2000 hrs and still daylight," Brandon moaned. "Don't know how we're suppose to sleep in this heat."

"Who's standing guard tonight?"

"Captain Wilkins ordered the second half of the leap frog unit to stand first guard," Buck said and crawled into his sleeping bag. "We take over at midnight."

He looked around to find Roosevelt looking back at him. "Goodnight Sarge."

"Goodnight Roosevelt," Bruce said and turned his back to the helter-skelter going on behind him and fell asleep again only to awaken by a messenger outside.

"Gas! Gas! Gas!"

Bruce searched through the mess at the end of his sleeping bag in search of his gas mask. His foul language blended well with the other men, as he swept the room with his flashlight to find them wrestling with their protective gear.

Captain Wilkins stepped into the room and gave the all-clear signal. "Fear has reared its ugly head again and we must be ready for the unexpected."

After the Captain and Sgt. Johnson left the room, Bruce laid out his suit, boots, charcoal-lined fatigues and gas mask at the foot of his sleeping bag for quick access.

Martinez rushed into the room. "Sheeit man," he

said. "Good thing that was a false alarm because this Mexican was caught with his pants down."

"Did you have your protective gear with you?" Brandon asked.

"Hell no," Martinez said. "I was butt naked and scared shitless."

"That's what the Captain was talking about, so we better get our ass in gear and be ready for anything," Brown said.

"Goodnight men," Bruce said and curled up in his sleeping bag again.

* * *

Chapter 94

The final hour of guard duty rolled around not a minute too soon as Bruce was more than ready to crash on the floor in his sleeping bag. "A man could set his watch to the daily sounds of early mortar fire around here," he thought aloud but before he could seize the moment of relaxation, he saw Captain Wilkins, Johnson and Sullivan running his way.

With a wave to Brandon, Wilkins ordered Johnson· to wake the others. In ten minutes tops a formation of 44 men, some half awake and others ready for sleep, were in formations and waiting to hear the cause for excitement.

"Alright men, loosen up. The 101st airborne ground forces are on the west bank of the Euphrates River under heavy Iraqi resistance and fighting their way in from the East. A call came in from Lt. Col. Masterson, requesting our assistance to close ranks on the onslaught of Iraqian troops heading our way," Captain Wilkins said and waved a hand toward the desert. "Our cargo supply helicopter has landed about a mile west of here and should be here soon with food supplies, mail, ammunition and two gun trucks."

Bruce turned in a westerly direction to see two covered transport trucks with one gun truck in front and one in back, headed in their direction with sand flying in all directions.

"Let's enjoy a hearty breakfast men, before our meeting with the enemy. Six Apache's heavily armed with missiles are waiting about a mile out for orders," Wilkins said. "The Iraqis we drove to the river will be coming our way again, with gun trucks, tanks and Lord only knows what else. Please take over, Johnson."

"Alright men, we have one hour and thirty minutes before our date with the enemy so chow down and don't be late," Sgt. Johnson said. "Squad dismissed."

After breakfast and fear of chemical weapons, the men packed their injectors of atropine in case of a nerve gas attack. The fighting dozen was now down to the fighting eight and ready to take this war game more seriously. "This is the real deal," Bruce said and turned to his partner. "Good luck Roosevelt."

"I'll watch your back and you watch mine," Roosevelt said with a man hug for his senior partner. "No way can they beat us."

"They sure as hell better not," Bruce said and returned the man hug.

The supply trucks pulled into the compound and before all else, war included would have to wait until after mail call. Bruce ran up for his mail and the package from his mother. He tore it open and pulled out two interceptor vests with ceramic plates and found a note.

Hello dear;

One for my son and the other for his partner, and here is your favorite candy bar. Remember when you were just a little guy, how much you loved these? Hope you still do.

Love you son,

Mom

Bruce pulled out the box of big hunks and handed one to Roosevelt.

"Hey amigo, my man," Martinez stepped up to stare at the candy bars. "My favorite candy. Do you have an extra one for this fine Mexican friend of yours?"

"Here you go Amigo, wrap those beautiful Mexican lips around this."

"Si Senior." He tore the sticky wrapper from around the candy and shoved the end of it in his mouth. "A little taste of heaven, Amigo and I must thank your ma'ma when I see her."

Bruce handed a candy bar to the other five men for a sweet taste before battle. It made him feel good and the love he felt for his mother was too big for words.

"Spread out men, your letters will have to wait until later, and good luck," Captain Wilkins voice sounded a bit on edge, before he flanked left away from the fighting eight.

Hunkered down on the far side of the schoolhouse to where they had a clear view of Main Street, both to the north and south and between the buildings across the street. He quickly replaced his flack vest with the one from his mother and looked around to find Roosevelt doing the same.

He looked to the left to see Brown, Buck, Martinez and Brandon and to the right; he found a new partnership between Longview and Davidson after losing their original partners. He felt the pain again of losing Richard.

Bruce felt the children at his back and looked over at Roosevelt, but before he could say anything, Roosevelt spoke to them in Arabic. With quick hugs and kisses to all eight men, the youngsters turned and rushed back into the schoolroom to wait and watch from the windows.

* * *

Chapter 95

Five hours and counting, the first Iraqis came into view from around the buildings to the east totally unaware of the armed and ready soldiers waiting for them. At about the same time Bruce aimed his weapon, the civilian clad men in front suddenly fell to the ground. The Iraqi soldiers left standing shot two of their own before the fighting eight could take them out.

Off in the distance, Bruce could see Iraqi gun trucks and tanks headed in their direction and before he could make up his mind to shit or get, he heard the hum of Apaches overhead and the ear splitting shriek of a whistling teakettle just seconds before the explosion.

The tank was no longer a threat and Buck's distance on the gun truck was dead on, but there was another with machine guns aimed in their direction. Buck's second grenade stopped it, but not until after the wild shot of the enemy explodes the window in back of them. The screams of the children were like a sharp knife to his heart.

There was so much going on around him, Bruce wasn't sure who was doing what, but for sure he had to check on the children and nudged his partner on the shoulder. "Cover me," he said and started for the door to the schoolroom but found Sullivan there ahead of him.

Hours of adrenalin rush later, just how much later Bruce wasn't sure, but the first sign of U.S. tanks, machine gun manned humvee's and a squad of gun toting infantrymen entered the city to maneuver around the wreckage left by the Apache's and Bucks grenade.

A drum roll couldn't be more fitting, he thought while watching the parade pull in between the buildings and onto the street. Bruce held up his hand for the men to hold their fire and stood his ground, hoping the

101st recognized them as being on the same team.

"Lawson, to the left, the 101st are blindsided to the twelve Iraqis with weapons raised and aimed in their direction," Brown hissed. "How about we surprise the bastards?"

"Sounds good to me," Bruce hissed back, but once Roosevelt sighted the Iraqis with his SAW, there was little left for the rest of them. Bruce put his rifle stock to the ground, but before he could push up, a little person leaned into his back and slipped tiny arms around his neck. A small voice in Arabic sounded in his ear.

"She said thank you Sarge for not killing her daddy," Roosevelt said.

She ran across the yard to one of the men lying on the ground and fell down beside him with her arm around his neck. "I completely forgot about the men on the ground," Bruce whispers to no one in particular. When the man pulls the little girl into his arms and smothers her face with kisses, he smiles and remembers his baby daughter.

He whirled around to see what Brown and Roosevelt were looking at. There stood six men with guns at their feet and hands behind their heads. Roosevelt yelled in Arabic and the men fell to their knees.

He looked around to the men marching in behind the humvees and jerked back, unable to believe his eyes. After a quick glance and seeing no threat around, he sprang to his feet and ran out to meet Webb.

*   *   *

Chapter 96

Bruce read a part of Samantha's letter again, the part about Sari's bout with the flu bug and felt a rush of overwhelming need to be home with his daughter. In a near run for the dining room and feeling a presence at his side hanging in stride for stride, he looked around to find Roosevelt with eyes straight ahead and apparently nothing to say at the moment.

The letter from Sam squeezed at his heart again, bringing with it the agony of Richard's death, the vision of his mangled body, the blood, oh Lord...help me with this! He wanted to strike out, to hit something and yell at the cussed pain to make it go to hell away.

Roosevelt picked up two cups, filled one for Bruce and one for himself. They sit side by side in silence for the longest time before either of them said a word. "Sarge," he stares down at his cup. "I know you must have received bad news and I shouldn't tell you mine, but I need someone real bad right now."

"Sorry Roosevelt, is your mother okay?" Bruce pulled himself out of the haze of pain surrounding him. "Did something happen to your mother?"

"No Sarge, it's Alice. She had a miscarriage." Roosevelt let his breath out slowly. "My baby, a little boy, he's dead."

"I'm so sorry, Roosevelt," Bruce said. "Damn death to hell. It's all around us and there's not a damn thing we can do about it."

"A bottle of whiskey might help."

"Perhaps," Bruce agreed and looked around when Webb settled on the bench alongside him with a cup of coffee in hand.

"Hey, you guys have this place fixed up pretty good," he looked around the dining hall and raised a hand to Sgt. Luke, who stood behind the counter grinning like a Cheshire Cat at Webb's compliment. "We have supplies, water tanks, cots, lumber and carpenters coming in behind us to undo the damage we did and build a couple of barracks for your outfit."

"You're kidding," Bruce smiled and looked around at Roosevelt for his take on the news to find him smiling from ear to ear.

"What time is dinner around here?"

"How about a sample plate of meat loaf, some mashed potatoes and gravy to go with it young man?" Sgt Luke yelled and motioned the three men to the empty plates.

"Aside from fighting the whole damn way we came through some pretty country. We really messed up this farmer's irrigation ditches, but taking a shortcut across his green fields saved time," Webb chuckled. "I felt bad about it but orders are orders." Webb stopped talking long enough to take a mouthful of his meatloaf and give Luke a thumb and finger okay. "It's beautiful along the Euphrates River. We marched through an oasis of palms most of the night until we arrived and took up our attack position there."

"There was nothing beautiful about our trip," Bruce said. "Desert, desert and more desert and if that wasn't bad enough, we ate dust for two days after we got here."

"I think everybody got a taste of that. You know the hardest thing about this war is how human shields are being forced to carry weapons and ordered to fight or die."

Bruce nodded in agreement to what Webb was saying. "How long will you be around?"

"Some of us will stay to help rebuild the city and see that you guys have something a hell of a lot better than you have now." Webb chuckled at being surrounded with man hugs from both sides.

"A third of our troop has been ordered to seize the Najaf airport," Webb looked at his watch. "Probably a done deal as we speak. It's imperative that we control the airport because with all the heavy cargo aircrafts loaded with machinery coming through here and whatever else we need to rebuild this holy city. Plans are to build barracks near the airport to use as our main base of operations for here and farther north. We will need a water treatment plant for here as well as the airport and work is to begin immediately."

"Water will make living around here a hell of a lot better," Bruce smiled his appreciation at Webb's news and looked around when Sgt. Luke sat down at the end of the table.

"Luke, this is the best damn meatloaf I ever tasted, better even than my mom's," Webb said and gave the cook a shoulder knuckle.

"Drop by whenever you got time on your hands and I'll let you sample one of my pot roasts," Luke chuckled.

"Sounds like a winner."

*   *   *

Chapter 97

Webb pulled the voice-activated radio out of his pocket and turned up the sound. The Lt. Colonel was giving the location of Iraqi trucks moving a stockpile of ammunition and orders to search and destroy.

Bruce grabbed Roosevelt and together they followed Webb outside. Captain Wilkins, Johnson and Sullivan were waving their arms with a shout of orders for the leapfrog unit to backup the 101st.

Bruce and Roosevelt fell in behind Johnson through the smoke from fires still smoldering from yesterday's bombardment. He turned to the hum of helicopters overhead and shortly thereafter, the sound of an explosion and a plume of black smoke rose above the city.

A number of secondary explosions followed as they

rushed the large municipal building and around the corner to where they could see the pickup trucks, mortar shells and rocket-propelled grenades reduced to a pile of rubble. Following the move of their superior officers, the fighting eight fell to their knees and faced off with the rush of unarmed Iraqis trying to escape the explosion of wild artillery shells.

"Hold it men, stay alert but hold your fire." Johnson bumped into the backside of Bruce when he went down on one knee. "The men are unarmed."

"What the hell we gonna do with the prisoners?"

Johnson turned to Bruce with a chuckle. "We'll let the 101st Airborne have them."

"Hey, Sgt. Johnson Sir," Martinez knelt down just in back of Bruce and cupped the back of his ear with his palm. "Do you hear what I hear, Senior? I do think the fat lady is singing?"

The four men shared another chuckle while Sgt. Johnson gave Martinez a shoulder bump. "I'd be surprised to find the singing fat lady here in Iraq."

Bruce looked around to see Brown, Buck and Brandon settle down in back of them while Davidson and Longview shuffled around to the far side of Sgt. Johnson.

"What now, boss?" Brown said.

"Let's backtrack, but stay alert, the Iraqis may have come up from behind us while we were busy," Captain Wilkins said, making his presence known. "Don't know about the rest of you, but I'm ready for a cup of coffee."

"Si, Captain Wilkins, Sir," Martinez said. "This worn out Mexican could go for a couple of Margarita's."

"I'm with you, man," Buck said and pretended to lick the salt off his lips.

∗　∗　∗

Chapter 98

Looking at his watch to find both hands on the twelve, Bruce welcomed the end of guard duty and followed the trail hell bent for his sleeping quarters. He stripped down to his shorts and was asleep before his head hit the pillow.

"Gas! Gas! Gas!"

Bruce held on to the dream of Lana, but when his mind became jumbled in the midst of a room full of grunts and groans and a blind search for chemical gear in the darkness, his beautiful lady slips away. "Son of a bitch," he muttered and sank down into his pillow, chemical gear and all.

"Sarge..."

He looked around to the sound of Roosevelt's voice

and flinched. "Yeah," he said, and sounding like he was in an echo chamber when he said it, Bruce stripped off the gas mask and tossed it to the foot of his sleeping bag.

"You been sleeping in that damn thing all night?"

"Looks like it," he laughed and shed the chemical suit to find his body wet with sweat.

"It's 0500 hrs Sarge and formation in thirty minutes."

Bruce raced for the showers and back again to toss his dirty clothes in the bunkhouse and join the line with a group salute when Johnson stepped up to front the formation.

After breakfast and taking advantage of down time, Bruce and Roosevelt wandered the streets and the bombed-out buildings. The barracks, offices and supply rooms not only made him aware of the chills using his spine for a playground, but he could actually smell and feel the ghosts of the Iraqi military still hanging around. "With a little elbow grease we can make these barracks a hell of a lot better than the one we're sleeping in now."

"Yeah, but who the hell's gonna clean up the bird shit," Roosevelt laughed.

"I suppose a no trespassing sign in pigeon and bat language to hang on the door is in order." Bruce laughed.

His mind on the rise and fall of the Iraqi Army, Bruce took note of the frown playing on the young man's face. "Do you think the United States will ever fall into enemy hands?"

They stepped out into the glaring sunlight before Bruce turned to his partner with an answer. "I suppose so, Roosevelt. Just hope I'm not around to see it." He looked up to see Webb jogging toward them.

"There you are," Webb called to them with a wave. "Been looking all over hell for you."

"I agree, tis a hell of a good name for this country, but I got something for you in the barracks," Bruce grinned at the curiosity in Webb's face. "We were just looking this place over and have already staked out a claim."

"Soon as the transports and carpenters get here, put them to work on it," Webb suggested. "But changing the subject, I came to tell about the Explosive Ordinance Detachment. They're due to arrive soon with the Rhino to remove IED's and sweep for land mines."

"We have a hell of a lot of them staked out already," Bruce said and pointed to the ones nearby. "I'd like to get my hands on the bastard responsible." He stepped into their barracks and laughed at Webb's expression. "It's not so bad when you don't spend much time in here."

Webb completed his inspection of the room and turned to Bruce for the surprise he had for him. "Well?"

Bruce reached into the box at the foot of his sleeping bag. "My locker," he says to Webb and held the big hunk behind his back.

"You do need barracks and beds would be a plus," he laughed and spied the candy bar. "A taste of home is just what this old boy needs."

"Thought so," Bruce laughed and handed one to Roosevelt. He peeled a part of the paper away from his and let his mouth have at it.

"The day after your unit left Udaira, the heat climbed to triple-digits and the dust storms started to swirl like crazy," Webb said and turned for the door. "The Lt. Col. has been invited to the Ali Mosque for a meeting with the Grand Ayatollah Thursday, so better be on my way for the training exercise, oh by the way, I heard about your wife's accident and would like to extend my condolence."

"Thanks Web and I suppose you heard about my friend Richard who was killed by a suicide bomber."

"Yeah, I did," Webb said and looked at his watch. "I lost a friend I'd known for 12 years shortly after we left Kuwait."

* * *

Chapter 99

What a difference eight months can make, Bruce thought as he looked around at the six new barracks. Two new buildings with twelve shower stalls in each one and serviced by a new water treatment plant situated between the compound and the airport. Ten porta poties were lined up in a three walled building with a roof. It was now time to fully concentrate on the job at hand, to search out and mark the location of new explosive devices on the map.

He sat on the rooftop of his barracks searching the area with his binoculars and stopped suddenly to sharpen the focus on a dog. He turned to Roosevelt and held the binoculars out to him. "What do you think? Is it dead or alive?"

"I'm not about to get close enough to find out," he laughed.

"Brown and Buck found six new devices yesterday morning," Bruce said and shook his head. "What's so damn frustrating is the terrorist, who plants these things all over hell is hid out somewhere laughing up his sleeve and waiting to activate a detonator that will forever end the lifestyle of loving families."

Roosevelt raised the binoculars to his eyes and turned in a circle. "Don't see him Sarge, but he could be any one of these Iraqis just milling around with nothing better to do."

Bruce was suddenly struck with an idea and backing down the ladder he took off in a search for Captain Wilkins to lay the idea on him. Twenty minutes later and still looking for the Captain, he caught sight of Sgt. Johnson and looked around to find Roosevelt jogging alongside step for step.

"What's the hurry men?" Johnson held his hand up. "Something on your mind?"

"Yeah, it's about these new IED's the Iraqis set up at night," he stopped to catch his breath and to make sure he had Johnson's attention.

"Go on Lawson, I'm listening."

"I think I've come up with a way to axe these bastards. What if, when we're on guard duty we hide out and wait in one spot rather than walking the perimeter?"

"That might work," Johnson rubbed his chin. "And just where are these lookout points?"

"Look around you Sgt. Johnson, the new roof tops. We could have men working the ground and the ladders while four of us cover the area from the rooftops with rifle sights and night vision glasses."

"I like it Lawson," Johnson looked up at how the rooftops covered the area. "We could shoot the assholes before they get lost in the crowd."

"Yeah, but we gotta make sure the bastard is not a walking IED with a belt of dynamite before we approach him. Could be a man waiting nearby with the detonator to take out his man and anyone else who happened to be around."

"This calls for a meeting of the minds Lawson. Let me get back to you after I take it to the Captain."

Roosevelt moved around to affront Bruce. "That's a brilliant idea! It would do my heart good to blow one of those lamebrain assholes away."

"The gift of freedom from terrorists and suicide bombers should make the people of Najaf sit up and take pride in their notice of our intentions," Bruce said and again moaned the loss of Richard. "Hope to hell they appreciate the cost of American lives in this venture."

The outcome of the meeting with the Captain was favorable in Bruce's search and destroy plan and at a little past dusk, Roosevelt, Buck and Brown were on the rooftop. Bruce spread out his sleeping bag and lay his chemical gear nearby as a safety precaution. Rooftops make for cool bedrooms in the summer, but with winter just around the corner he worries that it might be a dead give away to the plan.

The Captain's order of four men to a rooftop with two on guard while two sleeps, Bruce looked around at his three volunteers. They gave off a pretense of sitting around and having a friendly chat. Roosevelt and Buck however, were looking over each other shoulders, as was Brown and Bruce.

"What the hell are you doing Lawson?" Buck laughed. "Are you losing a little upstairs substance?"

"I figured hairs would work as good as straws," he said and pushed the fourth hair into his fist. "Short hairs get first choice to sleep or guard."

"Goodnight men," Buck said as he lay back on his sleeping bag.

"And happy hunting guys," Bruce said.

Roosevelt and Brown took up a squat shuffle to their designated look out post.

* * *

Chapter 100

Bruce felt someone brush against his sleeping bag and struggling to get away from the hand over his mouth he heard what sounded like Roosevelt. "Sssh," he whispered. "Come have a look."

He fumbled around for his night vision goggles and looked down to where the younger man was pointing. "Sure as hell," Bruce whispered. "I do believe the asshole is about to get caught in our trap." With the radio to his mouth, he quickly contacted Kemp on the ground. "Lone man heading for the north east corner of building C. Stay alert and remember men, take…"

The explosion caught Bruce unprepared for the turmoil it brought to his gut. " Kemp?" Anticipating the worse, a yell was near to surfacing. "You guys okay?"

Roosevelt crawled to the edge of the roof and looked over. "The bastard blew his guts out and took our guys with him. Here comes Sullivan now with a couple of men."

Bruce lay back with his arm across his eyes until he heard Sullivan's voice on the radio. "Stay your position Lawson, Kemp and Ness are dead. Your new replacements are Lopez and Fielding. New orders from the Captain, if in doubt take the enemy out."

"If you look southwest around building C here, you can see the IED he planted." Bruce rolled to his stomach. "Take a look around the dead man for a detonator or percussion cap."

"Buck and me will take guard Roosevelt, while you and Brown try to catch a little shuteye," Bruce said after filling them in on their new orders. He belly crawled to his observation point.

All looked quiet for 30 minutes or so and suddenly, dumbfounded by what he saw, Bruce could hardly believe what he was seeing. A lone man near the pile of explosives. "Pssst, Buck, look!"

"What the hell, is he...?"

"Don't know?" Without taking his eyes away from the action below, he made a wide sweep with his hand. "Look around the area for a man who appears to be watching this one."

"Don't see anyone Lawson."

"Maybe this is the guy with the detonator and is checking out the other guys work," Bruce said and radioed the men on the ground. "There's another man out there. When he moves away, let him have it between the eyes and approach with caution. Make sure the bastard is dead and stand at a distance while you look for a belt of explosives around his body. If he's clean, go in for a body search, look for the detonator."

"We found something Lawson, not sure what it is," Lopez said. "What now?"

"Push the man near the IED pile and see if you can detonate it, make sure you're at a safe distance." Bruce hid his face until after the explosion.

"He sure as hell won't be laying out booby traps again," Lopez said.

"What the hell happened?" Roosevelt crawled out of his sleeping bag for a look.

"The sumbitch set off an IED and blew himself up," Buck laughed.

"Good, one less asshole to worry about," Brown said and curled up on his sleeping bag.

"Yeah," Bruce said with a chuckle and realized the night has been good.

Guard duty over, Bruce crawled to the edge of the roof to see replacements on the way. He filled them in on what had taken place and the four men left the four newcomers up to take their place. He motioned the men to follow him. "How about we see if Luke left the coffee pot on," he said. "I want to check my e-mail and a cup of coffee might help to keep my eyes open."

"Sounds good to me Sarge,"

Surprised to find Luke up and sitting at a table, Bruce pointed to the coffee pot and upon Luke's nod, he filled his cup and shuffled across the room to sit down beside Luke. "What the hell you doing up this time of night?"

"The explosion woke me. Is everybody okay?"

"Two terrorist and two of our own are dead."

"Who?"

"Kemp and Ness, they were on the ground," Bruce said and climbed over the bench with his cup in hand. "I hear my computer calling me."

*   *   *

Chapter 101

Bruce X'd out Thursday April 6, 2004 on the calendar and grins. "My last day in Iraq," he mumbled before rushing off for the meeting at the dining hall. The fighting eight were already seated at the table. He squeezed into the seat Roosevelt held for him and turned his nose toward the kitchen. "Do you guys smell what I smell?"

"Sgt. Luke is baking a chocolate cake to honor four brave fighting men and their year of service in this God forsaken land," Buck rolled his eyes and grinned from ear to ear. "And three of us guys came over earlier to cover the ice with our butts while Corp. Joseph turned the crank on the ice cream maker."

"Chocolate cake was dad's favorite," Roosevelt said.

"Wish I could have met your old man," Longview said, looking almost as downtrodden as Roosevelt. "Have him take me under his wing and teach me a thing or two about guns."

"Oh si, senior Longview and don't forget the hunting," Martinez said and looked at Bruce. "Hey Lawson, how about letting this poor Mexican take your seat on the plane?"

"Don't think my daughter would appreciate such generosity," Bruce laughed and leaned into Roosevelt with a shoulder bump. "Gonna miss you partner."

"I'm happy for you Sarge so don't go worrying bout me," Roosevelt said. "Buck and me will be the meanest fighting machine, other than you and me of course, this army ever had."

Bruce joined the strained laughter and looked up to see Sgt. Johnson and Sullivan making their way across the floor. "Guess you four men know about the private meeting tomorrow night, why don't you stay around for another day and join the fun?"

"Don't think so, Sgt. Johnson," Brown said. "Lawson, Davidson, Hemp and I will probably be in Germany at about that time, so you guys just go ahead with your fun meeting," he shared a chuckle with the three men, who whole heartedly agreed with him.

Sgt. Luke stepped up to the table with a chocolate cake in hand. "Did I hear someone say party?" Corp. Joseph followed with his churned ice cream, while Roosevelt and Martinez retrieved bowls and spoons from the counter.

His mouth full of cake and ice cream, Bruce gave a thumbs up to Luke and Joseph. "I'm gonna miss hell out of you guys, no kidding." His smile was misty and the men around the table, wolfing down their desert, would forever remain a part of his fondest memories. "I love you partner." he said and laid his arm around Roosevelt's shoulder.

"What the hell was that?" Bruce yelled and looked to his senior officer.

"Some old dynamite they found in a falling down

warehouse," Sgt. Johnson chuckled. "Nothing to worry about,"

"It shook the whole damn building like when the suicide bombers took out the Iman Ali Shrine." Buck said. "Remember that day when they killed the Shiite leader?"

"Oh hell yeah," Davidson said. "To get the hell out of Najaf and save my ass was the first thought that came to mind."

"When the Iraqis pointed at us like we were to hell responsible it was a tossup as to whether to shit or get the hell out of there," Roosevelt said.

"Scared shit outta me and I'm not too proud to admit it," Longview said. "The trunk of that car wedged in the door looked almost like a part of the building." He looked to the other men for agreement. "The blood and guts scattered all over the court yard still to this day, interrupts my sleep."

Brown dropped his spoon in his bowl. "Longview please, we're eating cake here."

"When Sgt. Sullivan attempted to help the injured and the Iraqi police held him back I couldn't believe what I was seeing," Brandon said.

"And when the Iraqi police turned on Sgt. Sullivan scared shieet out of me," Martinez said. "Thought for sure they were gonna to throw your ass in jail, Amigo Sir."

Sullivan picked up his bowl and pushed away from the table. "Thank you men, I feel honored with all this concern for my safety," he said and knuckled punch Bruce on the shoulder. "Good luck men, some of us here still have work to do."

Sgt. Johnson stood up with his hand out to the four men leaving the country. "If I don't see you guys before you leave have a safe trip. Oh! By the way Lawson, how in the hell did you get to Camp Udaira?"

"Hell Sgt. Johnson, are you telling me you had nothing to do with the smooth transition?" Bruce chuckled and returned Johnson's wave when he walked off shaking his head.

"Remember to look at your e-mail when you get home," Roosevelt said.

"I'll do that Bro, yes indeedy." His pet name for Richard slipped out, but it felt good to lay it on the young man.

*   *   *

Chapter 102

Bruce looked out the window and smiled in recognition of speedboats on the Columbia River and water skiers trailing in their wake. Campers were spread on the banks along the Washington side and houses along the slip on the Oregon side. "No more tents for me, but all that water down there makes me want to get my boat on the water," he muttered and turned to his traveling companion.

"I hear you Lawson, I've had enough tents to last a lifetime."

"Me and Richard were pretty good on water skies. I talked Lana into giving it a try," he chuckled. "She came up out of the water like a pro, but I forgot to warn her about spreading her arms to take up the slack and she went down backwards. Never could get her back on them." Bruce looked out the window again to swallow the thickness in his throat. "Richard's wife was a natural, almost like she'd been born on water skies," Bruce chuckles with a bump to the shoulder of his traveling companion. "Hell Jim, maybe I'll get you on a pair of skies."

"Don't know about that, but I'll give it some thought."

Bruce was suffering second thoughts about his idea of sneaking into the office without calling Pops first. Worried and while at the same time, so excited he could hardly keep his seat belt fastened.

Memory of the fighting eight brought a smile to his face, but the four they left behind, the tears in Roosevelt's eyes when he left Iraq, brought a teary blur between him and the handsome brown face in the seat next to him. "I'm gonna miss those four guys we left behind, Brandon, Martinez and to partner Buck with Roosevelt was a good call. Hope they watch each other's back."

Brown reached for his handkerchief to blow his nose and dry his eyes as well. "They'll be okay Lawson, we trained them good and leaving your lap top behind was a good idea. Keep in touch and let me know what's going on with them."

"I'll do that Jim, but in the meantime why don't the two of us get together for a game of golf or better yet, do you bowl?"

"Never bowled a day in my life," Brown laughed. "But Golf? Hell yeah man, anytime."

"You got it," Bruce said and lay back in his seat mindful of Najaf city and how well it fared through the war. Yep, he smiled; Roosevelt will keep me up to date throughout the coming year, with maybe some news about the coming election.

"Hmmm," he murmured before closing his eyes to the grinding of the landing gear. He stole a quick peek to see the ground coming up fast and closed his eyes until after the wheels touched down on the runway.

"The folks meeting you?" Brown asked as they started to move forward.

"Big secret," Bruce whispered. "Gonna surprise them at the office."

"Hope to hell you don't give your ole man a heart attack," Brown laughed and gave Bruce cause to wonder again, if surprise was a good idea. "There's my wife, Lawson, come on over with me, I'd like you to meet Lila."

After the introduction and a quick hug for the beautiful black woman and a man hug for Brown, he promised to stay in touch and let him know what was happening in Najaf.

Rucksack on his back and duffel under his arm, Bruce rushed out of the airport to grab the first taxi parked at the curb. After a short conversation with the taxi driver about his tour of duty in Iraq, he sat back against the seat, closed his eyes and smiled, feeling better than he had in a very long time. He looked up when the driver slowed at the parking lot and directed him to the building on the right. "Pull up near the door," he said and pulling some bills out of his wallet, waved them over the driver's right shoulder.

"No way, Sergeant, my treat," he said and rushed around to the trunk for the duffle bags and rushed to set them just inside the door.

Bruce slammed the taxi door shut and met the driver on the way out. "Thanks man," he said and accepted the hand held out to him. Afraid of being recognized, he rushed inside and started for Samantha's office, but stepped back when she came around the corner.

Lord she looks beautiful, he thought and watching her come at him in leaps and bounds, he dropped his duffel and braced to catch her. He was surprised in a good way when her lips came down hard and full on his with a longing that well matched his. "Been a long time since I felt a kiss like that, my lady. Oh yes indeedy, a very long time."

"I just opened your email and you didn't say a damn thing about meeting you at the air port," she squealed and slid down the front of him.

"Lord that felt good," he teased, and squeezed her around waist as they shuffled toward the old man's office. Bruce stepped into the office and stopped in front of the desk

"What the hell!" the old man gasped and turned deathly white.

Bruce rushed around the desk, his heart pounding against his ribs. "Pops, you okay?" He knelt down and searched his face for pain.

"Pinch me son, is this for real or is it just another damn dream?"

"It's for real Pops, and I'm here to stay."

"Come into my office and help me clear my desk," Sam said and waved him toward the door. "I know a little girl who misses her daddy very much."

"Why don't I get Martin in here," Pops said and reached for the intercom. "When you've finished in your office Sam, call me and we'll all go home together."

Bruce rushed out of Pops office into the arms of his

black salesman. "Good Lord, you look great, but what the hell you doing carrying that damn thing on your back," BJ said and pulled the straps from around Bruce's shoulders.

"My rucksack has become so much a part of me I forget sometime that I still have it on." Bruce said and gave Billy Joe a shoulder punch. "Crazy huh?"

"I suppose you're dying to see your daughter so I'm out of here. She's one gorgeous little gal, Bruce." BJ calls back over his shoulder and with a wave he closed the door and waved again from outside the window.

"I'll call mom to let her know I'm in town, Sam, why don't you call the Elkington's. I want to see my daughter and I want to see her now."

* * *

Chapter 103

The door opened and standing there with two little arms reaching up and tiny hands in a pick me up wiggle was his daughter. "Up, up dady," she squeals and before Bruce could gather her into his arms, she began to cry.

"Shush shush little darling," he said and held her close to his chest to smoother her neck with noisy kisses. "Want to go with daddy to see Grandma Lawson?"

"Go bye bye Mam-maw," she giggles and waves at Grandma Elkington.

"Sari's only a year old, mother Elkington. How did you get her to walk and talk in the amount of time?"

"I can't take all the credit, son, papa here and Sam had a lot to do with it."

Leaving hugs with Grandma and Grandpa Elkington, Sam came into the room with an overnight bag for Sari. It had started to rain while they were inside and with his boonie hat on Sari's head, the three of them raced out to the car. Sam ran around to the passenger side and reached for Sari when Bruce opened the door to slide in behind the wheel. "I haven't done much driving while I've been gone. You sure you want this, me sitting behind the wheel?"

"You damn betcha," she settled in with Sari on her lap. "No time like the present to see what you got."

He tapped his daughter on the chin and squeezed Sam's hand. "It's good to be home and have two gorgeous females in the car with me."

"Having you home is like having a part of Richard home with me," she smiled through the tears in her eyes and laughed when Bruce reached up to brush away a tear of his own.

"We had some good times together, the four of us," he said. "Especially our last night in the motel. Tell me Sam, who the hell won that night, me or Richard?"

"Neither," Sam laughed. "Our expectations were waaay too high."

Bruce reached across the seat to tousle Sari's hair and laughed out loud when she scolded him. "No, dady!"

"She's a regular little bitching female," Sam laughed and combed the baby curls into place with her fingers.

Bruce returned Sam's smile and pulled into the folk's driveway. He looked toward the door to catch his mother letting the screen door slap her in the butt. With her feet off the floor, he carried the woman he loved most in the world, back into the house. "Is that you smelling sooo good or something else?"

"Must be what I have in the oven," she giggled and wiggled until her feet came to rest upon the carpet again. Backing away she looked her son over from top to bottom. "What sounds good dear, barbeque steaks or fried chicken?"

"We had an excellent cook, not so good as you, mother dear, but we ate well over there," he kissed her cheek and turned to the old man with a full man hug. "What I missed most over there was our daily routine at the office. The comradery over there was necessary in our day to day existence, but not nearly as much fun as the bull we spread around here."

"We have the rest of our lives to shoot the bull and have fun at the office, but right now, son, please tell your mama what you want for dinner."

Bruce raised his eyebrows at Sari. "Do we want steak or chicken?"

"Chi, dady," she giggles.

"You got it, fried chicken sounds good." He reached out for Sam and pulled her into the curve of his arm. "How about it? Stay for dinner?" He followed her glance to find his mother watching them and waiting for Sam's answer.

"Yes dear, please stay for dinner," mother said and carried the invitation a bit further. "Why don't you spend the night with us and ride to work with the men in the morning."

"I have my car Mrs. Lawson," Sam said and looked around for Bruce's reaction to the invitation. "I'll have to run home to pick up some clothes if I spend the night."

"I'll ride along with you after dinner." Bruce said. "Maybe stop in at the cemetery on the way." He looked around to see his mother drop the phone into its cradle.

"The Elkington's will be joining us for dinner tonight."

*　*　*

Chapter 104

Bruce turned into the driveway at the cemetery and stopped near Lana's grave to find the marker not at all like he remembered. He closed the car door and was only half conscious of Sam slipping her arm through his. The memory of Lana on their last night together was like a fist in the gut. He wanted to turn away, to hide the tears stinging his eyelids.

The grave marker to the left with Richard's name on it and the date of his death felt like another fist to the gut and the tears, like a tidal wave of emotions, gushed unashamedly down his cheeks and into the handkerchief he held to his face.

He felt Sam's head against his shoulder and grabbed her, their arms holding to each other while they moaned the loss of their loved ones. A tremor of weakness fell over him, his knees buckled and he fell to the ground, pulling Samantha down with him. "Why did this happen to us, Sam? What the hell did we do that was so bad...why Sam? Why did God take our loved ones?"

"Everything happens for the best, they say, but I have not found one good reason for this loneliness and a hurt that won't go away," Sam cried and held her hands out to the graves of Richard and Lana.

"I wanted to come home with Richard, to hold your hand in the same way you held mine, but with those damn shots Sgt. Sullivan gave me, Richard was already gone by the time I came out of it," Bruce said and pulled Sam to his side again. "I wanted to be the first to tell you, but everything happened so fast. I even missed the memorial service for the three men who were killed in the same blast as Richard."

"I really needed you, Bruce. Pops knew that and did all he could to help me through the ordeal. I have cried more since these two beautiful people died than in all my life put together. I come out here every day and talk to them. I want to touch both of them so bad," Samantha said and stopped to blow her nose. "I really lost it one day and got drunk. Your mother and Pops were so good about taking care of me when I had a hangover the next day. Pops gave me the day off."

"Pops is a man you can lean on when all else fails. Did he lay one on too?"

"No he was too busy taking care of me. He came with me several times to talk with Lana. He was proud of your wife, but I guess you already know that," Sam smiled across at him and pointed to the markers. "I bought these two plots for you and me, see your name beside Lana's, and mine there with Richard. All that's needed is the date. When I die, please fill in the date of my death and lay me out alongside my beloved and I will do the same for you if you should die first."

Bruce crossed his heart and reached for her hand. "I promise to abide by your wishes and if I die before you, the folks will take special care to carry out your wishes. And you my darling wife, the day will come when I will rest at your side."

The End

Printed in the United States
219415BV00001B/2/P

9 781438 938844